PENGUIN CLASSICS  DELUXE EDITION

PHILOSOPHY IN THE BOUDOIR

Donatien-Alfonse-François, MARQUIS DE SADE was born in 1740 into a family of extremely distinguished but impoverished aristocrats. At the age of twenty-three, Sade married Pélagie de Montreuil in a union that was arranged by his father for exclusively materialistic reasons. In 1771, in order to escape the scabrous reputation numerous sexual transgressions had earned him, the Sades moved to Provence and lived in a family chateau at La Coste that the Marquis had inherited from his father. After he had participated in several more scandalous debauches, Sade's own mother-in-law secured his imprisonment in 1777 from King Louis XVI. Sade would remain in jail for thirteen years, first at Vincennes, and then at the Bastille. While in prison, Sade wrote the first drafts of *Justine* and of *The 120 Days of Sodom*. Upon his release from prison in 1790, his wife refused to see him; some months later he set up a household with another woman. During the 1790s Sade published, in strict anonymity, several of his pornographic works, including *Justine, Philosophy in the Boudoir*, and *Juliette*. Sade enjoyed only a decade of freedom. In 1801, he was identified as the writer of *Justine* and was incarcerated at the insane asylum of Charenton on the grounds of libertine dementia. He died at Charenton in 1814, at the age of seventy-four.

JOACHIM NEUGROSCHEL has translated numerous books from French, German, Italian, Russian, and Yiddish. He has won three PEN translation awards and the French-American translation prize. He has translated Thomas Mann, Herman Hesse, and Leopold von Sacher-Masoch.

FRANCINE DU PLESSIX GRAY is a regular contributor to *The New Yorker*, and the author of numerous books of fiction and nonfiction, including *Lovers and Tyrants, Soviet Women, Rage and Fire, At Home with the Marquis de Sade, Simone Weil*, and *Them: A Memoir of Parents*. She lives in Connecticut.

MARQUIS DE SADE

Philosophy in the Boudoir

or,

The Immoral Mentors

Translated from the French by
JOACHIM NEUGROSCHEL

Introduction by
FRANCINE DU PLESSIX GRAY

PENGUIN BOOKS

PENGUIN BOOKS

Published by the Penguin Group
Penguin Group (USA) Inc., 375 Hudson Street, New York, New York 10014, U.S.A.
Penguin Group (Canada), 90 Eglinton Avenue East, Suite 700, Toronto, Ontario,
Canada M4P 2Y3 (a division of Pearson Penguin Canada Inc.)
Penguin Books Ltd, 80 Strand, London WC2R 0RL, England
Penguin Ireland, 25 St Stephen's Green, Dublin 2, Ireland
(a division of Penguin Books Ltd)
Penguin Group (Australia), 250 Camberwell Road, Camberwell, Victoria 3124,
Australia (a division of Pearson Australia Group Pty Ltd)
Penguin Books India Pvt Ltd, 11 Community Centre, Panchsheel Park,
New Delhi – 110 017, India
Penguin Group (NZ), 67 Apollo Drive, Rosedale, North Shore 0632, New Zealand
(a division of Pearson New Zealand Ltd)
Penguin Books (South Africa) (Pty) Ltd, 24 Sturdee Avenue,
Rosebank, Johannesburg 2196, South Africa

Penguin Books Ltd, Registered Offices: 80 Strand, London WC2R 0RL, England

This translation first published in Penguin Books 2006

18th Printing

Translation coypright © Joachim Neugroschel, 2006
Introduction copyright © Francine du Plessix Gray, 2006
All rights reserved

LIBRARY OF CONGRESS CATALOGING-IN-PUBLICATION DATA

Sade, marquis de, 1740–1814.
[Philosophie dans le boudoir. English]
Philosophy in the boudoir, or, The immoral mentors / Marquis de Sade ; translated from
the French by Joachim Neugroschel ; introduction by Francine du Plessix Gray.
p. cm—(Penguin classics deluxe edition)
ISBN 978-0-14-303901-3
I. Neugroschel, Joachim. II. Title. III. Title: Philosophy in the boudoir.
IV. Title: Immoral mentors. V. Series.

PQ2063.S3A7613 2006
843'.6—dc22   2006044775

Printed in the United States of America
Set in Sabon

Contents

Introduction

In 1795, under the Directory regime that followed the over-throw of Robespierre and was liberated from that tyrant's puritanical censures, there appeared in Paris a slim little volume, anonymously published, entitled *La Philosophie dans le Boudoir*. Its frontispiece portrays three nude persons disporting themselves in the following manner: a winsome female teenager stands on a pillow, her legs slightly spread out; kneeling in front of her and behind her, two handsome adults, a man and a woman, perform cunnilingus on those private parts of the girl's that are closest to them, while the woman, having glided her hand between the girl's legs, fondles the man's phallus.

The illustration would be a fitting one for the entire oeuvre of its author, the Marquis de Sade. For this is a pornographer who often seems more interested in the sheer mathematics of sexuality—how many persons create the erotically ideal daisy chain, what is the maximum of exploitable orifices in any given number of human bodies—than in the carnal act itself. The least cruel and most joyous of Sade's works, the one that most harmoniously blends sexology, comedy, and politics, *Philosophy in the Boudoir* is as obsessively concerned with numerology as any of Sade's texts. Its principal protagonists are Madame de Saint-Ange, a depraved aristocratic beauty who boasts of having enjoyed twelve thousand lovers in her twelve years of marriage, and of having once been fucked "ninety times in front and in back within twenty-four hours"; Dolmancé, an elegant sodomite repelled by the very notion of female genitalia, whose penis measures "at least six inches around"; and Madame de Saint-Ange's younger brother, known simply as "the Chevalier," an equally libidinous fellow whose sister is one of his favorite sexual partners. Incited by Madame de Saint-Ange, the three roués decide to play School of Vice for a day, and to corrupt an exquisite fifteen-year old, Eugénie de Mistival, indoctrinating her, in Madame de Saint-Ange's words, "with all the principles of the most unbridled libertinage." ("Fuck—in a word—Fuck!" Saint-Ange instructs her pupil. "That's why you were put upon this earth. . . . Or are you obsessed with immortality? Well, it's by fucking, my dear, that you will linger in the reminiscences of men.") Eugénie turns out to be a quick, enthusiastic study. And the trio—now turned quartet—of *débauchés*, who are briefly joined by members of the working class—a gardener and a butler whose sexual organs are of even more phantasmagoric proportions than those of their aristocratic counterparts—end up having the time of their lives.

"This little tongue that's found underneath," Saint-Ange teaches Eugénie at the beginning of her instructions, "is called the 'clitoris.'" The corruption of virtuous young virgins had been a staple of pornography since the Renaissance. And *Philosophy*'s narrative structure—a series of seven dialogues throughout which the three adult libertines praise the vices and activities long considered most heinous by "civilized" mankind: egotism, adultery, incest, sodomy, atheism, blasphemy, theft, even murder—is a pastiche of the didactic conversational form long used in erotic literature. Which all leads one to believe that Sade's intent, in this work, was clearly parodic. Even the book's epigraph—"May every mother get her daughter to read this book"—is a pun on the epigraph to a notoriously scurrilous antiroyalist pamphlet of 1791 that reads "The mother will proscribe the reading to her daughter."

Within a half hour of perusing *Philosophy in the Boudoir*, readers are bound to wonder what kind of man wrote this fiercely corrupt book. They might be surprised to know that notwithstanding his numerous sexual aberrations and his dreadful temper Donatien-Alfonse-François, Marquis de Sade, born in 1740 into a family of extremely distinguished but penurious nobles who were natives of Avignon, was in many ways a decorous, home-loving citizen. He loved children as long as they obeyed him; he adored dogs; he was an accomplished gardener and landscape designer; he delighted in family games such as blind-man's buff and musical chairs. A fastidious gourmet, he particularly fancied quail stuffed with grape leaves and very fresh cream of chard soups. He was most particular about matters of personal hygiene and liked to bathe every day (a habit totally foreign to his eighteenth-century contemporaries, who might have bathed twice a month at the most). Sade even had his priggish side: he threw violent fits of rage when his wife exhibited her décolleté; and, having confined his lust to opera girls and whores, he much prided himself on not being an adulterer—the term only applied, in those days, to those who dallied with married women.

Sade's love for domesticity might be traced to his youth, which was even more deprived of parental affection, or of role models, than that of most of his peers. His mother was a distant, glacial woman who so hated family life that she sought refuge in a convent soon after her son's birth. His merrily bisexual playboy father, an erstwhile diplomat, was one of the most notorious rakes of Louis XV's reign. His depraved uncle, Abbé de Sade, a priest at whose Provençal estate Sade spent much of his early youth, set the norm for the family by running a bordello in his house. By the time he was in his early twenties the young Marquis seemed determined to outshine his elders in debauch, and had already earned a reputation as a flagrant libertine.

Although Sade's marriage, at the age of twenty-three, to a very chaste, pious girl of the newly wealthy bourgeoisie, Pélagie de Montreuil, was arranged by his father for the crassest material reasons—to boost the Sades' pathetic finances—there was a most unusual aspect to his ménage: within a few months of their wedding the young Sades became very fond of each other, and developed close, affectionate bonds that were highly unusual in the context of the eighteenth century's prearranged nuptials. The quiet, straitlaced Marquise, who would bear Sade three children, would remain passionately in love with her husband for the next twenty-five years. She calmly accepted his various sexual exploits, which by the time he was thirty had already earned him a few short jail terms, and included such unsavory offenses as whipping women with knotted cords and committing apostasy with icons of the Roman Catholic Church. As for Sade, his numerous letters to his wife show that he remained childishly dependent on her, and was perpetually terrified of losing her esteem: upon falling into any scrape, his first plea to authorities was "Don't let my wife know." In one particularly affectionate letter to Pélagie he addresses her as "My poopsie," "Olympian Ambrosia," "Star of Venus," "my doggie," "my baby," "Muhammad's bliss," "violet of the Garden of Eden," "celestial Kitten." (In the hundreds of passionate letters Madame de Sade wrote to her husband during his jail terms, she most often addresses him as "my good little boy.")

In 1771, the Sades moved to Provence to escape the scabrous reputation the Marquis's sexual transgressions had earned him in Paris, and went to live in a family chateau at La Coste—a forty-minute drive, these days, from Avignon—that he had inherited from his father. A pinnacle of pale gray fieldstone that commands breathtaking views over the valleys of the Vaucluse, La Coste, which had belonged to the Sade clan for many centuries, is set on a flat, rocky two-acre plateau that surmounts its village like a hovering eagle. The feudal character of the locale—the conical hill surmounted by its phantasmagoric castle—struck some central chord of Sade's imagination: it is the site he would look on throughout his life as his true roots, the only real home he'd ever had. And it would not be outlandish to conjecture that the very aura and topography of his dwelling at La Coste may have further aroused him to defy the law, in sexual matters as in every other sphere of life. Sade often expressed great nostalgia for those anarchic eras of the early Middle Ages, before the rise of nation-states, when every warrior lord had total control over his vassals and was not constrained by the edicts of any other ruler (don't only think eighteenth century if you want to understand Sade, think also tenth century). One of the most interesting and least emphasized aspects of the Marquis's character was his hatred of Paris and of Versailles and his thorough disdain for his peers—the corrupt aristocracy of his own time, the very kind of folk (Saint-Ange, Dolmancé) whose mores he satirizes in *Philosophy in the Boudoir*. Indeed, his eventual demise would be in great part caused by the fact that he refused to network with his fellow nobles: this haughty aloofness from the French court and from any circles of power, an aloofness he shared with his very rustic, reclusive wife, left him without any base of support in those frequent cases when he got into trouble with the law.

For within a year of his move to his cherished Provençal home, Sade became a hunted man, the victim of his outlandish need for sexual experimentation. In his most outrageous debauch to date, he had traveled to the nearby metropolis of Marseilles to choreograph a particularly festive orgy with four prostitutes and his valet at which he passed out some sloppily concocted homemade aphrodisiacs. These treats caused the girls to feel rather ill for twenty-four hours. Two of them brought charges of sodomy and attempted poisoning against Sade, and a week later he received the first of many official warrants that would be issued by the kings of France—first Louis XV, then Louis XVI—for his arrest. He continued to live on the lam for the next few years, seeking refuge in Italy, or in the wilds of the Vaucluse. But in 1777, after a few more outrageous bacchanals, he was finally captured thanks to the cunning of the woman who would turn out to be his nemesis: his altogether remarkable mother-in-law, Madame de Montreuil, who had successfully lobbied Louis XVI for a lettre de cachet, or sealed letter. This was an arbitrary order of arrest and detention that could be issued and signed only by the king and could imprison the accused for life without any legal hearing. Madame de Montreuil, a pivotal character of the Sadean epic, would foster in Sade a rabid hatred of mother-figures that is most harshly reflected in the one brutal moment of *Philosophy in the Boudoir*—the liberated Eugénie's truly sadistic rape, at the end of the book, of her own mother.

Sade would remain in jail for thirteen years, first at Vincennes, and then at the Bastille. It is in prison that this renegade, who if left at liberty would have remained yet another tedious eighteenth-century *débauché*, became a writer: the first drafts of

Justine and of *The 100 Days of Sodom,* the latter of which features the most gruesomely scatological of his fantasies and fully displays the numerological obsessions symptomatic of many borderline psychopaths, were written at the Bastille. He was not released from jail until 1790, six months after the onset of the Revolution. He rushed to see his wife, only to learn that after having stood by him throughout his years of disgrace, Pélagie had decided never to see him again, a decision that filled Sade with great sorrow. He had come out of jail a hundred pounds fatter than he'd entered it, swearing that he was now disgusted by all "impure pleasures." Yet such was the obese codger's charm that within weeks of his release he found new happiness with citizeness Constance Quesnet, a quiet, diligent divorced seamstress who, notwithstanding his slovenly physique and total penury, offered Sade as much affection and fidelity as his wife ever had.

Like many other aristocrats—Mirabeau, Lafayette, de Noailles—the Marquis vigorously served the revolutionary cause, carefully hiding his aristocratic origins and using the nom de guerre of "Louis Sade." He even rose to considerable power in Paris's political circles, being regarded as one of the capital's most gifted orators. Since this consummate survival artist was at heart a constitutional Royalist, and shrewdly concealed his equal loathing for Robespierre and for the insurgent mobs, there was much chicanery in his pose of the dedicated revolutionary. But whatever the disparity between Sade's public behavior and his inner beliefs, the 1790s, chastely spent under Constance's tender care, were his most productive years. During that decade he published, in strict anonymity, several of his pornographic works, of which *Justine, Philosophy in the Boudoir,* and *Juliette* have remained the most famous. Though the Directory's nouveaux riches had a taste for the most scabrous pornography, *Philosophy in the Boudoir,* issued in 1795, soon after *Justine,* went relatively unnoticed at the time of its publication. It may well have been swamped by the profusion of literature, both chaste and profane, that flooded the book market when the Terror's stringent censorship rules were lifted—novels of Diderot and Madame de Staël, translations of texts by Goethe, Ann Radcliffe, and William Godwin, which soon became cult books. Moreover, *Boudoir* was mostly printed in expensive, very limited editions that ended up in the libraries of a few Thermidorian parvenus.

A sign of Sade's astounding productivity during those few years of liberty is that he also published, under his own name, over twenty excruciatingly chaste, excruciatingly boring plays, and a few equally virtuous and tedious prose fictions, of which he was immensely fond: one of the greatest ironies of the Sade saga is that his highest ambition in life was to be a popular, honorable playwright, on the Marivaux or Congreve model. He would never acknowledge having authored any of the pornographic works for which he has become famous, looking on them merely as the potboilers with which he sustained his efforts as a respectable author.

Sade enjoyed only a decade of freedom. Notwithstanding his numerous noms de plume, his authorship of *Justine, Philosophy in the Boudoir,* and *Juliette* was eventually suspected by the government of yet another very prudish French ruler, Napoleon. In 1801, upon the First Consul's orders, Sade was incarcerated at the insane asylum of Charenton on the grounds that his writings expressed—this was a phrase specifically devised by the French police for Sade's writings—a state of "libertine dementia." He was to spend his last thirteen years there. The ever-devoted Constance at his side, he died at Charenton in 1814, at the age of seventy-four, already a legend, and still denying that he had ever written a line of smut.

A note on the curiously mythical manner in which Sade handles historical particulars in the narrative of *Philosophy in the Boudoir*: just the way it presents a Utopia of permanent arousal totally out of sync, alas, with sex-as-we-know-it—Dolmancé remains tumescent for the entire day, the virile member of Madame de Saint-Ange's gardener is thirteen inches long, one reveler's sperm jets ten feet up into the air—so the book's action occurs in a surreally scrambled time frame; it merges aspects of the Ancien Régime and of the Directory. The novel's manners and physical setting are clearly of the former, pre-

1789 era: guests arrive in liveried coaches and address each other in the formal *vous*; Madame de Saint-Ange's prodigious gardener, the only character addressed in the *tu* form, is relegated to strictly erotic functions, and is sent out of the room when any serious ideas are discussed ("Go out, Augustin, this isn't meant for your ears. But don't get too far away. We'll ring for you when we need you"). Yet there is mention of the Constitution of 1795 and of the solidly bourgeois "respect for property" fundamental to the Directory era. This hybrid historical aura enables Sade to indulge in the boldest and most modernist literary ploy of his career: the insertion, mid-book, of a seventy-five-page polemical tract entitled "Français, Encore un Effort si vous voulez être Republicains"—"Frenchmen, Some More Effort if You Wish to Become Republicans"—that is read aloud, as an entr'acte to the debauch, by Madame de Saint-Ange's younger brother.

The very title of the tract, and its dual pastiche of clichés used by the hoi-polloi sansculottes and by Sade's bête noire, the priggish, learned Robespierre, suggests that the author meant it to be a parody of revolutionary principles. It might also be seen as Sade's ultimate revenge against the Enlightenment philosopher who had been Robespierre's principal mentor, Jean-Jacques Rousseau. The most perverse aspect of *Philosophy in the Boudoir*, in fact, may well be Sade's vicious subversion of Rousseau. His reversal of the philosopher's view of Nature's goodness, already articulated in *Justine*, is here given a political spin. Whereas the state institutions provided by Rousseau's Social Contract allow us to recapture some of the goodness and innocence we enjoyed in our original "Nature," Sade sees all governments as evil because they thwart and curb humankind's innate cruelty. According to Sade—here the argument grows increasingly fiendish—it is precisely that cruelty which we must retain and cultivate in order to be true to "Nature." "Cruelty . . . is the first sentiment that nature teaches us. A child breaks its rattle, bites its wet nurse's nipple, and strangles its pet bird, long before it reaches the age of reason. . . . Among savages, cruelty is far closer to nature than among civilized men." In Sade's view, only the institution of far "gentler" laws can create a gentler society. "But laws may be so mild, so few in number, that all men, no matter what their characters, can easily comply." In sum, Sade's views of human character are quite as pessimistic as those of Thomas Hobbes, whom he ardently admired, but lead him to radically opposite political conclusions—the institution of absolute license as against absolute authority.

Another roguish argument of "Some More Effort" is that the newborn French Republic, having been founded on the dreadful crime of regicide, can only survive if it continues to be based on all other forms of crime—calumny, theft, rape, incest, murder, "for it is already steeped in crime," Sade writes in a passage that hints at his fundamentally Royalist beliefs. "And if it wished to pass from crime to virtue—that is, from violence to gentleness—it would plunge into an inertia that would definitely spell its doom." What is equally scandalous about this passage of *Boudoir* is that it takes a pivotal fixation of the Ancien Régime's elite—the unleashed satisfaction of sensual appetites sought by Dolmancé and Saint-Ange—and places it at the heart of post-revolutionary political discourse. Since the political liberation brought by the French Revolution is meaningless without sexual freedom, the imperative of a truly republican state, Sade preaches in "Some More Effort," is the institution of public bordellos in which both sexes can satisfy their erotic drive. Fucking well will make you into a better republican (in the 1790s sense of that word) because it is "the secret possibility of exhaling the dose of tyranny that nature has put at the bottom of [our] hearts"—a despotism that, if left unfulfilled, might run the risk of being redirected unto another human being.

Like all of Sade's pornographic works, *Philosophy in the Boudoir* raises the problem of the author's intent. Is Sade writing on a level of subversive irony or of deliberately obscure subterfuge? Does he take any of these wacky ideas seriously? To what degree are his narratives incited by his buffooning exhibitionism, or by his desire to startle, shock, jolt the reader into considering some extremist positions on libertarian individualism? The social and sexual anarchy touted in *Philosophy in the*

Boudoir, its disavowal of private property, and its cordial support of theft totally contradict the decorous British-style parliamentary system this staunch elitist held to in real life, the feudal possessiveness he expressed for his own family domains, the often hysterical jealousy he even displayed concerning his wife. The only passages of *Boudoir* unquestionably written in earnest are the articulations of Sade's atheism ("we relegate [such a God] forever to the oblivion from which the infamous Robespierre wanted him to emerge"). But then earnestness and consistency are the last features we should expect from this bastard child of the Enlightenment. One of the most maddening and modernist aspects of Sade's writing is that he has programmed himself to foil most methods of decoding and typification. Having robbed us of all traditional pacts of trust between reader and writer, having also cracked, through his excesses, any traditional critical grid through which we might evaluate him, he forces us to play his own textual game, which works through principles of fluidity, indeterminacy, and—this can bear repeating—sadomasochistic traumatization. "We don't have to know whether our actions will please or displease the object serving us," Sade states in *Philosophy in the Boudoir* in what might serve as a summation of his aesthetic tenets. "We need only shake the mass of our nerves as violently as possible . . . [and] there is no doubt that since pain affects us much more sharply than pleasure, the shocks reacting upon our nerves . . . are likewise more violent; our nerves vibrate far more vigorously."

Philosophy in the Boudoir

or,

The Immoral Mentors

DIALOGUES
AIMED AT THE EDUCATION OF YOUNG LADIES

*May every mother get her daughter
to read this book.*

To the Libertines

Voluptuaries of all ages and sexes—it is to you alone that I offer this work. Nourish yourselves on its principles: they foster your passions; and these passions, with which cold and shabby moralists try to intimidate you, are simply the means used by nature to help human beings attain nature's goals. Listen solely to those delicious passions; their source is the only one that will lead you to happiness.

Lubricious women: may the voluptuous Madame de Saint-Ange serve as your ideal; take her example and despise everything that flouts the divine laws of pleasure, to which she was fettered an entire lifetime.

You girls who have been tied down too long by the absurd and dangerous bonds of an imaginary virtue and a disgusting religion: imitate ardent Eugénie. Destroy, trample, as swiftly as she, all the ridiculous precepts inculcated by moronic parents.

And you, lovable profligates, who since childhood have had no other restraints than your desires and no other laws than your caprices: may that cynic Dolmancé serve as an example. Go as far as he if, like him, you wish to travel all the flowery roads prepared for you by lubricity; convince yourself at his school that it is only by expanding the sphere of his leanings and fantasies, it is only by sacrificing everything to sensual delight that the miserable individual known as "man" and tossed reluctantly into this dismal universe can manage to sow a few roses amid the brambles of life.

First Dialogue

MADAME DE SAINT-ANGE,
CHEVALIER DE MIRVEL

MADAME DE SAINT-ANGE. Good day, dear brother. Well, and where is Monsieur Dolmancé? CHEVALIER. He'll arrive at four p.m. on the dot. We're not dining until seven. So as you can see, we've got all the time in the world for chatting. MADAME DE SAINT-ANGE. Do you know, dear brother, that I slightly regret both my curiosity and all the obscene plans that we have forged today? Honestly, dear friend, you are too indulgent. The more reasonable I should be, the more my accursed mind grows angry and licentious. You pass everything on to me, which only serves to spoil me. . . . I'm twenty-six, I ought to be devout, and yet I'm nothing but the most dissolute of women. . . . No one can imagine my fancies, dear friend, imagine what I would like to do. I used to think that sticking to women would keep me virtuous; that by concentrating my desires within my own sex, I would no longer pour them into your sex. Vain assumptions, dear friend! The pleasures I tried to deprive myself of assailed my mind all the more ardently; and I saw that if a person is born, like me, to debauchery, it is useless to apply restraints: fiery desires will soon shatter them. Ultimately, my dear, I'm an amphibious creature: I love everything, I enjoy everything, I want to try all kinds of pleasure.

But, dear brother, admit it: isn't it utterly nonsensical for me to wish to know Dolmancé, that singular man, who, you say, has never in his life been able to see a woman as prescribed by custom? A sodomite by principle, he not only idolizes his own sex, he also yields to our sex purely on condition that it will supply him with the treasured charms that he is accustomed to using among men. Dear brother, this is my bizarre fantasy: I wish to be the Ganymede of this new Jupiter, I wish to savor his tastes, his debaucheries, I wish to be the victim of his follies. So far, as you know, my dear, I have given myself in that fashion only to you, for complaisance, or to one of my servants, who, paid to treat me like that, did so purely out of greed. Today, it is neither complaisance nor caprice, it is solely my taste that determines my interest. . . .

I see an inconceivable difference between the conduct that has enslaved me and the conduct that will enslave me to that bizarre mania, and I would like to know that difference. I beg you: describe Dolmancé for me, so that I may have him firmly in my mind before I see him arrive. As you know, I've never met him except briefly the other day, in a house where I spent only a few minutes with him.

CHEVALIER. Dolmancé, dear sister, has just turned thirty-six. He is tall, with a beautiful face and very lively and vivacious eyes. Nevertheless, his features are slightly hard and wicked. He has the finest teeth in the world, his bearing and his posture are slightly effeminate—no doubt, because of his habit of frequently acting like a woman. He is extremely elegant, his voice is lovely, he is talented, and he is totally a philosopher.

MADAME DE SAINT-ANGE. I hope he doesn't believe in God.

CHEVALIER. Not on your life! He's the most renowned atheist, the most immoral man. . . . He practices the most thorough and complete corruption, and he is the wickedest and most nefarious person in existence!

MADAME DE SAINT-ANGE. How exciting this is! I'm going to be crazy about him! What are his tastes, dear brother?

CHEVALIER. You know his tastes. The delights of Sodom are dear to him both in the active role and in the passive. In his pleasures he likes only men; and if nevertheless he occasionally agrees to try a woman, it is on condition that she be obliging enough to exchange her sex with his. I've spoken to him about you, I've warned him about your intentions. He accepts the deal and, for his part, he reminds you of the conditions. I must caution you, dear sister: he will flatly refuse if you try and commit him to any other stipulation.

"What I consent to undertake with your sister is," he states, "an adventure, an escapade with which I rarely soil myself and only with many precautionary measures."

MADAME DE SAINT-ANGE. "Soil?! . . . Precautionary measures!" I'm crazy about the language of these lovable people! We women also have exclusive words, which prove, like those words, their profound horror of anything not accepted in the usual ritual among us. . . . Well, tell me, dear brother: did he have you? You're twenty and you have an adorable figure—you can, I think, captivate such a man!

CHEVALIER. I won't hide my follies from you—the follies I've had with him. You're too intelligent to rebuke me. Actually, I like women and I submit to those bizarre adventures only when a lovable man urges me strongly. There is nothing I won't do in such a case. I am far from that ridiculous arrogance that makes our young whippersnappers feel that such a proposition should be met with a good caning! Is man the master of his tastes? We must pity those who have such singular tastes, but never insult them: their lack is a lack in nature. They are no more the masters of arriving in this world with bizarre tastes than we are the masters of arriving bowlegged or shapely. Besides, is a man saying something disagreeable to you when he reveals his desire to enjoy you? Absolutely not! He's paying you a compliment! Then why respond with insult and abuse? Only a moron could think in those terms. No reasonable man will ever speak differently about this issue than I do. But the world is populated by dull imbeciles who believe that you are being disrespectful when you confess to them that you find them suitable for pleasures. Spoiled by women, who are always jealous of anything that seems to interfere with their feminine rights, such men imagine that they are the Don Quixotes of these ordinary rights, and they brutalize everyone who fails to acknowledge their full scope.

MADAME DE SAINT-ANGE. Ah, my dear! Kiss me! If you thought otherwise, you wouldn't be my brother! However, I implore you: give me a few details about this man's body and about his pleasures with you.

CHEVALIER. A friend of mine informed Monsieur Dolmancé

about the superb member with which you know I am provided. He advised the Marquis de V . . . to invite the two of us to dinner. Once I was in his home, I naturally had to exhibit what I possessed. At first, curiosity seemed to be Monsieur Dolmancé's sole motive; but when a gorgeous ass was turned toward me, and I was told to enjoy myself, I promptly saw that pleasure alone was behind that examination. I warned Dolmancé about all the difficulties of this enterprise; but nothing appeared to daunt him. "I can take a ram," he said to me, "and you won't even have the glory of being the most redoubtable of the men who've perforated the ass that I'm offering you!"

The marquis was there. He encouraged us, handling, fondling, kissing everything the two of us displayed to each other. I was ready, I wanted at least a few preparations.

"Not on your life!" the marquis said to me. "You'd give Dolmancé only half the sensations he's expecting of you! He wants to be stabbed, he wants to be ripped apart—!"

"He'll be satisfied!" I said, plunging blindly into the abyss.

And might you believe, dear sister, that I went to a lot of trouble? Not a bit! Enormous as my dick may be, it disappeared without a trace; it reached the bottom of his innards, and the guy didn't seem to feel a thing! I treated Dolmancé like a friend; the excessive delight he reveled in, his wiggling, his delicious exclamations—everything soon made me happy, and I inundated him.

No sooner was I out than Dolmancé turned around to me, as red and disheveled as a bacchante: "Do you see the state you've put me in, dear Chevalier?" he said, offering me a dry and unruly dick, very long and at least six inches around. "Oh, my love, I plead with you! Be so kind and serve me as a woman after serving as her lover; and let me say that in your divine arms I tasted all the pleasures of the special joy that I cherish so powerfully."

Finding as little to object to in one as in the other, I consented. The marquis, removing his trousers in front of me, asked me to be so kind as to leave a bit of man with him, while I would be a woman with his friend. I treated him like Dolmancé, who, repaying a hundredfold all the strokes I inflicted on the third member of our trio, showered the bottom of my ass with that magical liquid that I squirted into V . . .'s ass almost at the same time.

MADAME DE SAINT-ANGE. Dear brother, you must have enjoyed the greatest pleasure as lucky Pierre. They say it's enchanting.

CHEVALIER. My angel, it's certainly the best place to be in. But whatever they say, those are merely wild adventures that I will never prefer to the pleasure of women.

MADAME DE SAINT-ANGE. Well, my dear! In order to compensate you today for your delicate service of love, I'm going to stoke your ardor with a virginal girl who is more beautiful than Love itself.

CHEVALIER. Come on! With Dolmancé. . . . You're bringing a female to your home?

MADAME DE SAINT-ANGE. It's for an education. A little girl I met at a convent last year when my husband was away, taking the waters. At the convent, the girl and I could do nothing, we didn't dare—too many eyes were fixed on us. But we promised one another that we'd get together the moment it became possible. I was so overwhelmed by this desire that in order to appease it, I made the acquaintance of her entire family. Her father is a libertine . . . whom I captivated. The beauty is coming at last, I'm waiting for her. We're going to spend two days together, two delightful days. I'll use most of this time to educate the young person. Dolmancé and I will fill her pretty little head with all the principles of the most unbridled libertinage. We will set her ablaze with our fires, we will nourish her with our philosophy, we will inspire her with our desires; and since I want to join a bit of practice to theory, since I want to follow each lecture with a demonstration, I have chosen you, my dear brother, to cull the myrtles of Cythera, and Dolmancé to cull the roses of Sodom. I will have two pleasures at once: the enjoyment of those criminal delights, and the bliss of teaching them and inspiring a taste for them in the lovable and innocent girl that I am drawing into our snares. Well, Chevalier, is this project worthy of my imagination?

CHEVALIER. Your imagination alone could have spawned it.

It is divine, my dear sister; and I promise to do an excellent job of playing the enchanting role that you have cast me in. Ah, you little minx! How deeply you'll enjoy educating this child! What a delight to corrupt her, to suffocate in that young heart all the seeds of virtue and religion that were planted in her by her tutors! I swear, it's too crafty for me.

MADAME DE SAINT-ANGE. It's quite certain that I will spare nothing in order to pervert her, to degrade her, to overthrow all the false moral principles that have benumbed her mind. I want to devote just two lessons to make her as wicked as myself . . . as impious . . . as debauched. Warn Dolmancé, inform him when he arrives. Within seconds, the venom of his immoral doings, circulating in that young heart together with the venom that I inculcate, will uproot all the seeds of virtue that might germinate there but for us.

CHEVALIER. It would be impossible to find a better man: irreligion, impiety, inhumanity, libertinage trickle down from Dolmancé's lips as the mystical unction once trickled down from the lips of the famous Bishop of Cambrai. Dolmancé is the most profound seducer, the most corrupt man, the most dangerous. . . . Ah! My dear! If your pupil responds to her tutor's lessons, I can guarantee her quick doom.

MADAME DE SAINT-ANGE. It won't take long given what I know about her natural aptitude. . . .

CHEVALIER. But tell me, dear sister! Aren't you fearful about her parents? What if the little girl tattles when she returns home?

MADAME DE SAINT-ANGE. You needn't be afraid—I've seduced her father. . . . He is all mine. Must I finally confess to you? I submitted to him so he'd turn a blind eye. He is ignorant of my plans, and he would never dare investigate them. . . . I've got him in my clutches.

CHEVALIER. Your methods are horrible!

MADAME DE SAINT-ANGE. They have to be if they are certain to work.

CHEVALIER. Now please tell me: who is this young person?

MADAME DE SAINT-ANGE. Her name is Eugénie. She is the daughter of a man named Mistival, one of the richest merchants in Paris. The father himself is about thirty-six years old, the mother at most thirty-two, and the girl fifteen. Mistival is as licentious as his wife is devout. As for Eugénie, dear friend, it's no use my trying to describe her: she transcends my paintbrushes. Let it suffice for you to be convinced that neither you nor I have ever seen anything that delicious in the world.

CHEVALIER. If you can't paint her, then at least sketch her for me, so that I can more or less know whom I'll be dealing with, and so that I might more effectively picture the idol to which I must sacrifice.

MADAME DE SAINT-ANGE. Well, my friend, her chestnut hair, which can scarcely be clutched in one hand, descends all the way to the bottom of her buttocks; her complexion is a dazzling white, her nose slightly aquiline, and her eyes are a fiery ebony! . . . Ah, my dear! Those eyes are irresistible! You can't imagine all the follies those eyes have incited me to commit! . . . If you could only see the lovely brows that crown them, the appealing lids that line them! . . . Her lips are very small, her teeth superb, and everything so fresh! One of her beautiful features is the elegant way her wonderful head is attached to her shoulders, her noble manner when she turns it. . . .

Eugénie is tall for her age, she looks seventeen. Her figure is a model of elegance and finesse, her bosom delightful. . . . She has a pair of the loveliest breasts. Neither is large enough for a handful, but they are so sweet . . . so fresh . . . so white! . . . I've lost my mind twenty times when I've kissed them! And if you could have seen how she's responded to my caresses. . . . How those two big eyes have painted her mental state! My friend, I don't know what lies ahead! But to judge by what I know already, Olympus has never had a deity to match her!

Ah, I hear her coming. Leave us. . . . Go through the garden so you don't run into her. And be punctual for our rendezvous.

CHEVALIER. Your portrait of her guarantees my punctuality. . . . Oh, God! To go away! To leave you in the state I'm in! Farewell! . . . A kiss . . . a kiss . . . a single kiss, dear sister, to keep me at least until then. (*She kisses him, feels his penis through his trousers, and the young man hurries away.*)

Second Dialogue

MADAME DE SAINT-ANGE,
EUGÉNIE

MADAME DE SAINT-ANGE. Ah! Good day, my beauty. I've been fervently looking forward to your arrival—and you can readily infer my impatience if you read my heart.

EUGÉNIE. Oh, my darling! I was so eager to be in your arms that I thought I'd never arrive! One hour before leaving, I was terrified that everything might change! My mother was adamantly opposed to this delightful visit! She claimed that it was unsuitable for a girl of my age to go out alone. But, the day before yesterday, my father had mistreated her so severely that a single glance from him curtailed her resistance. She finally consented to what my father permitted, and I dashed over here. They've given me two days. Your carriage and one of your ladies must absolutely see me home the day after to-morrow!

MADAME DE SAINT-ANGE. What a brief period, my angel! It's scarcely enough time for me to express all the feelings you inspire in me. And besides, we have to chat. Don't you know that during this interview I must initiate you into the most secret mysteries of Venus? Will two days be enough?

EUGÉNIE. Ah, if I don't know everything by then, I'll remain. . . . I've come here to be taught, and I won't leave until I'm an expert.

MADAME DE SAINT-ANGE (*kissing her*). Oh, my darling! How many things will we do and say to one another! By the way, would you care for a bite, my queen? The lesson might go on for a long time.

EUGÉNIE. Dear friend, my sole desire is to listen to you. We already had lunch several miles from here, and I won't be hungry again until eight p.m.

MADAME DE SAINT-ANGE. Then let's go to my boudoir, we'll be more comfortable there. I've already warned my servants. Rest assured that no one will dream of interrupting us. (*They embrace as they pass into the boudoir.*)

Third Dialogue

MADAME DE SAINT-ANGE,
EUGÉNIE, DOLMANCÉ

The action takes place in a lovely boudoir.

EUGÉNIE (*very surprised to find a man, whom she didn't expect*). Oh, my God! This is treason, my dear friend.

MADAME DE SAINT-ANGE (*equally surprised*). What fluke brings you here now, Monsieur? I believe that you weren't scheduled to arrive until four p.m.

DOLMANCÉ. I always come as early as possible in order to enjoy my delight in seeing you, Madame. I ran into your brother. He felt I ought to attend the lessons you are to give Mademoiselle. And since he knew that this was the school where the courses would be provided, he secretly showed me the way—nor did he imagine that you would disapprove. As for him: knowing that these practical demonstrations won't be necessary until after the theoretical groundwork, he won't join us until later on.

MADAME DE SAINT-ANGE. Honestly, Dolmancé, you're playing a trick!

EUGÉNIE. Which I won't fall for, my good friend. This is all your handiwork. . . . You might at least have consulted me. . . . I'm so embarrassed that it will certainly interfere with all our plans.

MADAME DE SAINT-ANGE. I give you my word, Eugénie, that it was my brother who thought up this surprise all alone. But don't let it frighten you. I know Dolmancé to be a lovable person, and his level of philosophy that we need for your instruction is very useful for our plans. In regard to his discretion, I guarantee it as much as my own. So, my dear, familiarize yourself with the man most able to form you in the world and to guide you on the road to pleasure and happiness that we want to travel together.

EUGÉNIE (*blushing*). All the same, I'm very confused. . . .

DOLMANCÉ. Come on, beautiful Eugénie. Make yourself comfortable. . . . Modesty is an old-fashioned virtue, which, given your charms, you must certainly do without.

EUGÉNIE. But decency—

DOLMANCÉ. Another medieval custom, which is no longer valued today. It is so unnatural! (*DOLMANCÉ grabs EUGÉNIE and hugs and kisses her.*)

EUGÉNIE (*defending herself*). Stop that, Monsieur! Honestly, you lack respect!

MADAME DE SAINT-ANGE. Eugénie, believe me. Let's both of us stop being prudes with this charming man. I don't know him any better than you do. But look at the way I submit to him! (*She kisses him lecherously on the mouth.*) Imitate me!

EUGÉNIE. Oh, I'd love to! I don't know whom I'd rather emulate! (*She submits to DOLMANCÉ, who kisses her ardently with his tongue in her mouth.*)

DOLMANCÉ. Oh, what a delightful and delicious creature!

MADAME DE SAINT-ANGE (*also kissing her*). You little slut—do you believe I won't take my turn? (*At this point, DOLMANCÉ, holding both of them in his arms, flicks his tongue in and out for fifteen minutes, and the two women return the favor to him and to each other.*)

DOLMANCÉ. Ah, these preliminaries intoxicate me with their sensual delight! Ladies, you can take my word for it! This room is extraordinarily hot! Let's get comfortable! We can chat infinitely better.

MADAME DE SAINT-ANGE. I agree! Let's change into these gauze simars. They veil only the charms that must be hidden from desire.

EUGÉNIE. Honestly, my dear, you make me do such things! . . .

MADAME DE SAINT-ANGE (*helping her undress*). Utterly ridiculous things, right?

EUGÉNIE. At least very indecent things. I swear. . . . Oh! How you kiss me!

MADAME DE SAINT-ANGE. Your lovely bosom! It's a rose that's scarcely budded.

DOLMANCÉ (*viewing EUGÉNIE'S breasts without touching*

them). And that promises further charms . . . far more laudable charms.

MADAME DE SAINT-ANGE. More laudable?

DOLMANCÉ. Yes, yes, on my honor! (*While speaking, he prepares to turn* EUGÉNIE *around to examine her from the back.*)

EUGÉNIE. Oh, no, no, I beg you!

MADAME DE SAINT-ANGE. No, Dolmancé. I don't want you to see . . . an object to which you are now devoted, but which, once it's in your mind, you could easily discuss with sangfroid. We need your lessons, give them to us, and the myrtle leaves that you wish to pick will then shape your wreath.

DOLMANCÉ. Fine! But in order to demonstrate, to give this beautiful child her first lessons in libertinage, you must, at least, Madame, be willing to make yourself available.

MADAME DE SAINT-ANGE. Very well! As you can see, I'm stark naked. So teach away over my body as much as you like!

DOLMANCÉ. Ah, the beautiful body! . . . It is Venus in the flesh, embellished by the Graces!

EUGÉNIE. Oh, my dear friend. What charms! Give me time to make their acquaintance, let me cover them with kisses. (*She does so.*)

DOLMANCÉ. What excellent aptitude! A bit less ardor, beautiful Eugénie. All I ask of you at this moment is your attention.

EUGÉNIE. Fine, I'm listening, I'm listening. . . . It's just that she's so beautiful, so plump and dimpled, so fresh! Ah, how bewitching my dear friend is—don't you agree, Monsieur?

DOLMANCÉ. She's beautiful, assuredly . . . perfectly beautiful. But I am convinced that you are in no way inferior to her. . . . Come on, listen to me, my pretty little pupil, or else, if you are not docile, you may fear that I will use the rights to which I am so richly entitled as your instructor.

MADAME DE SAINT-ANGE. Oh, yes, yes, Dolmancé. She's all yours. She must be scolded thoroughly if she misbehaves!

DOLMANCÉ. I could easily go beyond mere rebukes.

EUGÉNIE. Oh, just heaven, you frighten me! And what would you do to me, Monsieur?

DOLMANCÉ (*stammering and kissing* EUGÉNIE *on her lips*). I'd punish you, chastise you, and that pretty little ass could readily answer to me for the errors of your mind. (*He smacks her through the gauze simar that* EUGÉNIE *is now wearing.*)

MADAME DE SAINT-ANGE. Yes, I approve of your plan, but not the rest. Let's begin our lecture. Otherwise what little time we've got to enjoy Eugénie will remain tangled in preliminaries, and the lesson won't be taught.

DOLMANCÉ (*touching each body part that he discusses*). Let me begin.

I won't speak about those globes of flesh. You know as well as I do, Eugénie, that they are indiscriminately called "bosom," "breasts," "tits." They are very useful for pleasure; a lover views them when enjoying; he caresses them, he fondles them. Some lovers even make them the center of their pleasure. With his member nestling between the two Venus mounds, the woman squeezes and compresses his member; and after some twisting and turning, a few men manage to discharge the delicious balm of life, which, when gushing forth, constitutes all the happiness of the libertines. . . . Now, as for this member, which we must talk about incessantly, Madame, isn't it time we discussed it with our pupil?

MADAME DE SAINT-ANGE. I think so, too.

DOLMANCÉ. Well, Madame, I'm going to stretch out on this sofa. You will place yourself near me, you will take hold of the subject, and you yourself will explain its features to our young pupil. (DOLMANCÉ *lies down, and* MADAME DE SAINT-ANGE *demonstrates.*)

MADAME DE SAINT-ANGE. This scepter of Venus that you see before you, Eugénie, is the primary agent of the pleasures of love. It is known par excellence as the "member." There isn't a single part of the human body that it doesn't enter. Always acquiescent to the passions of the person wielding it, the member soon nestles here (*she touches* EUGÉNIE's *cunt*). That's the ordinary route . . . the one used most but not the most agreeable one. In the quest for a more mysterious temple, it is often here (*she spreads her cheeks and reveals her asshole*) that the libertine seeks his pleasure: we will return to this enjoyment, the most delightful one of all. The mouth, the bosom, the armpits frequently offer him other altars for burning his incense. And whatever place he prefers, he strokes for a few moments and then shoots a white, sticky liquid, plunging the man into a delirium intense enough to procure for him the sweetest pleasures that he can expect in his lifetime.

EUGÉNIE. Oh, how I'd love to see this liquid pouring!

MADAME DE SAINT-ANGE. You could do so if I simply rub the member with my hand. See how it stiffens as I jiggle it! These movements are known as "masturbation," and, in libertine terms, these actions are called "jerking off."

EUGÉNIE. Oh, my dear friend! Let me jerk that gorgeous member!

DOLMANCÉ. I can't stand it any longer! Let her do it, Madame. Her ingenuousness is giving me an awful hard-on.

MADAME DE SAINT-ANGE. I am against this agitation! Be reasonable, Dolmancé! By reducing the activity of your animal drives, the outpouring of this semen will diminish the fire of your clarification.

EUGÉNIE (handling DOLMANCÉ's testicles). Oh, my dear friend! I'm so angry at the way you thwart my desires! And what about these little spheres? What are they used for and what are they called?

MADAME DE SAINT-ANGE. The technical word is indeed "balls," and the scientific term is "testicles." These balls contain the reservoir of that prolific semen that I have just spoken of. It is their ejaculation in the woman's uterus that produces the human species. But we won't focus on these details, Eugénie. They belong more to the realm of medicine than that of libertinage. A pretty girl should concentrate only on fucking, and never on bearing children. We will skip everything connected with the lowbrow mechanism of reproduction, and we will chiefly and uniquely align ourselves with the libertine delights, whose spirit never cares about breeding.

EUGÉNIE. But, my dear friend. I can barely clutch this huge member in my hand, and yet you assure me that it can penetrate a hole as small as the hole in your behind. The penetration must hurt the woman terribly!

MADAME DE SAINT-ANGE. Whether she's penetrated in front

or in back, if a woman is still unaccustomed to such treatment, then she'll always feel pain. It has pleased nature to help us achieve happiness only through pain. But once nature is vanquished, nothing can replace the pleasure felt by the woman; and the pleasure enjoyed during the penetration of her ass is incontestably preferable to all the delights that can be gained by the penetration in front. And besides: what dangers a woman avoids if her ass is pierced! There is less risk to her health, and no risk of pregnancy. For now, I don't wish to dwell any further on this type of joy. Our mentor will, Eugénie, soon amply analyze it; and, joining practice to theory, he will hopefully convince you, my dear friend, that of all the pleasures of enjoyment, this pleasure is the only kind that you should prefer.

DOLMANCÉ. I beg you, Madame, please hurry with your explanations, I can't hold out any longer. I'll discharge in spite of myself, and my fearful member will be reduced to nothing and will no longer serve you in your lessons.

EUGÉNIE. What, my dear friend? He'd shrink if he lost the semen you're talking about?! Oh, do let me make him lose it so I can see what becomes of it. . . . And then, I'd so much enjoy watching it gush!

MADAME DE SAINT-ANGE. No, no, Dolmancé! Stand up! You must see it as a reward for your efforts, and I can render your payment only after you've earned it.

DOLMANCÉ. Fine! But in order to convince Eugénie more effectively that everything we tell her about pleasure is true, would it be indelicate of you, say, to jerk her off in my presence?

MADAME DE SAINT-ANGE. Not indelicate at all. And I'll proceed all the more joyfully as this lewd episode is able to help our lessons. Lie down on this sofa, my dear friend.

EUGÉNIE. Oh, God! Oh, the delicious niche! But why all these mirrors?

MADAME DE SAINT-ANGE. By reflecting the positions in a thousand different images, the mirrors infinitely multiply the same delights in the eyes of the people enjoying them on this ottoman. That way, no part of either body can be concealed: everything must be exposed. And there are as many groups surrounding the people entangled in love, as many imitators of their pleasures, as many delightful tableaux whose lechery is intoxicating, and which can soon serve to crown our efforts.

EUGÉNIE. What a delicious invention.

MADAME DE SAINT-ANGE. Dolmancé, strip the victim yourself!

DOLMANCÉ. Nothing could be easier since it's a matter of removing that gauze in order to view those arousing charms naked. (*He strips her naked, and he initially peers at her behind.*) I'm going to see it—this divine and precious ass that I covet so ardently! . . . Damn it all! What fullness and freshness, what splendor and elegance! . . . I've never seen a more beautiful ass!

MADAME DE SAINT-ANGE. Ah, you rascal! Your very first homage confirms your leanings and your pleasures!

DOLMANCÉ. But can there be anything in the world as fabulous as that ass? Where would love find more divine altars? . . . Eugénie! . . . Sublime Eugénie! Let me shower that ass with the sweetest caresses! (*He fondles it and kisses it passionately.*)

MADAME DE SAINT-ANGE. Stop it, you libertine! . . . You're forgetting that Eugénie belongs to me alone! She is the sole payment for the lessons she awaits from you. It is only after receiving them that she will become their reward. Curb your ardor, or I'll be angry!

DOLMANCÉ. Ah, you slut! You're jealous! Well then hand me your ass; I'll shower it with the same homage! (*He removes* MADAME DE SAINT-ANGE'S *gauze simar and caresses her behind.*) Oh, how beautiful it is, my angel, and how delicious to boot! Let me compare both asses, let me admire them side by side: it's Ganymede next to Venus. (*He showers both behinds with kisses.*) Madame, in order to leave the magical spectacle of so much beauty before my eyes, couldn't you, in entangling one another, endlessly offer my vision those enchanting asses that I idolize.

MADAME DE SAINT-ANGE. Marvelous! Now then, are you satisfied? (*The two women intertwine in such a manner as to show their two asses to* DOLMANCÉ.)

DOLMANCÉ. It couldn't be better! This is exactly what I was asking you for. And now shake those gorgeous asses with all the fire of lechery! Make them rise and fall rhythmically. Let them follow the impressions moved by pleasure. . . . Good, good! That's delicious! . . .

EUGÉNIE. Ah, dear Madame. You give me such intense pleasure! . . . What's the name for what we're doing?

MADAME DE SAINT-ANGE. It's called "jerking," dear friend . . . for mutual pleasure. But listen: let's change positions. Examine my "cunt." That's what they call the temple of Venus. Scrutinize the cavern that's covered by my hand: I'm going to open it partway. The elevation that you see crowning it is known as the "mound" or "Venus mound." It gets hairy at fourteen or fifteen, when a girl starts having her period. The little tongue that's found underneath is called the "clitoris." That's where a woman's entire sensitivity is located; it's the source of mine. You couldn't tickle this part without having me swoon with pleasure. . . . Try it! Oh, you little slut! How well you do it! It's as if you'd never done anything else in all your life! . . . Stop! . . . Stop! . . . No, I tell you, I won't give in! Ah! Hold me back, Dolmancé! I'm about to lose my mind under the bewitching fingers of this pretty girl!

DOLMANCÉ. Perhaps, in order to cool your ardor—if possible—by varying it, you can jerk off Eugénie yourself! Hold back and let her submit on her own. . . . There! Yes! . . . In that position! This way, her pretty ass will slip under my hands. I'll "pollute" her lightly with one finger. . . . Submit, Eugénie. Abandon all your senses to pleasure. Let pleasure be the sole god of your existence. It is to pleasure alone that a girl must sacrifice everything, and nothing should be as sacred to her eyes as pleasure.

EUGÉNIE. Ah, I can feel that nothing in the world is as delicious. . . . I'm beside myself! I don't know what I'm saying or what I'm doing! . . . My senses are intoxicated!

DOLMANCÉ. Just look at how intensely the little slut comes! . . . Her anus is tight enough to slice off my finger! . . . What bliss it would be to fuck her up the ass right now! (*He stands up and shifts his cock to the girl's asshole.*)

MADAME DE SAINT-ANGE. Just be patient for another moment. We have to focus totally on educating this dear girl! . . . It is so sweet molding her.

DOLMANCÉ. Fine! You can see, Eugénie: after a more or less lengthy excitement, the testicles swell, and they emit a liquid that plunges a woman into the most delicious rapture. This pleasure is known as "ejaculate" or "come." If your good friend permits, I'll show you how much more energetically and imperiously this process takes place in men.

MADAME DE SAINT-ANGE. Wait, Eugénie. I'm going to teach you a new way of plunging a woman into the most extreme ecstasy. Pull your thighs far apart. . . . Dolmancé, you can see that, by placing her in this fashion, I'm exposing her asshole! Lick her there while I lick her cunt, and, if possible, let's make her faint three or four times in a row. Your Venus mound is enchanting, Eugénie. How I love to kiss this down! . . . Your clitoris, which I now see more clearly, is only slightly formed, but very sensitive. . . . How you wriggle! . . . Let me open a bit further! . . . Ah! . . . You are definitely a virgin! . . . Tell me the effect you're going to produce when our two tongues slip simultaneously into your two openings. (*Their tongues do so.*)

EUGÉNIE. Oh, my darling! It's wonderful! It's a sensation that's impossible to depict! It would be very difficult to say which of your two tongues is more intoxicating!

DOLMANCÉ. In the position I've placed myself in, my cock is very close to your hands, Madame. Would you be so kind as to jerk it, while I slurp this divine asshole. Slip your tongue farther in, Madame. Don't just lick her clitoris. Let that delicious tongue penetrate all the way to her womb: that's the best way to hasten the ejaculation of the come.

EUGÉNIE (*stiffening*). Oh, I can't anymore, I'm dying! Don't desert me, my friends. I'm about to faint! . . . (*She reaches an orgasm between her two instructors.*)

MADAME DE SAINT-ANGE. Well, my darling, how do you feel after the pleasure we've given you?

EUGÉNIE. I'm dead, I'm shattered. . . . I'm devastated! . . . But please explain two words that you've used and that I don't understand. First of all: what does "womb" mean?

MADAME DE SAINT-ANGE. It's a sort of vase resembling a bottle: its neck embraces the man's member and receives the come produced in the woman by the oozing of the glands, and in the man by the ejaculation, which we'll show you. And the blending of these liquids generates the seed that brings forth either a boy or a girl.

EUGÉNIE. Ah! I understand. This definition also explains the words "semen" or "come," which I didn't quite grasp. And so it's the union of those two juices that's necessary for the formation of the fetus?

MADAME DE SAINT-ANGE. Definitely. Even though it's been proven that the fetus owes its existence purely to the man's come. But, launched alone, this come would never succeed without blending with the woman's come. The come that *we* furnish serves only to elaborate. It doesn't create, it merely helps creation without causing it. Some modern scientists actually claim that this come is useless. Hence, the moralists, who are always guided by scientific discoveries, have concluded, with great likelihood, that in this case, the child formed with the father's blood owes his filial love purely to his father. This assertion seems quite probable, and even though I'm a woman, I won't try to fight it.

EUGÉNIE. Dear friend, in my heart I feel the proof of what you're saying, for I'm crazy about my father, but.I feel that I hate my mother.

DOLMANCÉ. There's nothing astonishing about your predilection. I've felt the same way. I still haven't gotten over my father's death; but when I lost my mother, I lit a bonfire! . . . I despised her with all my heart! Don't be afraid to adopt those same feelings, Eugénie. They are quite natural. Formed, as we are, purely by the blood of our fathers, we owe absolutely nothing to our mothers. Besides, they merely submitted to the act, while other fathers instigated it. Hence, our fathers wanted our birth, while our mothers simply acquiesced. What a difference in the emotions!

MADAME DE SAINT-ANGE. A thousand more reasons support your feelings, Eugénie. If there is any mother in the world who deserves to be despised, it is assuredly *your* mother! Ill-tempered, superstitious, sanctimonious, grumbling . . . and revoltingly prudish! I would bet that this straitlaced creature has never made a faux pas in all her life. . . . Ah! My darling! How I hate virtuous women! . . . We'll come back to this topic.

DOLMANCÉ. Wouldn't it now be necessary for Eugénie, guided by myself, to learn to repay what you have just lent her—to jerk off in front of me?

MADAME DE SAINT-ANGE. I consent, I even find it useful. And during the process, you no doubt wish to see my asshole, Dolmancé?

DOLMANCÉ. Madame, can you doubt the pleasure with which I will pay it my sweetest tribute?

MADAME DE SAINT-ANGE (*presenting her ass cheeks to DOLMANCÉ*). Well, do you find me *comme il faut* like this?

DOLMANCÉ. You're marvelous! That way I can repay you with the same services that were so beneficial to Eugénie. Now, you silly thing! Place your head between your friend's legs and let your pretty tongue give her the same care that you have just obtained from her. By all means! In this position, I can possess both your assholes! I'll fondle Eugénie's hole while I rim her beautiful friend's hole. There. . . . Great! . . . Look how smoothly we act together!

MADAME DE SAINT-ANGE (*swooning*). I'm dying, God damn it! Dolmancé, how I love to touch your gorgeous dick while I come! I would like it to inundate me with juice! Jerk me! . . . Lick me! . . . God damn it! Oh, how I love to be a whore when my sperm ejaculates like that! It's over! I can't anymore! . . . The two of you have overwhelmed me! . . . I don't believe I've ever had so much pleasure in all my born days!

EUGÉNIE. How glad I am to be the cause. But there's a word, dear friend, a word that escaped you and that I don't understand. What do you mean by that expression "whore"? I apologize, but I'm here to learn.

MADAME DE SAINT-ANGE. The word "whore," my lovely, refers to those freely available victims of male debauchery, women who are always ready to submit, either for their temperament or for their profit. They are happy and respectful creatures who are stigmatized by public opinion but crowned by pleasure. More crucial to society than any prudes, they have the courage to serve it and to sacrifice the good reputation that society dares to deprive them of unjustly. Hurray for the women who feel honored by that title! They are truly lovable, the only real philosophers of the Enlightenment! As for me, my darling, I've been working a dozen years to merit that title, and I can assure you: far from taking offense, I find it amusing. Moreover, I love being called a whore while I'm getting fucked. This insult gets me hot!

EUGÉNIE. Oh, I understand that, my dear, and I wouldn't be angry if I were called a whore, much less if I deserved it! But doesn't virtue oppose such misconduct, and aren't we affronting virtue by behaving as we are?

DOLMANCÉ. Ah! Renounce all virtues, Eugénie! Is there a single sacrifice we can make to those false deities that's worth a minute of the pleasures we savor while outraging them? Why, virtue is nothing but a chimera, whose cult consists of perpetual immolations, countless revolts against the inspirations of the temperament. Can such processes be natural? Does nature advise us to do something outrageous? Don't be the dupe, Eugénie, of those women who you hear are virtuous. It is not, if you like, the same passions as we whom they serve—they've got other ones, which are often far more horrible. These passions are pride, ambition, greed, frequently just the coldness of a temperament that never counsels them. I ask you: Do we owe anything to such creatures? Don't they follow purely the impressions of vanity? Is it therefore better, wiser, more appropriate to sacrifice to egotism rather than to the passions? For myself, I believe that either is as valid as the other. The person who harks only to the latter voice is probably more rational, because reason alone is the organ of nature; whereas the former voice is the voice of stupidity and prejudice. A single drop of come ejaculated by this member, Eugénie, is more precious to me than the sublimest acts of a virtue that I despise.

EUGÉNIE. (*The participants have grown a bit calmer; the women, in their gauze simars, are half reclining on the sofa, and* DOLMANCÉ *is near them in a large easy chair.*) But there are different kinds of virtue. For instance, what do you think of piety?

DOLMANCÉ. What can that virtue mean for someone who does not believe in religion? And who really believes in religion? But let's tackle it systematically, Eugénie. Don't you call religion the pact linking man to his Maker and committing him, by way of worship, to display his gratitude for the existence he receives from that sublime Creator?

EUGÉNIE. "Religion" couldn't be defined better.

DOLMANCÉ. Good! If it is demonstrated that man owes his existence purely to the irresistible plans of nature; if it is proved that he has existed on this globe as long as the globe itself; that, like the oak tree, like the lion, like the ores in the bowels of this globe, man is a creation dictated solely by the existence of this globe and owes nobody—whoever it may be—any gratitude for his existence; if it is attested that this God, regarded by fools as the Creator and single producer of everything we see— that this God is merely the *ne plus ultra* of human reason, merely the phantom invented the moment that reason sees nothing further; if it is shown that the existence of this God is impossible, and that nature, always acting, always moving, has itself devised what fools like to give nature gratuitously; if it is certain that—assuming this inert creature exists—it must definitely be the most ridiculous of all creatures, since it functioned for only one day, next tarrying in loathsome inaction for millions of centuries. Now assuming it existed as described for us by the religions, it would assuredly be the most detestable of beings, since it introduced evil into the world, whereas its omnipotence could prevent it. If, I say, all this were proved as incontestable, do you believe, Eugénie, that the piety linking man to this moronic, inadequate, ferocious, and despicable Creator would be a highly crucial virtue?

EUGÉNIE (*to MADAME DE SAINT-ANGE*). What? Honestly, my dear friend! Is the existence of God really just a fantasy?

MADAME DE SAINT-ANGE. And a contemptible fantasy to boot!

DOLMANCÉ. A person must have lost his mind to believe in God. The product of either fear or weakness, this abominable phantom, Eugénie, is useless for the system of the earth. It would even be infallibly harmful. You see, its will, which must be just, could never ally itself with the injustice essential to the laws of nature. It would constantly have to wish for goodness, which nature desires only as compensation for the evil that serves its laws. It would have to act continuously, and nature, one of whose laws is that perpetual motion, could only rival and perpetually resist it. But, people will argue, God and nature are one and the same. Wouldn't that be absurd? The created thing cannot be equal to the being that creates it: Can the clock be the clockmaker? People will then argue: nature is nothing, it is God that is everything. More stupidity! There are necessarily at least two entities in the universe: the creating agent and the created individual. Now, who or what is that creating force? This is the only problem that needs to be solved; it is the only question that needs to be answered.

If matter acts and moves through arrangements that are unknown to us; if motion is inherent in matter; if, because of its energy, motion alone can ultimately create, produce, preserve, maintain, balance, in the immense plains of space, all the globes whose sight amazes us, and whose uniform and invariable courses fill us with respect and admiration, why do we need to seek a force that is foreign to all those things, since this active faculty is found essentially in nature itself, which is nothing but matter in action? Will your deific chimera explain anything? I challenge anyone to prove it. Supposing I'm wrong about the inner faculties of matter: I merely face a single difficulty. What do you accomplish by offering me your God? You simply give me one more difficulty. And why should I, for not understanding something, accept something that I understand even less? Should I try to examine, to depict your dreadful God with the help of dogmas of the Christian religion? . . . Let's see how Christianity portrays me. . . .

What do I see in the God of this infamous cult but a barbaric and inconsistent being, who creates a world one day, then repents its construction the next day? What do I see but a weak being who can never succeed in forming man according to his will? This creature, although deriving from him, dominates him. And this creature can offend him, thereby deserving eternal tortures! What a weak being that God is! Come on! He managed to create everything we see, and yet he is unable to shape a man in his own image? But, you will reply, If man had been created like that, he wouldn't have any merit. What a platitude! And why is it necessary for man to merit something from his God? If God had made him totally good, man could never have done any evil, and only then would the work be worthy of a God. Giving man a choice is tempting him. Now God, in his infinite prescience, certainly knew what the results would be. That is, For no apparent reason, God dooms the creature that he himself has molded. What a horrible God this God is! What a monster! What a scoundrel—more deserving of our hatred and our implacable vengeance! Nevertheless, dissatisfied with such a sublime task, God drowns man in order to convert him; he burns man, he curses him. None of these things change him. A more powerful being than this villainous God—namely, the Devil—who has forever preserved his dominion, forever defied his Maker, endlessly manages, through his seductive skills, to debauch the flock reserved for himself by the Lord. Nothing can overcome the power that this demon has over us.

Then how do you picture the horrible God for whom you are sermonizing? He has but one son, an only son, whom he acquired through some kind of interaction; for since man fucks, he wanted his God to fuck, too; he sends out that respectable portion of himself from heaven. We imagine perhaps that this sublime creature will appear on celestial rays, in the midst of the cortege of angels, in sight of the entire universe. . . . Nothing of the sort! The God who has come to save the earth is heralded in the bosom of a Jewish whore inside a pigsty! Such is the noble pedigree ascribed to him. But will his honorable mission compensate him? Let's follow this personage for a moment. What does he say? What does he do? What sublime mission will he assign us? What mystery will he reveal? What dogma will he prescribe? And finally, what deeds will expose his greatness?

First, I see an incognito childhood, a few services—highly libertine, no doubt—performed by this scamp for the priests of the temple in Jerusalem; next, a disappearance of fifteen years, during which this wretch poisons his mind with all the reveries of the Egyptian school, something he finally brings back to Judea. No sooner does he reemerge there than his madness erupts and he says he is the son of God, the equal of his father; he expands this alliance with another phantom, which he calls the Holy Ghost; and these three figures, he assures us, can only be one! The more this ridiculous mystery confounds reason, the more this rascal declares that it deserves to be adopted . . . and the greater the danger in denying it! The imbecile guarantees that it was to save us all that, albeit God, he became flesh in the bosom of a human child; and the dazzling miracles that he works will soon convince the universe! At a feast of drunkards, the scalawag is indeed said to change water into wine; in a desert, he feeds a couple of ne'er-do-wells with hidden provisions that his followers have prepared; one of his comrades pretends to die, and our imposter resuscitates him; he climbs a mountain and, in front of only two or three friends, he carries out a hocus pocus that the worst trickster would be ashamed of today.

While vehemently cursing all the people who don't believe in him, the rogue promises heaven to all the morons who will listen to him. Since he's illiterate, he writes nothing; since he's stupid, he says little; since he's weak, he does even less. And when the magistrates finally grow tired of him and impatient with his very rare but seditious speeches, the charlatan lets himself be crucified after assuring his wretched followers that each time they invoke him, he will descend to them and let them eat him! He is tortured, he puts up with it. His papa, that sublime God, whom he dares to herald, doesn't help him in the least. So the rascal is treated like the worst of the scoundrels whom he was so worthy of leading.

His henchmen gather. "We are doomed!" they say. "And all our hopes are dashed if we don't save ourselves by means of a glorious feat! Let's get the guards around Jesus drunk. Then we'll carry off his corpse and we'll announce that he's risen from the dead! The method is certain! If we can manage to make people believe this knavery, our new religion will be bolstered and propagated. It will seduce the entire world! . . . Let's get to work!"

The trick succeeded. They pulled it off! For how many rascals has boldness failed to replace merit?! The corpse was carried away; fools, women, and children shouted as much as they could: "A miracle!" And yet, in this town where great miracles had just occurred, in this town which was stained with God's blood, no one was willing to believe in that God; not a single conversion transpired! Furthermore, it was all so uneventful that not a single historian bothered to mention it! Only the disciples of this imposter figured they would profit from the fraud—but not right away.

This consideration was so essential that they let several years flow by before they made use of their notorious swindle; finally, they erected their nauseating doctrine on that wobbling edifice. People like any change. They were weary of the despotism of emperors, and so a revolution became necessary. Those swindlers were listened to, they made rapid progress; that's the history of all errors. Soon the altars of Venus and Mars were changed into the altars of Jesus and Mary; the imposter's life story was published; this shallow novel found dupes; he was made to say a hundred things that he had never even thought. A few of his preposterous statements promptly became the basis of his morals; and since this new dogma was preached to the poor, charity became its first virtue. Bizarre rites were established under the name of "sacraments," and the most unworthy and most abominable of all is the way a crime-ridden priest enjoys the virtue of several magic words that enable him to make God arrive in a piece of bread.

There is no doubt about it. This dreadful cult would have been doomed at its very birth, without resources, if it had been attacked by merely the weapons of scorn, which it deserved. But its foes decided to persecute it; so it grew. The outcome was unavoidable. Even if we tried to cover it with ridicule today, it would not collapse! The adroit Voltaire never used any other weapons; and of all writers, he can take credit for making the highest number of proselytes.

In short, Eugénie, that is the history of God and religion. See for yourself how to assess these fables, and make up your own mind.

EUGÉNIE. My choice isn't difficult. I despise all those disgusting reveries. And this God, to whom I stuck out of weakness or ignorance, is now nothing for me but an object of horror!

MADAME DE SAINT-ANGE. Swear to me that you'll stop thinking about him, that you'll never occupy yourself again with him, that you'll never in your life invoke him for even an instant, and never return to him for the rest of your days.

EUGÉNIE (*throwing herself on* MADAME DE SAINT-ANGE'S *breasts*). Ah! I'll swear my oath in your arms! Isn't it easy for me to see that what you demand is for my own good, and that you don't want such reminiscences ever to trouble my tranquillity?

MADAME DE SAINT-ANGE. Could I have any other motive?

EUGÉNIE. But, Dolmancé. Isn't it the analysis of the virtues that has led us to the examination of the religions? Let's get back to that analysis. Mightn't this religion, ludicrous as it may be, contain certain prescribed virtues that could contribute to our happiness?

DOLMANCÉ. Very well! Let's examine! Will it be chastity, Eugénie, that virtue denied by your eyes although you are entirely its very image? Will you revere the obligation to battle all the drives of nature? Will you sacrifice all of them to that vain and ridiculous horror of never having had a weakness? Be fair and reply, my lovely friend: Do you believe you can find all the pleasures of the opposite vice in that absurd and dangerous purity of the soul?

EUGÉNIE. No, I don't want any honor. I don't feel the slightest need to be chaste, I'm extremely fond of the opposite vice. But, Dolmancé, couldn't charity and benevolence constitute happiness in a few sensitive souls?

DOLMANCÉ. Eugénie, may we be spared the virtues that produce only ingratitude! And don't be fooled, my charming friend. Benevolence is more a vice of pride than a true virtue of the soul. A person comforts his fellowmen purely in order to show off and never simply to do a good deed. He'd be quite angry if the amount of alms he's just been given weren't generally made known as far as possible. Nor should you imagine, Eugénie, that this action has as good an effect as one pictures it. I personally envisage it only as the greatest of swindles. It accustoms the pauper to assistance, which saps his energy. He no longer works if he expects your charity. And should he fail to receive it, he becomes a thief or a killer. I hear on all sides that beggary must be abolished, yet people do anything humanly possible to increase it. Do you wish to have no flies in your chamber? Then don't strew any sugar—it attracts flies. Do you wish to have no paupers in France? Then don't hand out alms. And above all, close down the poorhouses. If a man is born in misery and finds himself without those dangerous resources, he will employ all the courage, all the power he has received from nature to free himself from his native condition, and he'll stop pestering you. Close them down, tear them down pitilessly—those detestable houses that shamelessly harbor the fruits of this pauper's libertinage, those dreadful cesspools that daily vomit a disgusting swarm into society, a horde of those new creatures whose only hope is your purse. What's the good, I ask, of maintaining such individuals so carefully? Are we afraid that France might get depopulated? Ah! That's something we should never fear!

One of the top vices of this country is its far too extreme overpopulation, and it is wrong to assume that these superfluous inhabitants are a source of wealth for the state. Actually, these supernumerary existences are like parasitical branches, which, living at the expense of the tree trunk, ultimately exhaust it. Remember, every time a country's population is larger than its means of existence, its government will languish. Examine France, and you'll see that such is the case here. What is the result? We can see it. The Chinese, who are smarter than we, make sure not to be overwhelmed by a copious population. There is no haven for the shameful fruits of their debauchery. They abandon that terrible outcome like the consequences of digestion. Nor are there poorhouses in China—they are totally unknown. Everyone works, everyone is happy, nothing drains the poor man's energy. And everyone can say, like Nero: *Quid est pauper?* What is a pauper?

EUGÉNIE (*to* MADAME DE SAINT-ANGE). Dear friend, my father thinks absolutely along the same lines. He has never given charity in all his life. And he never stops scolding my mother for the alms she donates. She was in the Maternal Society, in the Philanthropic Society—and goodness knows what other societies. He forced her to leave them by threatening to restrict her to the tiniest allowance if she decided to relapse into such stupidity.

MADAME DE SAINT-ANGE. There is nothing more ludicrous and also more dangerous, Eugénie, than all those associations. It is to them—the free schools and the poorhouses—that we owe our dreadful upheaval today. Never give alms, my darling, I beg you.

EUGÉNIE. Don't worry! My father demanded the same thing of me long ago. And charity hardly tempts me to flout his orders . . . to defy the urges of my heart and your desires.

DOLMANCÉ. Let's not divide that share of sensitivity that we've received from nature—stretching it means eradicating it. What do I care about other people's sufferings? Don't I have enough misery of my own without burdening myself with the misery of others? May the hearth fire of that sensitivity never illuminate anything but our own pleasures! Let's be sensitive to whatever delights them, and let's be absolutely inflexible about the rest. This attitude of the soul results in a sort of cruelty that is sometimes not without its charm. One cannot always do evil. So if we can't always create this pleasure, we can nevertheless replace this sensation with the caustic little malice that we never do good.

EUGÉNIE. Oh, my God! How your lessons excite me! I think I'd let myself be killed now rather than perform a good deed!

MADAME DE SAINT-ANGE. And if you had the chance to perform an evil deed, would you be willing to carry it out?

EUGÉNIE. Hold your tongue, seductress. I won't answer your question until you've finished my lessons. It seems to me, Dolmancé, that, after all you tell me, nothing on earth matters less than whether one does good or evil. So then, must only our leanings and our temperaments be respected?

DOLMANCÉ. Believe me, Eugénie, the words "vice" and "virtue" supply us only with local meanings. There is no action, however bizarre you may picture it, that is truly criminal; or one that can really be called virtuous. Everything depends on our customs and on the climates we live in. What is considered a crime here is often a virtue a few hundred leagues away; and the virtues of another hemisphere might, quite conversely, be regarded as crimes among us. There is no atrocity that hasn't been deified, no virtue that hasn't been stigmatized. Because of these purely geographic differences, we pay little heed to men's esteem or contempt. These are futile and ridiculous sentiments, and we should transcend them—indeed, fearlessly prefer their scorn, if only the actions through which we merit them provide us with sheer delight.

EUGÉNIE. Still, mustn't certain actions be so dangerous and so intrinsically evil that they should be generally viewed as criminal and punished as such from one end of the universe to the other?

MADAME DE SAINT-ANGE. There is no such action, my love, no such action—not even rape or incest, not even murder or parricide.

EUGÉNIE. What? These horrors have been excused in some places?

DOLMANCÉ. They have been honored there, crowned, considered excellent, while in other places, humanity, candor, charity, chastity—why, all our virtue were regarded as monstrosities.

EUGÉNIE. Please explain these things. I demand a brief analysis of each of these crimes, starting, I beg you, with your opinion of the libertinage of girls, then the adultery of wives.

MADAME DE SAINT-ANGE. Now listen to me, my dear Eugénie. It's nonsense to say that the moment a girl leaves her mother's bosom she becomes the victim of her parental will and continues to be this victim until her final breath. It is precisely in a century when the rights of man have been so carefully widened and deepened that girls must stop believing themselves to be the slaves of their families. The fact remains that these parental powers are absolutely chimerical. Let's heed nature in regard to such an important subject, and let the laws of animals, which, after all, are far closer to nature than we, serve as examples for a moment.

Do the fatherly duties of animals extend beyond their primary physical needs? Don't the fruits of the pleasures of males and females possess all their freedom, all their rights? Do their parents even recognize them once their offspring can walk and can feed themselves on their own? And do their offspring, in turn, honestly believe they owe anything to the parents who have given them life? Certainly not! Then by what right are human children compelled to perform other duties? And what establishes these duties if not paternal greed and ambition? Now, I wonder if it's just for a girl, who is starting to feel and reason, to submit to such restraints? Isn't it prejudice alone that prolongs the wearing of those chains? And is there anything more ludicrous than the sight of a fifteen- or sixteen-year-old girl, blazing with desires that she is obliged to squelch, and waiting—in worse than hellish torments—to please her parents? Haven't they already made her adolescence miserable, and now, aren't they sacrificing her maturity by immolating her, in her perfidious greed and against her will, to a husband, who has nothing lovable about him or who has everything hateful? No and no again, Eugénie! Such bonds will soon disappear. As soon as a girl attains the age of reason, she should leave her paternal home after receiving a governmental education. She must then, at fifteen, be her own mistress and become whatever she wishes. Will she devote herself to vice? Who cares? Aren't the services that a girl renders by consenting to the happiness of all those who ask her—aren't these services infinitely more desirable than the ones for which she isolates herself and offers herself only to her husband? A woman's fate is to be like a she-wolf, a bitch: she must belong to everyone who wants her. We are quite blatantly outraging the destiny that nature imposes on a woman if we absurdly fetter her to a solitary marriage.

Let's hope that people will open their eyes and that, in achieving the freedom of all individuals, they won't forget the fate of unhappy girls. But if girls, lamentably, are forgotten, then they themselves should surpass habit and prejudice and boldly trample the shameful chains that hold them down. In this way, they will soon triumph over custom and opinion. Having grown wiser by being freer, man will sense the injustice of scorning those who proceed in this fashion, and for whom the action of yielding to natural impulses, viewed as a crime in a captive nation, can no longer be viewed as a crime in a free nation.

Therefore, Eugénie, assume that these principles are legitimate, and smash your fetters—cost what it may! Despise the vain rebukes of a moronic mother, to whom you owe nothing but hatred and disdain. If your father, who is a libertine, desires you, then all well and good! Let him enjoy you but not shackle you! If he tries to enslave you, break the yoke. Any number of girls have done this with their fathers. Fuck—in a word—fuck! That's why you were put upon this earth! There is no barrier to pleasure outside of your own strength and will; no exception beyond place, time, and person. All hours, all areas, all men must serve your sensual delight; continence is an impossible virtue, which nature, violated in its rights, instantly punishes with a thousand miseries. As long as the laws are what they are today, we have to wear several veils. Public opinion forces us to do so. But let's make amends in silence for this cruel chastity that we are compelled to sport on the outside.

I advise a girl to have a good friend, a woman, who, untrammeled and in society, can help the girl to secretly taste those worldly pleasures. At the very least, the girl should attempt to enthrall the spies who surround her. Let her beg them to prostitute her, promising to give them all the money they could derive from these sales. Either these spies themselves or the women they find—the so-called procuresses—will soon fulfill the girl's wishes. She can then throw dust in the eyes of all the people around her: brothers, cousins, friends, parents. She ought to submit to all of them if that's necessary for concealing her behavior. Indeed, if it's demanded of her, the girl should even sacrifice her leanings and her preferences. An amorous intrigue that displeases her, and to which she submits purely out of self-interest, will soon lead her to a more agreeable situation—and she'll be launched in society. But she should never return to the prejudices of her childhood. Threats, exhortations, duties, virtues, religion, advice—the girl should trample them underfoot. And she must stubbornly reject and despise everything that tends only to clap her in irons again—in short, everything that doesn't contribute to keeping her in the lap of lewdness.

It is nonsensical of our parents to predict that libertinage will cause misery. There are thorns everywhere, but roses bloom over them on the road of vice. It is only on the muddy paths of virtue that nature won't ever allow roses to blossom. The sole reef to fear during the voyage of vice is the opinion of other people. But where is the girl of vital spirit who, after a little reflection, cannot transcend this despicable judgment? The pleasures of esteem, Eugénie, are nothing but spiritual delights, which are suitable purely for certain minds, while the pleasures of *fucking* please everyone. Indeed, its seductive allures soon compensate for the illusory scorn that a person has a hard time escaping while braving public opinion; yet a few smart women

have cared so little about it that they've created one more pleasure. Fuck, Eugénie, fuck away, my dear angel! Your body belongs to you, to you alone. You are the only person in the
world who has the right to enjoy your body and to let anyone
you wish enjoy it. Profit from the happiest time of your life. The happiest years
of our pleasures are only too brief! If we are lucky enough to
have enjoyed them, then delicious memories will console us
and amuse us in our old age. Did we waste those years? . . . Bitter regret, dreadful remorse will devour us and join the torments of old age, whereby tears and brambles will accompany
the disastrous approach of the coffin.

Or are you obsessed with immortality? Well, it's by fucking,
my dear, that you will linger in the reminiscences of men. People soon forgot Lucretia, while the Theodoras and the Messali-
nas are still the topics of the sweetest and most frequent
conversations in life. Now, Eugénie! Would it be possible not to
prefer a course that, while crowning us with flowers down
here, lets us hope for worship quite beyond the grave? How, I
ask you, can we not prefer this course to the one that, making
us vegetate stupidly on earth, promises us nothing but scorn
and oblivion after we die?

EUGÉNIE (to MADAME DE SAINT-ANGE). Ah, my dear love,
how intensely these seductive discourses set my mind ablaze and
captivate my soul! I'm in a state that's difficult to depict. . . .
Tell me, my darling, can you introduce me to some of those
women who (confused) will prostitute me if I ask them to do so?

MADAME DE SAINT-ANGE. Until you are more experienced,
this concerns only me, Eugénie. You have to count totally on
me in this regard and even more so on all the precautions I'll
take to conceal your deviations. My brother and this reliable
friend who is instructing you will be the first men to whom
you'll submit. We'll find others after them. Don't worry, dear
friend. I'll let you fly from pleasure to pleasure, I'll plunge you
in a sea of delight, I'll overwhelm you, my angel, I'll satiate you!

EUGÉNIE (throwing herself into MADAME DE SAINT-ANGE'S
arms). Oh, my darling, I adore you! Go on! You'll never find a
more willing pupil than I. However, didn't you tell me in our

earlier conversations that it's hard for a young woman to hurl herself into libertinage without this being noticed by the husband whom she will have to take later on?

MADAME DE SAINT-ANGE. That's true, my dear. But there are secret methods that will heal all breaches. I promise to acquaint you with them. And then, even if you've fucked like Antoinette, I'll make you as virginal as when you first came into the world.

EUGÉNIE. Ah! You're wonderful! Come on! Let's continue with our lessons! Hurry up and teach me how a married woman should act in such a case.

MADAME DE SAINT-ANGE. In whatever state a woman may be, my darling—whether girl, woman, or widow—she must never have any other goal, any other occupation, any other desire than to be fucked from dawn till dusk. It's toward that single end that nature has created her. But if, to fulfill that objective, I demand that she trample all her childhood prejudices, if I require her strictest disobedience to her family's orders, the most verified scorn of all parental advice, you will agree, Eugénie, that, of all the chains to break, the one I would shatter first is certainly marriage.

Imagine a girl, Eugénie, who has just emerged from her paternal home or from boarding school. Imagine that, although totally ignorant and totally inexperienced, she is obliged to pass suddenly into the arms of a man she has never seen; she is obliged, in front of an altar, to swear obedience to this man, a fidelity all the more unjust because, in her heart of hearts, she often has the greatest desire to break her word. Is there, Eugénie, a more dreadful fate? Yet there she is tied, whether or not she likes her husband, whether he treats her with affection or cruelty. His honor depends on her oath. He is sullied if she transgresses it. She must either lose her way or patiently bear her yoke, even if she dies of grief.

Oh, no, Eugénie. No! That's not what we were born for! Those absurd laws are the handiwork of men, and we must not submit to them! Is a divorce capable of satisfying us? Absolutely not! Who can guarantee that we will more assuredly find in a second marriage the happiness that eluded us the first time around? Let us therefore compensate in secret for all the constraints of these absurd bonds. After all, we can be quite certain that such disturbances, to whatever excesses we can drive them, are natural; far from outraging nature, they are nothing but a sincere tribute to nature. We obey its laws if we yield to the desires that nature alone has placed in front of us; and we outrage nature if we resist it.

Men therefore regard adultery as a crime, which they have dared to punish by taking our lives. Yet adultery, Eugénie, is nothing but the assertion of a natural right that the fantasies of those tyrants would never contest. But isn't it horrible, our husbands say, that we are expected to cherish and embrace the fruits of your deviations as our own children? That is Rousseau's objection. And it is, I grant you, the only vaguely conceivable objection for attacking adultery. But isn't it ever so easy to submit to libertinage without fearing pregnancy? And isn't it even easier to destroy a pregnancy if it should occur imprudently? For now, however, since we'll be returning to this topic later on, let's stick to the basic issue. We will see that, plausible as it might sound initially, this objection is purely illusive.

First of all, so long as I sleep with my husband, so long as his semen flows to the bottom of my womb, then even if I sleep with ten men at the same time, nothing can ever prove to him that the resulting baby isn't his. It may belong to him or it may not. And in case of uncertainty, he cannot and must not ever have any scruples about acknowledging this creature as his, since he has cooperated in producing it. If it *can* belong to him, then it *does* belong to him. And any man who is rendered unhappy by suspicions about his paternity will have misgivings even if his wife is a vestal virgin. You see, it's impossible to rely on a woman; even if she's behaved herself for ten years, she can stop one. So if a husband has a suspicious character, he will remain distrustful in every case, and he can never be sure that the baby he's hugging is truly his. Now, if he can be distrustful in every case, then there's nothing wrong with confirming his suspicions from time to time. It would neither increase nor diminish his state of happiness or spiritual unhappiness, and everything would remain exactly as if his suspicion were justified.

Let's suppose that the husband is totally mistaken and that he's caressing the fruit of his wife's libertinage. Why is that a crime? Don't we share all our assets? In this case, what harm is there if I add to the household and bring in a child who is destined to inherit a portion of those common assets? The child will receive my portion and steal nothing from my tender spouse. I regard my child's portion as coming from my dowry; so neither the child nor I will take anything from my husband. Had this child been his, by what right would his child share my assets? Wouldn't it be insofar as I'd given birth to him? Well, the child would enjoy his part by virtue of that same intimate relationship. It's because this child belongs to me that I owe him a portion of my wealth.

What can you reproach me for? The child receives his share. —But you're deceiving your husband; this double dealing is atrocious! —No, it's tit for tat! That's all! I was duped first, by the chains he forced on me. I'm getting even! What could be simpler? —But it's a flagrant insult to your husband's honor! —Bah! That's a prejudice! My libertinage does not concern my husband in any way! My mistakes are personal. This may have been scandalous a century ago, but we've shaken off that chimera today, and my husband is no more stigmatized by my debaucheries than I am stigmatized by his. I could fuck the whole world without leaving a scratch on him! This alleged injury is merely a fable that can't possibly exist. Take it or leave it! My husband is either a jealous brute or a sensitive man. If he's brutal, then the best thing I can do is get even with him for his conduct. If he's sensitive, then I can't harm him. As a decent man, he should be happy that I'm enjoying my pleasures. There is no sensitive man who doesn't enjoy seeing happiness in the person he adores. —But if you loved him, would you want him to act the same way? —Ah! How miserable the woman who takes it upon herself to be jealous of her husband! If she loves him, she should be content with whatever he gives her, and she mustn't try to restrain him. Not only will she fail to hold him back, but he'll soon despise her. If I'm reasonable, I'll never be distressed by my husband's debaucheries. Let him likewise be reasonable with me, and peace will reign in the household.

Let's sum up:

Whatever the effects of adultery, children that were not the husband's might be introduced into the household; still, as the wife's offspring, they can certainly lay claim to part of her dowry. If the husband is informed about their true paternity, he must view them as though they were her children from a previous marriage. If he is uninformed, then he can't be unhappy, for you can't be unhappy about a misfortune that you're unaware of. If such adultery has no consequences, and if the husband doesn't know about it, then no legal expert could prove that a crime had been perpetrated. At this point, a wife's adultery is an act that is perfectly beyond the husband's ken, and perfectly good for the wife, who delights in it. Should the husband discover the adultery, it can't be wicked now, for it wasn't wicked before, and it can't have altered its character. There is no misfortune other than the husband's discovery; however, this problem is purely his own, it can't regard his wife in the least.

The men who once punished adultery were executioners, tyrants, jealous types, who took everything personally, and who unjustly figured that it was a crime merely to offend them—as though a personal insult could ever be viewed as criminal, and as though the word "crime" could ever be applied to an action that, far from outraging nature and society, obviously served both.

Still, there are cases in which adultery is easy to prove and thus it becomes embarrassing for the wife without, however, becoming more criminal. One such example is when the husband is impotent or has leanings that block reproduction. Since she comes, but her husband never comes, then, no doubt, her excesses grow all the more apparent. But should that bother her? Absolutely not! Her sole precaution is to avoid making a baby or to abort it if that precaution fails. Should her husband's perverse affections oblige her to compensate for his neglect, she must, without repugnance, satisfy his leanings no matter what they may be. She must then make him realize that such complaisance really deserves certain benefits, and that she requires total freedom in exchange for what she has granted him. The husband then refuses or consents. If he consents, as

mine has done, then the wife can live life to the fullest, without
the slightest misgivings, and she must agree all the more to con-
descend graciously to his whims. If the husband refuses, then
the wife can virtually wear a thicker veil and fuck tranquilly in
its shadow. Is the husband impotent? Then the couple should
separate, but every wife must still live life to the fullest. She
fucks in any case, my darling, for we are born to fuck; and, when
fucking, we are following the laws of nature, and every human
law that flouts natural laws merely deserves our contempt.

A wife is quite deceived if bonds as absurd as marital ties
prevent her from giving in to her leanings, if she fears either
getting pregnant or offending her husband or, still more vainly,
damaging her reputation! So you've just seen it, Eugénie, yes,
you've just felt how deceived she is, how she basely sacrifices
both her happiness and all the pleasures of life, immolates them
to the most ridiculous prejudices. Ah! She must fuck, fuck with
impunity! Will a little bogus glory, a few thoughtless religious
hopes make up for her sacrifices? No, and no again! In a coffin,
virtue and vice intermingle. After a few years, does the public
exalt virtues more than it condemns vices? No, no, and no
again! And the miserable wife, who has lived without pleasure,
expires, alas, with no compensation!

EUGÉNIE. How persuasive you are, my angel, how you triumph over my prejudices, how you destroy all the wrong principles that my mother has instilled in me! Ah! I wish I could get
married tomorrow so that I might instantly put your maxims
into practice. How seductive they are, how correct they are,
and how I love them! One thing bothers me though in what
you say, dear friend, and since I don't understand it, I beg you
to explain it to me. In his orgasms, your spouse, you claim, be-
haves in such a way as to prevent his having any children. Then
what, I wonder, does he do to you?

MADAME DE SAINT-ANGE. My husband was already old when
I married him. Right on our wedding night, he informed me
about his bizarre fantasies and he assured me that he would
never interfere with mine. I swore to him that I'd obey him, and
ever since that night the two of us have lived in the most delicious freedom. My husband's pleasure consists in his getting

sucked, and this is the very singular accessory that accompanies it: stooped over him, with my buttocks straight above his face, I ardently pump the come from his balls while I have to shit into his mouth! . . . And he devours my turds! . . .

EUGÉNIE. What an outlandish desire!

DOLMANCÉ. No desire can be termed outlandish, my dear; all desires can be found in nature. When nature created human beings, it delighted in differentiating their sexual leanings as much as their faces; and we should no more be astonished by the diversity of our features than by the diversity that nature has placed in our affections. The desire that your friend has just brought up is utterly in fashion. An endless number of men, especially those who are getting on in age, indulge in it prodigiously. If someone demanded it of you, Eugénie, would you refuse?

EUGÉNIE (blushing). After the maxims that have been inculcated in me here, could I refuse anything? I ask you to forgive only my surprise; this is the first time I've heard about all these obscenities. I first have to grasp them, but I think my instructors must be certain that the distance between solving the problem and carrying out the procedure will never be greater than the distance they demand themselves. So, be that as it may, my darling, you found your freedom by acquiescing to his complaisance?

MADAME DE SAINT-ANGE. Total freedom, Eugénie! I for my part have done anything I've liked without his putting any obstacles on my path. However, I haven't taken a lover; I love pleasure too much for that. Unhappy the woman who attaches herself. One sole lover can spell her doom, while ten acts of libertinage repeated day after day, if she likes, would instantly vanish into the night of silence.

I was rich: I paid young men, who fucked me without knowing me. I surrounded myself with charming footmen, who were bound to taste the sweetest pleasures with me if they were discreet and who were sure to be dismissed if they so much as breathed a word. You have no idea, my darling angel, of the torrents of joy into which I plunged. That is the conduct I will always prescribe for all women who wish to imitate me. During the twelve years that I've been married, I've been fucked by perhaps more than ten or twelve thousand people. . . . And I'm considered virtuous in my social circles! Another wife would have taken a lover, and the second lover would have sealed her fate!

EUGÉNIE. This maxim is the best, and I will be sure to follow it. Like you, I have to marry a rich man, especially one with bizarre leanings. . . . But tell me, my dear. Is your husband strictly bound to his desires? Will he never demand anything else of you?

MADAME DE SAINT-ANGE. During these twelve years, he has never gone back on his word for a single day except when I've had my period. I'm then replaced by a very pretty girl whom he wanted me to take in, and everything runs as smoothly as can be.

EUGÉNIE. But he can't stick to just that one pleasure. Don't other women contribute to bringing more external variety into his love life?

DOLMANCÉ. You can bank on it, Eugénie. Madame's husband is one of the biggest libertines of his time. He spends more than a hundred thousand crowns a year on the perversions that your friend has just depicted for you.

MADAME DE SAINT-ANGE. To tell you the truth, I suspect it. But who cares about his debaucheries? Doesn't their huge number sanction and obscure my own?

EUGÉNIE. I beg you, please detail the methods by which a young woman, married or not, can avoid pregnancy. For I must admit to you that I dread conceiving a child either with the husband I must marry or on the road of libertinage. You indicated one such method when you described your husband's leanings. However, this way of coming, which can be very agreeable for the man, doesn't strike me as being pleasant for the woman. I'd like you to teach me how we can have pleasures that are free of the risk I fear.

MADAME DE SAINT-ANGE. A girl never runs the danger of conceiving a child if she doesn't let the man slip his shaft into her pussy. She must take care not to come in this way; instead, she must indiscriminately offer her hand, her mouth, her breasts, or her asshole. If she chooses her asshole, she'll get lots of pleasure, even more than anywhere else, while the other methods are blissful for the man.

Let's proceed to the first of these methods—I mean using the hand, Eugénie, just as you watched it a few minutes ago. You shake your friend's member as if you were pumping it; after a number of strokes, the semen comes spurting out. During this time, the man kisses you, caresses you, and with that liquor he covers the part of your body that he likes the most. Do you want him to shoot between your breasts? Then you stretch out on the bed, you place the male member between your breasts, you squeeze them together, and after some shaking the man shoots his load, inundating your breasts and perhaps your face. This method is the least pleasurable of all, and it is suitable only for a woman whose experienced throat has already acquired enough flexibility to squash and compress the male member. Coming in the mouth is infinitely more agreeable for both the man and the woman. The best way to enjoy it is for the woman to lie down in the opposite direction of her fucker. He slips his cock into her mouth, and, with her head between his thighs, he gives her tit for tat as he introduces his tongue into her cunt or against her clitoris. If they utilize this position, they have to grab one another's buttocks and tickle one another's assholes—actions that are always necessary for sensual delight. Hot and imaginative lovers will then swallow the come ejaculated into the woman's mouth, and she will delicately enjoy the pleasure of mutually passing this precious liquid into her innards and thereby heinously deviating it from its normal destination.

DOLMANCÉ. This method is mouth-watering, Eugénie; I highly recommend it to you. It is truly alluring to thumb one's nose at reproduction and to thwart what morons call the laws of nature. Sometimes the thighs or the armpits also provide a haven for the male member, offering it nooks in which its semen might be lost without risk of conception.

MADAME DE SAINT-ANGE. Some women insert sponges into their vaginas, and these sponges receive the sperm, preventing it from spurting into the vessel and thereby propagating. Other women make their fuckers use a small pouch of fine Venetian skin, known vulgarly as a "condom." The semen pours in without risk of reaching its goal. However, of all these approaches, the one through the ass is, no doubt, the most delicious.

Dolmancé, I'll leave it up to you to hold forth about it. Who can do a better job of portraying a delight that you'd give your eyeteeth to defend?

DOLMANCÉ. I admit my foible. In all the world, there is, I agree, no more pleasurable way to come. I adore it in either sex. Still, a young boy's ass, I must concur, gratifies me more than a young girl's. Men who yield to that passion are called "buggers." And if a man is a bugger, Eugénie, he must bugger all the way. Fucking a woman's ass is a halfway measure; nature wants a man to carry out this fantasy in another man. And so it's particularly for a man that nature has given us this ecstasy. It's absurd to say that this mania is unnatural. Can it be censured if nature inspires it in us? Can nature dictate something that degrades it? No, Eugénie, no! We serve nature in this way as in other ways, and perhaps in an even saintlier fashion. Propagation is merely a concession on the part of nature. How can nature prescribe as a law an act that strips nature of the rights of its omnipotence? After all, propagation is merely a consequence of nature's initial aims; and even if our species were totally wiped out, new constructions, nature's handiwork, would again express nature's original intentions—in an act far more flattering for its pride and its power.

MADAME DE SAINT-ANGE. Do you realize, Dolmancé, that your philosophy will actually prove that you'll be doing nature a favor with the complete extinction of the human race?

DOLMANCÉ. Who can doubt it, Madame?

MADAME DE SAINT-ANGE. Oh, heavenly justice! Then wars, plagues, famines, massacres are nothing but necessary accidents of natural laws, and man, the agent or victim of these horrors, is no more a criminal as an agent than a sufferer as a victim?

DOLMANCÉ. Man is certainly a victim when he cringes under the strokes of misery. But a criminal? Never! We'll get back to all these issues. Meanwhile, since sodomite pleasure is now the topic of our conversation, let's analyze it for our beautiful Eugénie.

In her most usual position for this delight, the woman lies belly-down on the edge of the bed, her buttocks wide apart, her head as low as possible. For an instant, after the debauchee is entertained by the view of the beautiful ass that she offers, he slaps it, kneads it, sometimes even whips it, pinches it, bites it. Then his mouth wets the darling hole that he is about to pierce and that he prepares with the tip of his tongue. He lubricates his engine with saliva or pomade and gently presents it to the hole he wishes to penetrate. His one hand conducts it, while his other hand keeps the blissful ass cheeks apart. The instant he feels his member enter, he must push ardently, making sure to gain ground. Sometimes the woman suffers if she's new and young. But ignoring her pains that soon change to pleasures, the fucker must push his dick, gradually and energetically, until he achieves his goal—until, that is, his pubic hair precisely rubs the circumference of the anus he is fucking. He must then follow his route swiftly; all the thorns have been gathered, only the roses remain. Next he should complete transforming into pleasure the residue of pain still felt by his fuckee. If the latter is a boy, the fucker should grab the boy's cock and jerk it. If it's a girl, the fucker should tickle her clitoris. The blissful titillations he arouses by prodigiously tightening his victim's anus will double the agent's pleasure. And the agent, overwhelmed with joy and pleasure, will soon shoot a thick and abundant semen to the bottom of that delightful ass, a semen incited by so many lubricious details. Now, there are some who don't want the victim to come; we'll explain that presently.

MADAME DE SAINT-ANGE. Allow me in turn to be a pupil for a moment, Dolmancé, and let me ask you something. In what state should the victim's ass be in order to bring complete pleasure to the agent?

DOLMANCÉ. The ass must be full, quite assuredly. It is essential for the victim to feel a thorough need to shit, so that upon reaching the turd, the tip of the fucker's cock digs in and, more hotly and more softly, deposits the come that prods him and sets him ablaze!

MADAME DE SAINT-ANGE. I'd be worried that the victim would feel less pleasure.

DOLMANCÉ. Wrong! This pleasure is such that nothing can possibly interfere with it, and the person who serves it is transported to seventh heaven. There is no pleasure like it, no other pleasure can completely satisfy the two people yielding to it, and it's hard to go back to a different method once you've tried this one. Those, Eugénie, are the best ways of finding pleasure with a man and not risking pregnancy. For you enjoy—rest assured—not only submitting your ass to a man, as I've just described, but you also suck his dick, jerk it, and so forth. Why, I've known many licentious women who made these episodes more charming than vaginal orgasms. Imagination stimulates pleasure. In these kinds of pleasures the imagination rules everything—it is the real motivation! Now don't we enjoy ourselves by way of the imagination? Don't we delight in the most piquant pleasures through our imaginations?

MADAME DE SAINT-ANGE. Fine! But Eugénie must be careful. The imagination serves us only when the mind is absolutely free of any prejudice. A single prejudice suffices to cool off the imagination. This whimsical part of the mind is so unbridled as to be uncontrollable. Its greatest triumphs, its most eminent delights consist in smashing all the restraints that oppose it. Imagination is the enemy of all norms, the idolater of all disorder and of all that bears the color of crime. Listen to the singular response of an imaginative woman who was cold about fucking with her husband:

"Why so icy?" he asked her.

"Goodness!" said that remarkable creature. "It's because what you're doing is so simple!"

EUGÉNIE. What a maddeningly wonderful reply! . . . Ah, my dear friend! How deeply driven I feel to know those divine impulses of an unbridled imagination! You couldn't imagine how we've ever gotten together . . . only since that instant—no, no, my dear friend, you couldn't envision all the sensual delights that my mind has toyed with. . . . Oh! How well I understand evil now! How deeply my heart now desires it!

MADAME DE SAINT-ANGE. May the horrors, the atrocities, the most odious crimes no longer astonish you, Eugénie. The foulest, the filthiest, the most forbidden things are always the most exciting. . . . They always unleash the most delicious orgasms.

EUGÉNIE. What incredible deviations the two of you must have indulged in by now! How gladly I'd hear the details!

DOLMANCÉ (*kissing and fondling the girl*). Beautiful Eugénie, I'd rather have you experience a hundred times over what I'd like to do to you than tell you what I've already done.

EUGÉNIE. I don't know if it would be very good for me to expose myself to all those things.

MADAME DE SAINT-ANGE. I wouldn't advise you to do so, Eugénie.

EUGÉNIE. Well, then, I'll leave those details to Dolmancé. However, you, my dear friend, I beg you to describe for me the most extraordinary thing that you have ever done in your life.

MADAME DE SAINT-ANGE. I was once fucked by fifteen men in a row; I got banged ninety times in front and in back within twenty-four hours.

EUGÉNIE. Those are mere debaucheries, tours de force. I bet you've done far more bizarre things.

MADAME DE SAINT-ANGE. I've been to a brothel.

EUGÉNIE. What is a "brothel"?

DOLMANCÉ. A brothel is a public house, where, for an agreed-on price, a man can find young and pretty girls prepared to satisfy his passions.

EUGÉNIE (*to* MADAME DE SAINT-ANGE). And you surrendered there?

MADAME DE SAINT-ANGE. Yes, I was like a hooker. For an entire week I gratified the fantasies of several lechers, and I witnessed some rather peculiar leanings. I followed the same principle as the notorious Empress Theodora, the wife of Emperor Justinian. I accosted passersby on street corners, on public promenades, and as for the money I earned by my hooking, I spent it on lottery tickets.

EUGÉNIE. Darling, I know your mind. You've gone much further than that.

MADAME DE SAINT-ANGE. Can one go any further?

EUGÉNIE. Yes, yes, yes! And this is how I picture it. Didn't you tell me that our most delightful spiritual sensations derive from the imagination?

MADAME DE SAINT-ANGE. I did say that.

EUGÉNIE. Well, if we let the imagination wander, if we grant it the freedom to transgress the ultimate boundaries prescribed by religion, decency, humanity, virtue—indeed, all our alleged duties—then wouldn't the deviations of our imaginations be prodigious?

MADAME DE SAINT-ANGE. No doubt.

EUGÉNIE. And wouldn't the imagination provoke us even more because of the immensity of its deviations?

MADAME DE SAINT-ANGE. Absolutely!

EUGÉNIE. If that's true, then we ought to give our imagination free rein and send it to the most inconceivable things: the more excited we wish to become, the more intense stimuli we wish to feel. The further the mind wishes to go, the more blissful we will be—

DOLMANCÉ (*kissing her*). Delightful!

MADAME DE SAINT-ANGE. How much progress the little slut has made in so little time! But do you know, my charming girl, that one can go very far on the route that you are tracing for us?

EUGÉNIE. I'm quite aware of that! And since I don't set up any barriers for myself, you can see that I have an inkling of where we believe we are heading.

MADAME DE SAINT-ANGE. Toward crimes, my little bitch, toward the blackest and most dreadful crimes.

EUGÉNIE (*in a low and broken voice*). But you claim there's no such thing as a crime, and their descriptions are meant only to fire the imagination. They are never carried out.

DOLMANCÉ. Yet it's so nice to carry out the ideas we come up with.

EUGÉNIE (*blushing*). So people do commit crimes. . . . Or do you wish, my dear mentors, to persuade me that you've never carried out your ideas?

MADAME DE SAINT-ANGE. I've sometimes done so.

EUGÉNIE. There we are!

DOLMANCÉ. What a mind!

EUGÉNIE (*pursuing her course*). So I'm asking you what you've come up with and what you've then carried out.

MADAME DE SAINT-ANGE (*stammering*). Eugénie, some day

I'll tell you my life story. But for now, let's continue our instruction. . . . Otherwise you may get me to say things. . . .

EUGÉNIE. Goodness, I see you don't love me enough to bare your soul to me that far. Then I'll wait as long as you wish. Meanwhile, let's get back to our details. Tell me, darling, who is the happy mortal whom you made the lord of your deflowering?

MADAME DE SAINT-ANGE. My brother. He's worshipped me since childhood. Starting in our earliest years, we often amused ourselves without reaching a goal. I promised I'd surrender to him the instant I married. I kept my word. Luckily, my husband didn't injure me. My brother picked the first fruits. We kept indulging in our affair without hindering each other. Indeed, each of us plunges into the most divine excesses of gratification. We even enjoy mutual help: I procure him women, and he introduces me to men.

EUGÉNIE. What a delicious arrangement! But isn't incest a crime?

DOLMANCÉ. Can we regard the most beautiful natural union as a crime, a union that nature prescribes and so warmly recommends? Just think, Eugénie. After the great disasters that have afflicted our planet, how could the human species have reproduced itself if not through incest? Don't we find the proofs and the examples in the very books respected by Christianity? Could the families of Adam and Noah have survived in any other way? Noah, like Adam, was merely a restorer of the human race. A dreadful upheaval left Adam alone on the earth, just as the same thing happened to Noah. However, Adam's tradition was lost, whereas Noah's was retained. Analyze, investigate the mores of the universe. You will see incest permitted everywhere, regarded as a wise law that is meant to buttress the family bonds. If love, in a word, is born from resemblance, where can love be more perfect than between brother and sister, between father and daughter? A misunderstood policy, generated by the fear of making some families too powerful, bans incest from our way of life. But let's not delude ourselves; if an edict is dictated merely by egotism or ambition, we shouldn't call it a natural law. Let's examine our hearts. That's where I usually send our moralistic pedants. If we interrogate this sacred organ, we'll learn that there is nothing more delicate than the carnal union of families. We must stop blinding ourselves to a brother's feelings for his sister, a father's feelings for his daughter. It's no use their veiling those emotions behind a lawful tenderness. The most violent love is the only sentiment that fires their feelings, it's the only sentiment that nature has put in their hearts. So let's fearlessly double, let's triple the delights of incest, and let's convince ourselves that the closer the object of our desires may be to us, the more charming our pleasure.

A friend of mine lives with the daughter he sired with his own mother. Just a week ago, he deflowered a thirteen-year-old boy, the fruit of his relationship with that daughter. Several years from now, that same boy will wed his mother. Those are my friend's wishes. He's arranged a similar fate for this couple, and I know he's planning to enjoy the fruits of this marriage, for he is young and hopeful. You can see, my tender Eugénie, what a mass of crime and incest would have soiled my honest friend if there were any truth to the prejudice against these practices. In a word, I personally go by the following principle: If nature actually prohibited the bliss of sodomy, incest, masturbation, etcetera, would nature make them all so pleasurable? Nature cannot possibly tolerate things that truly outrage it.

EUGÉNIE. Oh, my divine mentors! I see that, according to your principles, there are very few crimes on earth. We can peacefully surrender to all our desires, bizarre as they may appear to the morons who are offended and alarmed by everything, and who stupidly mistake social institutions for the divine laws of nature.

But, my friends, won't you at least admit that certain procedures are absolutely revolting and decidedly criminal even though they are determined by nature? I'm willing to agree that nature, which is singular in its productions and varied in the leanings it gives us, can sometimes compel us to perform cruel actions. Yet what if, for argument's sake, we yielded to these depravities and capitulated to the inspirations of this bizarre nature to the point of killing another human being? You would then concede—at least, I hope so—that such an action would be a crime?

DOLMANCÉ. We are a long way from conceding anything of the sort, Eugénie. Since destruction is a primary law of nature, nothing destructive could be a crime. How could nature ever be outraged by an action that serves it so well? Besides, the destruction that man boasts about is nothing but an idle dream. Murder is in no way destruction. The person who murders is simply varying forms by returning certain elements to nature— elements that nature's skillful hand instantly uses to complete other beings. Now, since creation is nothing but delightful for the person who submits to it, the murderer therefore provides a delight for nature. He supplies raw materials that nature promptly employs; and this action, which morons are foolish enough to rebuke, is nothing but a merit in the eyes of this universal agent. It's our arrogance that dares to set nature up as a crime. Since we consider ourselves the supreme creatures in the universe, we stupidly imagine that every injury suffered by this sublime creature would inevitably be an enormous crime. We believe that nature would perish if our marvelous species were wiped off the face of the earth. Yet by returning the creative faculty that nature yields to us, we would restore an energy that we lose through propagation.

And how inconsistent, Eugénie. What? An ambitious sovereign can destroy the enemies that interfere with his striving for greatness—annihilate his enemies without any scruples and without a second thought. . . . By the same token, cruel, arbitrary, and dictatorial laws can justify the slaughter of millions of victims every century. . . . And yet we feeble and unhappy individuals are not allowed to sacrifice a single being to our whims or our vengeance? Is there nothing so barbarous, so ridiculously bizarre? And shouldn't we, under the guise of deepest mystery, take ample revenge for our ineptitude? (*Since this article is treated more extensively below, we have limited ourselves here to providing a few bases for the system that we will soon develop.*)

EUGÉNIE. Definitely! . . . Oh, how seductive your morals are, and how I enjoy them! . . . But Dolmancé, tell me in good faith: Haven't you sometimes fulfilled your cravings in this respect?

DOLMANCÉ. Don't force me to expose my faults. Their number and their quality would easily make me blush. Perhaps I'll confess them to you some day.

MADAME DE SAINT-ANGE. In wielding the sword of the law, that scoundrel has often used its blade to satisfy his passions.

DOLMANCÉ. May I have no other reproaches to endure!

MADAME DE SAINT-ANGE (*throwing her arms around him*). Divine man! . . . I adore you! . . . How much spirit and courage to have, like you, tasted all the pleasures! Only a genius has the honor of smashing all the barriers of ignorance and stupidity. Kiss me! You're bewitching!

DOLMANCÉ. Be frank, Eugénie. Have you never wished death on somebody?

EUGÉNIE. Oh, yes, yes, yes. And every day for a long time now, I have to deal with an abominable creature, who, I wish, were dead.

MADAME DE SAINT-ANGE. I bet I can guess who.

EUGÉNIE. Whom do you suspect?

MADAME DE SAINT-ANGE. Your mother.

EUGÉNIE. Oh! Let me hide my embarrassment in your bosom!

DOLMANCÉ. Voluptuous creature! I want to have my turn overwhelming you with caresses, as the reward for energy of your heart and your delicious mind. (*DOLMANCÉ covers her with kisses and slaps her buttocks lightly. He has an erection. MADAME DE SAINT-ANGE grabs and jerks his dick. From time to time, his hands stray across her bottom, which she offers him lecherously. Upon coming to slightly, DOLMANCÉ continues.*) But couldn't we carry out this divine idea?

MADAME DE SAINT-ANGE. Eugénie, I detested my mother as much as you despise yours, and I never wavered.

EUGÉNIE. I lacked the means.

MADAME DE SAINT-ANGE. You mean the courage.

EUGÉNIE. Alas! So young, too!

DOLMANCÉ. But now, Eugénie! What would you do now?

EUGÉNIE. I'd do anything. . . . Give me the means and you'll see!

DOLMANCÉ. You'll have the means, Eugénie, I promise you—but on one condition.

EUGÉNIE. And what condition would that be? Or rather, what condition can there be that I'm not ready to accept?

DOLMANCÉ. Come here, my little scoundrel, come into my arms. I can't hold out any longer. Your charming behind must be the price for the gift I'm promising you. One crime must pay for the other! Come here! ... Or rather, the two of you hurry up and let billows of come drench the divine fire that enflames us!

MADAME DE SAINT-ANGE. Let's put a little order into those orgies, if you please. We need order even at the height of ecstasy and infamy.

DOLMANCÉ. Nothing could be simpler. The most important goal, I feel, is for me to come and simultaneously offer this charming little girl the most pleasure that I can. I'm going to stick my cock into her ass while you hold her in your arms and jerk her as hard as possible. By means of the position I put you in, she'll give you tit for tat: you'll kiss each other. After several thrusts in this child's ass, we'll vary the tableau. I'll then fuck you up the ass, Madame. Eugénie, on top of you with your head between her legs, will present me with her clitoris to lick. That way, I'll get her to pour out her juice a second time. Next I'll plumb her anus again. You'll hand over your ass instead of the cunt she offered me—that is, you'll insert her head between your legs just as she'll have done. I'll suck your asshole just as I'll have sucked your pussy. You'll come, so will I—while my hand embraces the lovely little body of our bewitching novice, tickling her clitoris to drive her up the wall.

MADAME DE SAINT-ANGE. Good, my dear Dolmancé. But won't you be lacking something?

DOLMANCÉ. My dick up her ass? You're right, Madame.

MADAME DE SAINT-ANGE. Let's forgo it this morning. We'll make up for it tonight! My brother will assist us, and our pleasures will be infinite. Let's get to work!

DOLMANCÉ. I'd like Eugénie to jerk me for a moment. (*She does so.*) Yeah! That's it. ... A bit faster, my darling. ... Always keep it bare—that vermillion head! Never cover it up. ...

The tighter you draw the string, the more easily you induce the erection. If you're jerking a dick, you must never peel back the foreskin. . . . Fine! . . . This way you yourself prepare the state of the penis that is going to perforate you. . . . Do you see how it makes up its mind? . . . Give me your tongue, you little slut! . . . Put your buttocks on my right hand, while my left hand tickles your clitoris.

MADAME DE SAINT-ANGE. Eugénie, do you want him to taste even greater pleasures?

EUGÉNIE. Definitely. . . . I'll do anything to help.

MADAME DE SAINT-ANGE. Fine! Take his dick in your mouth and suck it for a few moments.

EUGÉNIE (*doing it*). Like this?

DOLMANCÉ. Ah, what a delicious mouth! What heat! . . . It's as enchanting as the most beautiful ass! You skillful and voluptuous ladies—never withhold this pleasure from your lovers. You will chain them to you forever! . . . Oh, God damn it! . . . God fuck! . . .

MADAME DE SAINT-ANGE. What blasphemy, my friend!

DOLMANCÉ. Give me your ass, Madame! . . . Yes, give it to me, so I can kiss it while getting sucked! And don't be surprised by my blasphemy! One of my greatest pleasures is to curse God when I get stiff. My mind, which is then exalted a thousand times over, seems to loathe and scorn this disgusting chimera all the more. I'd like to find a way to rail against it more nastily or rant against it more abusively. And when my cursed reflections finally convince me that this object of my hatred is invalid and nauseating, I lose my temper. At such an instant, I'd like to restore the phantom so that my rage is at least based on something concrete.

Emulate me, my charming lady, and you will recognize the increase that such discourses unfailingly impose on your senses. But God damn it! . . . I see that, blissful as I may be, I must withdraw totally from that divine mouth. . . . Otherwise I'd leave my semen there! . . . Come on, Eugénie, take your place. Let's carry out the tableau that I've drawn, and let's all three of us plunge into the most voluptuous intoxication. (*The tableau is arranged.*)

EUGÉNIE. My dear friend, I'm so terrified that your efforts may be useless! Our age difference is too big.

DOLMANCÉ. I sodomize younger persons than you daily. Just yesterday, a little seven-year-old boy was devirginized by this cock within less than three minutes. . . . Courage, Eugénie, courage! . . .

EUGÉNIE. Ah, you're tearing me apart!

MADAME DE SAINT-ANGE. Handle her with kid gloves, Dolmancé. Don't forget that I'm responsible for her.

DOLMANCÉ. Jerk her well, Madame. It'll be less painful. Besides, everything is settled now. I'm down to her hair.

EUGÉNIE. Oh, God! It's not painless! . . . Look at the sweat that covers my forehead, dear friend. . . . Oh, God! I've never felt such horrible pain! . . .

MADAME DE SAINT-ANGE. You're half deflowered, darling! That makes you a woman now. And a woman can buy this glory with a little torment. Besides, don't my fingers calm you down?

EUGÉNIE. How could I endure it without them? Tickle me, my angel. . . . I sense that pain is imperceptibly turning into pleasure. Push! . . . Push! . . . Dolmancé. . . . I'm dying! . . .

DOLMANCÉ. Oh! Fucking God! God damn it! Fucking Trinity! Let's switch! I can't stand it any longer! . . . Your butt, Madame, I beg you! Put yourselves instantly in the positions I've prescribed for you! (*They arrange themselves, and* DOLMANCÉ *continues.*) There's less pain here. . . . How deep my cock penetrates! . . . Honestly, this gorgeous ass is no less delicious, Madame! . . .

EUGÉNIE. Am I in the right position, Dolmancé?

DOLMANCÉ. You're marvelous! This pretty little virgin cunt is offering itself to me with such delight. I'm a culprit, a delinquent—I know! Such charms are scarcely meant for my eyes. But the desire to give this child her first lessons in lust will carry the day over all other considerations. I want to make her semen gush. . . . I want to make her come if possible. . . . (*He licks her.*)

EUGÉNIE. Ah! I'm dying of pleasure, I can't resist! . . .

MADAME DE SAINT-ANGE. And I'm coming! . . . Ah! Fuck, fuck, fuck! . . . Dolmancé, I'm coming!

EUGÉNIE. So am I, darling. . . . Ah! My God! He sucks me so
wonderfully! . . .

MADAME DE SAINT-ANGE. Then swear, you little slut! . . . Just
swear! . . .

EUGÉNIE. God damn it! I'm coming! . . . I'm in the sweetest
intoxication! . . .

DOLMANCÉ. To your place! . . . To your place, Eugénie! . . .
I'll be the victim of all these shifts of places. (*EUGÉNIE gets into
her position again.*) Ah! Good! I'm back in my starting loca-
tion. Show me your asshole, Madame, so I can rim it at
will. . . . How I love to kiss an ass after fucking it! . . . Ah! Let
me rim it thoroughly, while I spurt my seed to the bottom of
your friend's asshole! . . . Would you believe it, Madame? This
time my cock slid in painlessly! . . . Ah! Fuck! Fuck! You can't
imagine how it's squeezed, how it's squashed! . . . Good fucking God! What bliss! Ah! I'm done for! I can't hold back any
longer! . . . My gism is shooting . . . and I'm dead! . . .

EUGÉNIE. He's killing me, too, my darling, I swear it. . . . .

MADAME DE SAINT-ANGE. The little whore! How promptly
she'll get used to it!

DOLMANCÉ. I know an endless number of girls of her age
whom nothing in the world could induce to come in any other
way. It only hurts the first time. Once a woman has tried it, she
won't go for anything else. . . . Oh, God! I'm worn out! Let me
catch my breath—at least for a few moments.

MADAME DE SAINT-ANGE. That's a man for you, my dear! No
sooner does he glance at you than his desires are satisfied! This
exhaustion leads men to disgust, and disgust soon leads them
to contempt.

DOLMANCÉ (*coldly*). Ah! What an insult, divine beauty! (*He
embraces both of them.*) The two of you were made purely for
tributes, no matter what our condition.

MADAME DE SAINT-ANGE. In any event, console yourself, my
Eugénie. If they have the right to neglect us because they're satisfied, don't we have the same right to scorn them when their
behavior forces us to do so? If Tiberius, on Capri, sacrificed the
objects of his passions, Zingua, queen of Africa, likewise immolated her lovers.

DOLMANCÉ. Nevertheless, these perfectly simple excesses, with which I'm, no doubt, familiar, will never occur among us. There's an old saying: "Dog doesn't eat dog!" And banal as it may be, it's still correct. You needn't be scared of me, my darlings! I may cause you to do great harm to others, but I will never harm you myself.

EUGÉNIE. Ah! No, no, my dear lady! I can answer for him! Dolmancé will never abuse the privileges we give him in regard to us. I believe he has the honesty of a roué—the finest integrity there is. But let's lead our mentor back to his principles of conduct and, I beg you, let's return to the great plan that inspired us before we calmed down.

MADAME DE SAINT-ANGE. What, you slut! You're still thinking about that! And here I thought that it came purely from the excitement of your mind.

EUGÉNIE. It's the most definite thrill of my heart, and I won't be content until this crime is committed.

MADAME DE SAINT-ANGE. Ah, my oh my! Spare her! Remember that she's your mother!

EUGÉNIE. A nice title!

DOLMANCÉ. You're right. Did her mother think about Eugénie when she brought her into the world? The hussy let herself get fucked because she enjoyed it, but she was quite far from envisioning a daughter. So let Eugénie do whatever she likes to that woman! Let's give her free rein, and let's content ourselves with assuring her that no matter how extreme her excesses, she'll never be guilty of any crime.

EUGÉNIE. I abhor her, I detest her—a thousand reasons legitimize my hatred. I have to take her life no matter what the price!

DOLMANCÉ. Very well, Eugénie. Since your resolutions are unwavering, you will be satisfied—I swear it. But allow me to offer you some advice, which you should absolutely take to heart before acting. Never so much as hint at your secret, my darling, and, above all, proceed alone. Nothing is more dangerous than having accomplices. We must always suspect even those whom we consider to be closest to us. "Either we ought never," said Machiavelli, "to have collaborators, or else we should get rid of them after they've served us."

That's not all. Deception is indispensable for what you are contemplating. Ingratiate yourself more than ever with your victim, Eugénie, before immolating her. Pretend to sympathize with her or console her. Cajole her, share her sorrows, swear to her that you adore her. Stop at nothing until she's convinced. In such cases, deception can't go far enough. Nero caressed Agrippina on the very boat on which she was to drown. Emulate his example, use any imposture, any double-dealing that your mind comes up with. Lies are necessary for a woman—and it's above all when she wishes to swindle that lies become obligatory for her.

EUGÉNIE. These lessons will be retained and practiced by me, no doubt. But if you please, let's probe more deeply into the deception that you advise women to employ. Do you feel that fraud is unconditionally essential in the world?

DOLMANCÉ. Certainly! I don't know of anything more essential. An undeniable truth can prove how indispensable fraud can be—everyone employs it. Let me therefore ask you: How can a sincere individual get along in a society of deceitful people? Now, is it true, as is claimed, that virtues have some use in the civil world? If so, then how can one be like many people who don't have the will, the power, or the gift of any virtue whatsoever? How, I ask you, can't you expect such a person to be essentially obligated to put up a false front in order to obtain, in his turn, a bit of the portion of happiness that his rivals steal from him? And indeed, is it definitely virtue or the appearance thereof that becomes really crucial for a member of society? Let's not doubt that appearance alone suffices: If he possesses appearance, then that's all he needs. Since a social being regards other members of society in only a shallow fashion, isn't it enough for them to show us a disguise?

We must also make it very clear that the practice of virtues is useful only to the person who possesses them. Other people derive so little from them that, so long as the individual who must live with us seems virtuous, it doesn't matter whether or not he is actually virtuous. Deception, incidentally, is nearly always a sure means of gaining success. The deceptive person necessarily acquires a sort of priority over the man who deals with him or squares with him: he persuades him by dazzling him with a false exterior. From that moment on, he is successful. If I perceive that I've been tricked, then I blame myself, and my trickster has an even freer hand since I'm too proud to complain. His superiority grows and grows; he'll be right when I'm wrong; he'll advance while I stay put; he'll get rich while I get ruined. Always, finally, beyond me, he'll soon have public opinion on his side. At that point, it's no use my indicting him, nobody will listen to me. So let's boldly and endlessly cultivate the most notorious deception. Let's view it as the key to all graces, all favors, all reputations, all riches, and, at our leisure, let's calm the minor grief at making dupes with the piquant delight of being mischievous.

MADAME DE SAINT-ANGE. I think that was infinitely more than was needed to say about this issue. Eugénie is convinced, and now she must be appeased and encouraged. She'll act when she wishes. I imagine that we should continue our discourse on the different sexual refinements of lascivious men. This must be a vast domain—let's move across it. We've just initiated our trainee into several mysteries of practice. Let's not forget theory.

DOLMANCÉ. The wayward details of male passions, Madame, are scarcely appropriate subjects for a young girl who, above all like Eugénie, is not destined to become a prostitute. Eugénie is going to marry eventually, and, on that assumption, we can wager ten to one that her husband won't share those lecherous delights. If he does enjoy them, however, then her conduct must readily be as follows: lots of sweetness and compliance; otherwise, lots of duplicity and indemnity in secret. Those few words say everything.

Nevertheless, your Eugénie may desire several analyses of male pleasures in libertinage. If so, then let's sum them up in three groups: sodomy, sacrilegious fantasies, and a taste for cruelty.

That first passion, sodomy, is universal today. We are going to add a few reflections to what we have already stated. Sodomy is divided into two classes: active and passive. The man who fucks an ass—whether a boy's or a woman's—is committing active sodomy. But when the man gets fucked up the ass, then he's being a passive sodomite. People have often wondered which of these two kinds of sodomy is the more gratifying. It is assuredly the passive manner, since a man then enjoys both sensual pleasures: front and back. It is so delightful to change your gender, so delicious to imitate a hooker, to surrender to a man who treats you like a woman, to call him your male lover, to acknowledge yourself as his mistress! Ah, my friends! What sheer bliss!

But, Eugénie, let's confine ourselves here to specific advice that can serve only a woman who, by changing into a man and following our example, wishes to enjoy this delicious pleasure. I've just familiarized you with those attacks, Eugénie, and I've seen enough to convince myself that some day you'll go very far along that route. I can only counsel you to make such progress across the loveliest paths of the Island of Cythera, and I'm perfectly sure that you'll heed my advice. I'm going to stick to merely two or three counsels, which are essential to everyone who wants to enjoy purely this type of gratification or who wants to be the same.

First off, make sure you always jerk your clitoris while you're being sodomized. No two joys complement one another like these. Next, avoid the bidet and the rubbing of linen when you've been fucked up the ass. It's good if the breach is always open. The results are desires, titillations that are quickly snuffed out by the striving for cleanliness. You can't imagine how long the sensuous delights can last. So when you're amusing yourself in this fashion, Eugénie, avoid acids—they inflame the hemorrhoids, making any insertions in the asshole painful. Don't let several men in a row come inside your hole. This fusion of sperms may be pleasurable in the imagination, but it's often bad for your health. Keep pushing out those different emissions as they spurt.

EUGÉNIE. Well, if a man comes in front, isn't that a crime?

MADAME DE SAINT-ANGE. Please don't imagine, you silly thing, that there is anything the least bit wrong with using any method whatsoever to reroute a man's semen from its highway. After all, propagation is not the be-and-end-all of nature; it is simply tolerated by nature. And if we don't profit from this tolerance, then nature's intentions are carried out far more effectively. Eugénie, you must be the sworn enemy of this tedious propagation and you must endlessly divert this perfidious liquid, even in marriage. For the rank spread of this fluid serves only to ruin a woman's figure, to deaden the stirrings of delight in her, to make her wither, grow old, and to damage her health. Get your husband accustomed to the loss of his semen, offer him all the roads that can lead the tribute away from the temple. Tell your husband that you hate children, beg him not to make any offspring. Be extremely careful, my love. Let me tell you: I despise propagation so intently that I would stop being friends with you the moment you became pregnant. If, however, this misfortune strikes you through no fault of your own, notify me in the first seven or eight weeks of your pregnancy, and I'll let it flow out very gently. Don't be scared of infanticide, it's an imaginary crime. A woman is always the mistress of what she carries in her womb, and there is as little wrong with destroying this kind of material as there is with purging the other kind with medicaments, if we feel the need.

EUGÉNIE. But what if the expectant woman has reached her time?

MADAME DE SAINT-ANGE. Even if the baby had already seen the light of day, we would still have the right to destroy it. For there is no greater certainty on earth than a mother's rights over her children. There is no nation that hasn't recognized this truth; it is based on reason, on principle.

DOLMANCÉ. This right is given in nature. . . . It is incontestable. The absurdity of the deific system is the source of all those gross blunders. The imbeciles believed in God, convinced as they were that we owe our existence purely to him, and that the instant an embryo reaches maturity, it is animated by a little soul emanating from God. These morons, I tell you, must have regarded the destruction of this tiny creature as a capital offense, because it stopped belonging to mankind. It was now the work of God, it belonged to God: Could a human being dispose of it with a clear conscience?

However, since the torch of philosophy has scattered all those hypocrisies, since the divine chimera has been trampled underfoot, since we are better instructed in the laws and secrets of physics and have developed the principle of generation, and since this purely material mechanism offers our eyes nothing more astonishing than the growth of a seed of grain, we have left human blunders and returned to nature. In expanding the measure of our rights, we have finally come to realize that we were perfectly free to take back what we had given only reluctantly or accidentally, and that it was impossible to require any individual whomsoever to become a parent if he didn't wish to do so. We also acknowledge that it was of no special consequence whether one creature more or less lived on the earth. In short, we became as certain the masters of this lump of flesh—however animated—as we are the masters of the nails we cut from our fingers, or the outgrowths we remove from our bodies, or the digestives we expel from our innards; that's because they all come from us and they all belong to us, and we are the sole owners of whatever derives from us.

When I explained to you, Eugénie, the insignificance of a murder on this earth, you must have grasped the unimportance of anything pertaining to infanticide—even if the victim is already endowed with reason. So there's no use my rehashing my clarification. Your outstanding intelligence will add your evidence to mine. The history of the mores of all the nations in the world will show you the universality of this custom and convince you that it is pure nonsense to regard this utterly indifferent action as wicked.

EUGÉNIE (*first to* DOLMANCÉ). I can't tell you how persuasive you are! (*Next, to* MADAME DE SAINT-ANGE.) But tell me, my dear, have you ever used this remedy you offer me to destroy a fetus inside a womb?

MADAME DE SAINT-ANGE. Twice, and each time with the greatest triumph. I must admit that I passed the test only in the initial stage of pregnancy, while two women I know applied that same remedy halfway through, and they assured me that they were equally successful. So, my darling, you can count on me if the occasion arises. But I urge you to avoid ever needing this solution in the first place: prevention is the safest method.

Now let's resume the roster of lubricious details that we've promised this girl. Go ahead, Dolmancé, we've reached the sacrilegious fancies.

DOLMANCÉ. I assume that Eugénie has come too far from her religious errors. By now she must be profoundly convinced that anything linked to ridiculing the objects of the cult of fools must be totally inconsequential. These fancies are so insignificant that they must actually excite only very young minds, for which the breaking of any barrier provides sensual pleasure. It's a sort of minor criminal court that inflames the imagination, and that can, no doubt, be amusing for a few moments. But I find that these delights are bound to turn bland and cold once you've had time for learning and for persuading yourself of the nullity of the objects of which the idols we jeer at are paltry depictions. In the enlightened philosopher's eyes, the profaning of hosts, relics, icons of saints, the crucifix—these actions merely signify the same as the defacement of a pagan statue. Once you've condemned these execrable knickknacks to disdain, you must leave them there and forget about them. Among all these things, it's good to preserve only blasphemy—not that blasphemy contains more reality. For the instant that there is no God, why bother reviling his name? You see, it's essential to utter coarse and filthy words in the intoxication of pleasure, and blasphemous language powerfully incites the imagination. Nothing is to be spared. You must decorate these words with the greatest luxury of expressions. They must be as scandalous as possible, for scandalizing is very sweet. It involves a slight triumph over pride—a triumph that shouldn't be scorned. I confess, ladies, that this is one of my secret pleasures—there are few spiritual delights that animate my imagination more strongly. Try it, Eugénie, and you'll see the results.

Above all, you must display a tremendous impiety when you're among people of your own age, who are still vegetating in the murkiness of superstition. You must flaunt libertinage and free-thinking. Dress like a slut and expose your bosom. If you and the other girls go to secret places, tuck up indecently. Let them deliberately view the most furtive parts of your body; and demand the same of them. Seduce them, preach to them, make them grasp the silliness of their prejudices. Make them, as the phrase goes, fall. Curse with them like a man. If they're younger than you, take them by force, enjoy them and corrupt them, either by example, or by advice, or, in short, by whatever you believe can do the best job of perverting them.

You should likewise be extremely uninhibited with men, show off religiosity and insolence together with them. Far from being scared of the liberties they'll take, you must covertly grant them anything that entertains them without compromising yourself. Let them feel you up, jerk them off, have them jerk you. Go so far as to offer them your ass. But since a woman's fanciful honor greatly depends on her virginity, be less accessible with it. Once you're married, don't take a lover. Instead, hire some lackeys or pay a few trustworthy men. From that moment on, everything must be concealed. You must never sully your reputation. Without arousing suspicion, you've found the art of doing whatever you like. Now let's continue.

The delights of cruelty are the third group that we have undertaken to analyze. Nowadays, these delights are very widespread among men, and this is the argument men employ to justify them: "We want to be greatly excited," they say. "That's the goal of every man who submits to pleasure. And we want to reach this goal with the most potent methods. Starting from that premise, we don't have to know whether our actions will please or displease the object serving us. We need only shake the mass of our nerves as violently as possible. After all, there is no doubt that since pain affects us much more sharply than pleasure, the shocks reacting upon our nerves when we arouse this agonizing sensation in another person are likewise more violent; our nerves vibrate far more vigorously. The shocks reverberate in us more energetically, they circulate our animal drives more vehemently. Now, since these drives establish themselves in the lower regions of the body by means of their intrinsic retroactive motion, they also inflame the organs of pleasure and prepare them for the acts of passion."

In women, the effects of pleasure are always deceptive. Moreover, it is very difficult for an old and ugly man to produce those results in the first place. What if they succeed nonetheless? The effects are then feeble, and the nervous shock is a lot less forceful. We must therefore choose pain, because its effects cannot mislead, and its sensations are keener.

But, we protest to the men infatuated with this mania, pain afflicts your neighbor. Is it charitable to do evil unto others for your own satisfaction? The rogues will reply as follows. Since, in the act of pleasure, they are accustomed to viewing themselves as everything and the others as nothing, they are convinced that, according to natural impulses, the rogues quite obviously prefer what they feel to what they don't feel. Who cares, they dare to say, about our neighbor's pains? Do we feel them? No. Quite the opposite! We have just demonstrated that those pains engender a delicious sensation. On what grounds should we worry about an individual who doesn't matter to us in any way whatsoever? On what grounds should we spare someone a pain that's never cost us a tear—when we are certain that this pain will bring us enormous pleasure? Have we ever sensed a single natural impulse that advises us to give others priority over ourselves? And isn't everyone out for himself in the world? You speak fancifully to us about nature, which tells us to do unto others as we would have them do unto us. However, this absurd counsel has always come to us from men, and weak men at that. A powerful man would never utter such nonsense.

It was the early Christians who, persecuted day after day because of their mindless attitude, yelled at whoever wanted to hear them: "Don't burn us! Don't flay us! Nature says that we should do unto others as we would have them do unto us!"

Imbeciles! How could nature, which always advises us to enjoy ourselves, which never arouses other stirrings in us, other inspirations—how could nature, a moment later, with unprecedented inconsistency, assure us that we should never enjoy ourselves if it means hurting other people? Ah! Let's believe it! Let's believe it! Eugénie! Nature, the mother of us all, never speaks to us except about ourselves. Nothing is as egotistical as nature's voice. And what we hear most sharply in that voice is the holy and immutable advice to enjoy ourselves, no matter what it costs others. But, people will object, the others may try to avenge themselves. . . . Fine! Then might alone will make right! If that's the case, we'll find ourselves in an initial state of war and permanent destruction for which nature's hand created us, and it is only in this state that our existence is advantageous for nature.

That, my dear Eugénie, is how those people reason. And on the basis of my studies and my experiences, I will add that cruelty, far from being a vice, is the first sentiment that nature teaches us. A child breaks its rattle, bites its wet nurse's nipple, and strangles its pet bird, long before it reaches the age of reason. Cruelty is imprinted in animals, in which, as I believe I've told you, the laws of nature are more legible and energetic than in us. Among savages, cruelty is far closer to nature than among civilized men. It would therefore be ridiculous to regard cruelty as a deprivation of nature. This mentality, I repeat, is all wrong. Cruelty is inherent in nature. We are each born with a dose of cruelty, which is modified only by education. But education isn't part of nature. Education harms the sacred effects of nature just as cultivation harms trees. Go to your orchard and compare two trees: one has been abandoned to the care of nature, the other has been artificially cultivated and restrained. You'll then see which is the more beautiful tree, you'll see which supplies the better fruit. Cruelty is nothing but human energy that hasn't yet been corrupted by civilization. Hence, cruelty is a virtue and not a vice. Get rid of your laws, your punishments, your mores, and cruelty will stop having dangerous effects. It will never act without our managing to repel it with the same methods. It is in the state of civilization that cruelty becomes dangerous, because the injured party nearly always lacks either the strength or the means to resist the injury. However, if an uncivilized condition reacts to the strong man, it will be repelled by him; and if it reacts to the weak man, injuring merely a being who yields to the strong man according to the laws of nature, then the uncivilized condition will not suffer the slightest disadvantage.

We will not analyze the cruelty indicated in the lewd pleasures of men, Eugénie. You can more or less see the various excesses to which those delights can bring someone, and your ardent imagination must let you easily grasp that there should be no limits in a firm and stoic soul. Nero, Tiberius, Heliogabalus immolated babies in order to get an erection. Marshal de Retz, Charolais, Condé's uncle, also committed lust murders. In his investigation, de Retz avowed that he knew no more powerful bliss than the torture inflicted by him and his chaplain on little children of both sexes. Seven or eight hundred immolated corpses were discovered in one of his castles in Brittany. This is all understandable, as I've just proved to you. A man's constitution, his organs, the flow of his vital liquids, the energy of his animal spirits—these are the physical causes that simultaneously produce a Titus or a Nero, a Messalina or a Chantal. We should no more take pride in virtue than repent vice, no more accuse nature of letting us be born good than creating us evil. Nature has acted according to its goals, its plans, and its needs. We must submit. I will therefore examine only female cruelty, which is always far more active than male cruelty, the powerful reason being the hypersensitivity of a woman's organs.

In general, we differentiate two sorts of cruelty. One sort emerges from stupidity, which, never rational, never analyzed, puts the stupid person on the same footing as a wild beast. Stupidity offers no pleasure, since the person disposed to stupidity is insensitive to any studied nuances. The brutalities committed by such creatures are seldom dangerous. It is always easy to escape their clutches.

The other sort of cruelty, produced by the acute sensitivity of the organs, is known only to extremely delicate creatures; and the excesses to which this sensitivity is driven are merely refinements of their delicacy. It is this delicacy which, all too quickly blunted by its excessive finesse, rearouses itself by utilizing all the resources of cruelty. But how few people grasp these distinctions! . . . And how few do we sense! Yet they exist, they are indisputable.

Now this second kind of cruelty is affected more often by women. Study women thoroughly. You will see whether it wasn't their hypersensitivity that led them here. You will see whether it's not their overactive imaginations, their mental forces that make them evil and ferocious. All these women are enchanting. Nor does a single member of this species fail to turn heads if such is her aim. Unfortunately, the rigidity, or rather absurdity, of our mores leaves them little scope for their cruelty. These women are forced to hide, to mask, to conceal their proclivities behind open acts of charity, which they detest to the bottom of their hearts. It is only behind the darkest veil, with the greatest precautions, and with the help of several reliable friends, that these women can submit to their inclinations. And since there are many such females, there are, consequently, many miserable females. Would you care to meet them? Announce a cruel spectacle: a duel, a fire, a battle, a gladiator combat. You will see those women come running. However, these occasions are too infrequent to nourish their frenzies; they contain themselves and they suffer.

Let's have a quick survey of women of this kind.

Zingua, queen of Angola, the cruelest of women, slaughtered her lovers after they enjoyed her. She often had warriors clash before her and she became the winner's prize. To gratify her bloodthirsty soul, she entertained herself by condemning all pregnant women under thirty to be stacked up in a lime pit. (See *The History of Zingua, Queen of Angola*, by a missionary.)

Zoe, wife of a Chinese emperor, had no greater pleasure than watching executions of criminals. For lack of criminals, she immolated slaves while fucking with her husband, and the intensity of her orgasm was proportionate to the agonies that these poor wretches endured. It was Zoe who, refining the tortures she inflicted on her victims, invented the famous hollow bronze pillar, in which the sufferer was placed and roasted.

Theodora, Justinian's wife, enjoyed watching men turned into eunuchs. And Messalina jerked off while men were pumped dry in front of her.

The Floridians made their husbands' members swell up, and then the wives put tiny insects on the glans, which caused horrible pains. Several wives clustered around one man and tied him up in order to reach their goal more definitely. When they sighted the Spaniards, the women held their husbands while those barbaric Europeans slaughtered them.

Madame Voisin and Madame Brinvilliers poisoned their victims for the sole pleasure of committing a crime.

History, in short, offers us thousands upon thousands of cases of female cruelty. And since these stirrings correspond to women's natural tendencies, I wish they grew accustomed to active flagellation, a method employed by cruel men to appease their ferocity. Some women do use flagellation, I know. But it's not as widespread among them as I'd like it to be. If this possibility were opened to female barbarism, society would greatly benefit. For, unable to be wicked in this manner, they are wicked in another. And thereby spreading their venom in the world, they are the despair of their husbands and their families. These women refuse to do a good deed when the occasion arises, they refuse to help an unfortunate. Such a rejection gives, if you like, impetus to the ferocity in which some women are naturally trained. But this impetus is feeble and often far too remote from the female need to do worse. There are, no doubt, other methods with which a both sensitive and ferocious woman could pacify her stormy passions. But those methods are dangerous, Eugénie, and I would never dare advise you to apply them. . . .

Oh, God! What's wrong, my dear angel? Madame, just look at the state your pupil is in! . . .

EUGÉNIE (*jerking off*). Oh, gracious God! You're making my head whirl. . . . That's the effect of your fucking discourse!

DOLMANCÉ. Help, help, Madame! Are we going to let this gorgeous child come off without our help?. . .

MADAME DE SAINT-ANGE. Oh, that would be unjust! (*Taking the girl in her arms.*) Adorable creature, I've never seen a sensitivity like yours, I've never met such a delicious person! . . .

DOLMANCÉ. Take care of the front part, Madame. My tongue will graze her pretty little asshole, while I lightly slap her ass cheeks. That way, she'll come off seven or eight times in our hands.

EUGÉNIE (*very aroused*). Ah! Fuck! It won't be difficult!

DOLMANCÉ. In your current positions, my ladies, I see that the two of you can take turns sucking my dick. It would excite me so much that I would devote far more energy to the pleasures of our enchanting pupil.

EUGÉNIE. My darling, I'll compete with you for the honor of sucking this beautiful cock. (*She clutches it.*)

DOLMANCÉ. Ah, what bliss! . . . What delicious heat! . . . But Eugénie, will you behave properly when things come to a head?

MADAME DE SAINT-ANGE. She'll swallow . . . she'll swallow. . . . I guarantee it! And besides, if, out of childishness . . . or goodness knows what reason . . . she neglected the duties imposed here by lust—

DOLMANCÉ (*very animated*). I would never forgive her, Madame, I would never forgive her! . . . An exemplary punishment . . . I swear to you that she'd be whipped . . . whipped till I drew blood! . . . Ah, God damn it! I'm shooting! . . . My come is flowing! . . . Swallow it, swallow it, Eugénie! Don't waste a single drop! . . . And you, Madame, take care of my ass; it's offering itself to you. . . . Don't you see it gaping—my fucking ass? . . . Don't you see it begging for your fingers? . . . Fuck it to hell! My ecstasy is complete. . . . You'll fist-fuck my ass! Ah! Let's pull ourselves together, I can't anymore . . . That enchanting girl has sucked me like an angel . . . .

EUGÉNIE. My dear and adorable tutor, I haven't spilled a drop. Kiss me, my love, your come is now at the bottom of my bowels.

DOLMANCÉ. She's delightful. . . . And how wildly the little slut came! . . .

MADAME DE SAINT-ANGE. She's inundated! Oh, God! What do I hear? . . . Someone's knocking. Who can be disturbing us here? . . . It's my brother! How imprudent! . . .

EUGÉNIE. My darling! This is treason!

DOLMANCÉ. Without precedence, isn't it? Don't be scared, Eugénie! We work only for your pleasures.

MADAME DE SAINT-ANGE. Ah! We'll convince her soon enough! Come here, my brother, and laugh at this little girl, who's hiding so as not to be seen by you.

Fourth Dialogue

CHEVALIER. Beautiful Eugénie, I beg you, don't have qualms about my discretion. It is total. You have my sister and my friend here, and they can both vouch for me.

DOLMANCÉ. I can see only one possibility for ending this ridiculous ceremonial at a single blow. Look, Chevalier, we're educating this pretty girl. We're teaching her everything that a demoiselle of her age should know. And in order to do a better job of it, we always add a bit of practice to theory. She needs to see a shooting dick. This is the point we've reached. Would you like to set an example?

CHEVALIER. This proposal is assuredly too flattering for me to refuse, and Mademoiselle has charms that will quite swiftly determine the effects of the desired lesson.

MADAME DE SAINT-ANGE. Well, then, let's go for it! Let's get down to business right away!

EUGÉNIE. Oh! You're really going too far! You're exploiting my youth to a terrible extent. . . . Whom will Monsieur take me for?

CHEVALIER. I'll take you for an enchanting girl, Eugénie . . . for the most adorable creature that I've ever known. (*He kisses her and fondles her charms.*) Oh, God! What sweet and fresh delights! What captivating joys! . . .

DOLMANCÉ. Less words, Chevalier, and let's have far more deeds! I'll direct the scene—it's my right. The purpose of this scene is to show Eugénie the mechanism of ejaculation. But since it would be difficult for her to observe such a phenomenon with sangfroid, the four of us will position ourselves face to face and very close together. You will jerk your young friend, Madame, and I'll take care of Chevalier. When the issue is male masturbation, a man understands it infinitely better than a woman does. Since he knows what he enjoys, he knows what he has to do to other men. Okay, let's get into our places! (*They arrange themselves.*)

MADAME DE SAINT-ANGE. Aren't we too close together?

DOLMANCÉ (*taking hold of* CHEVALIER). We can't be too close together, Madame. Eugénie's face and bosom must be flooded with evidence of your brother's virility. You must shoot right in her face. As master of the pump, I'll direct the gushes in such a way that she'll be absolutely covered with gism. Meanwhile, jerk her carefully on all the lewd parts of her body. Eugénie, surrender your total imagination to the ultimate surges of perversion. You must appreciate that the most beautiful mysteries of your imagination will be revealed to your eyes. Trample all restraint underfoot; modesty has never been a virtue. Had nature wanted us to hide certain areas of our bodies, it would have done so itself. But nature created us naked. So it means us to go naked. And any contrary procedure absolutely outrages natural laws. Children, who as yet have no concept of pleasure, and therefore no need to intensify pleasure through modesty, display themselves stark naked.

And we at times encounter something even more singular. There are countries whose inhabitants dress modestly without being modest in their customs. In Oraiti, the girls go about clothed, but they hike up their skirts when told to do so.

MADAME DE SAINT-ANGE. What I like about Dolmancé is that he never wastes time. Watch him operate while he lectures. Watch him complacently examine my brother's incredible ass. Watch Dolmancé voluptuously jerk that young man's beautiful dick. . . . Come on, Eugénie, let's get to work! The pump pipe is erect. It's about to inundate us.

EUGÉNIE. Ah, my dear friend! What a prodigious member! I can barely stick it in! Oh! My God! Are they all that huge?

DOLMANCÉ. Eugénie, you know that mine is a lot smaller. Such devices are terrifying for a young girl. You realize that it won't perforate you without risk.

EUGÉNIE (*already jerked by* MADAME DE SAINT-ANGE). I'll brave all of them to enjoy them all! . . .

DOLMANCÉ. And you'd be right! A girl should never be scared of such a thing! Nature indulges, and the torrents of pleasures that nature overwhelms you with must soon make up for the minor pains that herald them. I've seen younger girls than you endure even bigger cocks. The largest obstacles are surmounted with courage and patience. It's foolish to imagine that girls must be deflowered by cocks that are as small as possible. On the contrary, I'm of the opinion that a virgin must submit to the most gigantic apparatus she encounters. That way, with the ligaments of the hymen soon torn, the sensations of pleasure will surge in her more quickly. It's true that once she's accustomed to this regime, she'll have a difficult time returning to mediocrity. But she's rich, young, and beautiful, she'll find as many big tools as she likes. Still and all, if she is offered smaller cocks, and she nevertheless wants to use them, she can always slip them up her ass. . . .

MADAME DE SAINT-ANGE. No doubt about it! And in order for her to be even happier, she ought to use both holes at once. The voluptuous thrusts that shake the man who fucks her cunt will hasten the ecstasy of the man who fucks her ass. Then, flooded with come, she shoots hers while dying of delight.

DOLMANCÉ. (*We must point out that he keeps masturbating during the dialogue.*) It strikes me that two or three more cocks must enter your tableau, Madame. Couldn't the woman in the position you've just described have a dick in her mouth and one in each hand?

MADAME DE SAINT-ANGE. She can have one in each armpit and one in her hair. She can have thirty around her if that's possible. At such a moment, she should have nothing but, touch nothing but, devour nothing but dicks all around her, and they must inundate her at the same instant in which a man comes himself! Ah, Dolmancé! Whatever fucker you may be, I bet you haven't equaled me in these delicious battles of bliss. I've done everything that's possible in this area.

EUGÉNIE (*still jerked by* MADAME DE SAINT-ANGE *as* CHEVALIER *is jerked by* DOLMANCÉ). Ah, Madame! . . . You're making my head whirl! . . . What! I could surrender . . . to so many men at once! Ah! What delights! . . . You're jerking me so

wonderfully, dear friend! . . . You are the very goddess of pleasure! . . . And that gorgeous cock! How it swells up! . . . How
its majestic head bulges and turns vermillion! . . .

DOLMANCÉ. It's close to shooting!

CHEVALIER. Eugénie . . . my sister. . . . Come here. . . . Ah!
What divine breasts! . . . What sweet and fleshy thighs! . . .
Shoot! Shoot both of you! My come will join in! . . . It's
pouring! . . . Oh! God in heaven! (*During this ejaculation,*
DOLMANCÉ *makes sure to direct the waves of his friend's sperm*
upon the two women—especially EUGÉNIE, *who is inundated.*)

EUGÉNIE. What a beautiful spectacle! . . . How noble and
majestic it is! . . . I'm totally covered! . . . It's even spurted into
my eyes! . . .

MADAME DE SAINT-ANGE. Wait, my dear! Let me gather these
precious pearls. I'm going to rub them into your clitoris to
make you come faster.

EUGÉNIE. Oh, yes! My darling, yes! A delicious idea! . . . Do
it, and I'll swoon in your arms!

MADAME DE SAINT-ANGE. Divine child! Kiss me a thousand
times and a thousand more! . . . Let me suck your tongue! So I
can inhale your delightful breath when it is fired by the flames
of pleasure! . . . Oh! Fuck! I'll come myself! . . . My brother!
Finish me off—I beg you! . . .

DOLMANCÉ. Yes, Chevalier! . . . Yes, jerk your sister!

CHEVALIER. I'd rather fuck her. I'm still stiff!

DOLMANCÉ. Shove in my dick while you present me with your
ass! I'll fuck you during this blissful incest! Eugénie, armed
with this dildo, will fuck my ass! Since she is destined to eventually play all the different roles of lust, she must practice fill-
ing them equally during the lessons we give her.

EUGÉNIE (*grabbing a dildo*). Oh! Gladly! You'll never find
me in default regarding perversion! Lust is now my only god,
the single measure of my conduct, the sole basis of all my actions. (*She thrusts the dildo into* DOLMANCÉ's *ass.*) Is this right,
my dear mentor? . . . Am I doing it properly? . . .

DOLMANCÉ. You're marvelous! The little slut is fucking my
ass like a man! . . . Fine! It seems to me that the four of us are
perfectly bound together. All we need do now is let go!

MADAME DE SAINT-ANGE. Oh, I'm dying, Chevalier! ... It's impossible for me to get accustomed to the delicious jerking of your gorgeous dick! ...

DOLMANCÉ. Damn it! Your charming ass gives me so much pleasure! ... Ah! Fuck! Fuck! Let's all four of us come simultaneously! ... God damn it! I'm dying! I'm perishing! ... I've never come so blissfully in all my life! Have you shot your load, Chevalier?

CHEVALIER. Look at that cunt! It's smeared with my semen!

DOLMANCÉ. Ah, my friend! If only I had as much gism up my ass!

MADAME DE SAINT-ANGE. Why don't we rest? I'm dying.

DOLMANCÉ (*kissing EUGÉNIE.*) This enchanting girl has fucked me like a god!

EUGÉNIE. I really felt your pleasure.

DOLMANCÉ. If you're a libertine, every excess triggers pleasure, and the best thing a woman can do is to multiply those excesses beyond the very limits of possibility.

MADAME DE SAINT-ANGE. I've placed five hundred louis d'or in escrow with a notary. They will go to any individual who teaches me a passion that I don't know and that can plunge my senses into an ecstasy that I haven't yet enjoyed.

DOLMANCÉ. (*The conversationalists have adjusted their clothes and are now absorbed in their conversation.*) That's a bizarre idea, and I'll grasp it. But I doubt, Madame, whether the singular pleasure that you are seeking can resemble the meager delights that you have just tasted.

MADAME DE SAINT-ANGE. What do you mean?

DOLMANCÉ. Upon my honor, I know of nothing more tiresome than a cunt. And once, like yourself, a person has enjoyed the ass, I don't see how he can return to other pleasures.

MADAME DE SAINT-ANGE. Those are old habits. When one thinks like me, one wishes to be fucked all over. And whatever body part is punctured by the cock, one is happy to feel it there. However, I do share your opinion, and I bear witness to all voluptuous women that the bliss they feel when an ass is fucked surpasses by far the sensations they feel when a cunt is fucked. You can rely on that woman in Europe who has experienced both methods the most: I can assure you that there is no comparison whatsoever, and that any woman will find it difficult to revisit the front side once she has tried the backside.

CHEVALIER. I don't quite agree. I'll certainly attempt anything you want, but for my personal taste the only thing I truly like in a woman is the altar to which nature pays its homage.

DOLMANCÉ. Why that's the ass! If you carefully scrutinize nature's laws, my dear Chevalier, you'll see that nature has never indicated any altar for our homage but the asshole. Nature allows other possibilities, but it prescribes that aperture. For God's sake! If nature didn't intend to have us fuck the ass, then would nature have so precisely adjusted the hole to the forms of our members? Isn't this orifice round like them? What enemy of common sense can imagine that nature can have created an oval hole for a round member? The intention can be read on this discrepancy of form. Nature thereby reveals clearly that, by fostering a merely tolerated propagation, nature would unfailingly dislike the all-too-frequent sacrifices in this part of the body. But let's get on with Eugénie's education. She has just comfortably witnessed the sublime mystery of an orgasm, and I would now want her to learn how to direct its surges.

MADAME DE SAINT-ANGE. It would cost her some effort, given how exhausted the two of you are.

DOLMANCÉ. I agree. That's why I'd like to take a young and very robust boy in your household or from the countryside. He'd serve us as a model, and he could demonstrate whatever we teach.

MADAME DE SAINT-ANGE. I've got just the boy for you.

DOLMANCÉ. Could that happen to be a young, deliciously shaped gardener around eighteen or twenty years old? I just saw him working in your vegetable patch.

MADAME DE SAINT-ANGE. Augustin! Yes! Exactly! His member is thirteen inches long and eight and a half inches around.

DOLMANCÉ. Oh my God! What a monster! And does it shoot? . . .

MADAME DE SAINT-ANGE. Oh! A torrent! . . . I'll go get him!

Fifth Dialogue

DOLMANCÉ, THE CHEVALIER, AUGUSTIN,
EUGÉNIE, MADAME DE SAINT-ANGE

MADAME DE SAINT-ANGE (*bringing* AUGUSTIN). Here's the man I told you about. Come on, my friends! Let's have some fun! What would life be without pleasure? . . . Come here, you fool! . . . Oh, you idiot! . . . Would anyone believe that I've been struggling to break in this big swine for six months now without any success?

AUGUSTIN. Damn it, Madame! Yet at times you do say that I'm starting to behave a little, and whenever you've got some fallow land, you let me have it! . . .

DOLMANCÉ (*laughing*). Oh, charming! . . . Charming! . . . The dear boy! He's as frank as he's unsullied. . . . (*Pointing to* EUGÉNIE.) Augustin, here's a flower bed that's lying fallow. Do you want to take care of it?

AUGUSTIN. Ah! God help us, Monsieur! Such yummy morsels aren't meant for us.

DOLMANCÉ. Get to it, Mademoiselle!

EUGÉNIE (*blushing*). Oh, goodness! I'm so embarrassed!

DOLMANCÉ. Get rid of that cowardly feeling. All our actions, especially those of perversion, are inspired by nature, and so no action, whatever you may think up, is shameful. Come on, Eugénie! Be a whore with this young man! Remember that a girl's challenge to a boy is always an offering to nature, and that the female sex never serves nature better than when it prostitutes itself to the male sex. In short, you were born to get fucked, and the girl who rejects nature's goal for her doesn't deserve to see the light of day.

Why don't you yourself lower this young man's trousers to the very bottom of his gorgeous thighs? Roll up his shirt under his jacket so that both his front side and his backside—which, parenthetically, is very beautiful—are at your disposal. . . . One of your hands should now grab this ample piece of flesh, which, I see, will soon frighten you with its form. Your other hand should fondle his buttocks and tickle the orifice of his ass. . . . Yes, like that . . . (*To show* EUGÉNIE *what it's all about, he pokes* AUGUSTIN *himself.*) Don't ever cap this rubicund head, don't ever cover it while you come. Keep it naked. Tighten the skin till its tearing point. . . . Well! Can you already see the effects of my lessons? And you, my child! I beg you! Don't stay like that with clasped hands! Isn't there something you can do with them? . . . Fondle your gorgeous breasts, your gorgeous buttocks. . . .

AUGUSTIN. Sir, couldn't I kiss this demoiselle who gives me so much pleasure?

MADAME DE SAINT-ANGE. Fine! Kiss her, you imbecile, as much as you like! Don't you kiss me when I sleep with you?

AUGUSTIN. God help us! That gorgeous mouth! How fresh it is! . . . I feel as if my nostrils were on the roses in our garden. (*Pointing to his hardening cock.*) Well, do you see the effect it has, Monsieur!

EUGÉNIE. Oh, God! Look at it growing! . . .

DOLMANCÉ. Your movements must now become more regular, more powerful. . . . Let me replace you for an instant and observe what I do. (*He jerks* AUGUSTIN.) Do you see that these movements are firmer and yet softer? . . . Here, take it back and, above all, don't cover it. . . . Good! There it is in all its force. Now let's determine whether it's true that his cock is bigger than the Chevalier's.

EUGÉNIE. There's no doubting it. You can see that I can't get my hand all the way around it.

DOLMANCÉ (*measuring*). Yes, you're right. Thirteen inches long and eight and a half around. I've never seen a cock mightier than this one. That's what I call a superb dick. And you make use of it, Madame?

MADAME DE SAINT-ANGE. Every single night that I'm out here in the country.

DOLMANCÉ. But you stick it in your ass, I hope?

MADAME DE SAINT-ANGE. A bit more often than in my cunt.

DOLMANCÉ. Damn it! What lecherous delight! . . . Well, quite truthfully, I don't know whether I could stand it.

MADAME DE SAINT-ANGE. Don't make your hole tighter than it is, Dolmancé. Augustin's cock will fit in your ass as nicely as it does in mine.

DOLMANCÉ. We'll have to see. I feel sure that my Augustin will do me the honor of spearheading a bit of sperm in my behind. And I'll definitely pay him back. But let's get on with our lesson.

Come on, Eugénie. The serpent is about to spurt its venom. Prepare yourself. Focus your eyes on the head of this sublime member. And when, to signal its prompt ejaculation, you see it swell up and turn the most beautiful purple, your movements will acquire all the energy they are capable of. Your fingers, which tickle the anus, must bore into it as deeply as possible. You must submit totally to the libertine you're entertaining. Look for his mouth so that you may suck him. Your charms must, so to speak, fly toward his hands. . . . He's coming, Eugénie! This is the moment of your triumph.

AUGUSTIN. Ah! Ah! Ah! Mademoiselle! I'm dying! . . . I can't stand it anymore! Jerk harder, I beg you! . . . Ah! God damn it! My eyes are blurring! . . .

DOLMANCÉ. Harder, harder, Eugénie! Don't spare him! He's ecstatic! . . . Ah, what a flood of sperm! . . . And how vigorous his spurts! Look at the traces of his first gush. The sperm jumped more than ten feet! Fucking God! The room's filled with it! . . . I've never seen anyone come like that! And you say he fucked last night, Madame?

MADAME DE SAINT-ANGE. Nine or ten times, I believe. We stopped counting long ago!

CHEVALIER. Beautiful Eugénie, you're covered with sperm!

EUGÉNIE. I want to be inundated! (To DOLMANCÉ.) Well, mentor, are you satisfied?

DOLMANCÉ. Very satisfied, for a beginner. But there are a few incidentals you've neglected.

MADAME DE SAINT-ANGE. Just wait. They can only be the fruits of inexperience. As for me, I confess that I'm very satisfied with my Eugénie. She shows evidence of the finest aptitudes, and I think that we must now have her enjoy another spectacle. She must see the effects of sticking a cock in an ass. Dolmancé, I offer you my ass. I'll lie in my brother's arms, he'll fuck my pussy, you'll fuck my ass, and Eugénie will prepare my dick. She'll thrust it into my ass and regulate all the movements. She'll study these movements in order to familiarize herself with this procedure, and then she herself will submit to the same enormous dick of this Hercules.

DOLMANCÉ. I look forward to it, and that pretty little derriere will soon be ravaged before our very eyes by our good Augustin's violent shaking. While waiting, I approve of your suggestion, Madame. But if you want me to treat you well, permit me to insert the following clause. I'll make Augustin get hard again in two shakes of my wrist, and he'll fuck my ass while I sodomize you.

MADAME DE SAINT-ANGE. I strongly endorse this arrangement. It's to my advantage, and for my pupil it will be two excellent lessons instead of one.

DOLMANCÉ (*grabbing hold of AUGUSTIN*). Come here, my big boy. Let me reanimate you. . . . What a handsome fellow! . . . Kiss me, dear friend. . . . You're still smeared with sperm, and sperm is what I ask of you! . . . Ah! God damn it! . . . I have to rim him while I jerk his dick! . . .

CHEVALIER. Come here, my sister! In order to carry out Dolmancé's plans and yours, I'll stretch out on this bed. You'll lie in my arms, showing him your gorgeous buttocks and spreading them as far as possible. Yes, there we have it! We can start whenever you like.

DOLMANCÉ. Wait, not yet. First I have to fuck your sister's ass since Augustin is going to slip it into me. Next I'll unite you, let my fingers tie you together. Let's not ignore a single rule. Remember that a pupil is watching us and that we owe her very precise lessons. Eugénie, please jerk my dick while I work on the gigantic tool of this ne'er-do-well. Keep my cock stiff while I lightly defile your ass cheeks. (*She obeys.*)

EUGÉNIE. Am I doing it right?

DOLMANCÉ. Your movements are still too soft, Eugénie.

Squeeze that dick a lot harder. Masturbation is agreeable only because it constricts more than the sexual act does. So for the tool, the participating hand must become infinitely tighter than any other part of the body. . . . Better! That's better! . . . Spread your cheeks a bit more so that at each thrust the head of my cock touches your asshole. . . . Yes! That's it! Meanwhile jerk your sister, Chevalier! We'll be yours in a minute. . . . Ah! Good! My man is hardening! . . . Let's go, Madame, prepare yourself! Open that sublime ass to my impure ardor. Guide the harpoon, Eugénie. It has to be your hand that steers it to the crack! It must be your hand that drives it in. Once your harpoon is inside, you'll grab Augustin's harpoon and you'll fill my entrails. Those are the duties of a novice, who receives a lot of instruction in that way. That's why I'm having you do it.

MADAME DE SAINT-ANGE. How do you like my ass cheeks, Dolmancé? Ah, my angel! If you only knew how much I desire you, how long I've been waiting to be ass-fucked by a bugger!

DOLMANCÉ. Your wishes will be granted, Madame. But allow me to stop for an instant at the feet of the idol. I want to worship it before I plunge down to the bottom of its sanctuary. . . . What a divine ass! . . . Let me kiss it! . . . Let me lick it thousands upon thousands of times! . . . Here it is, the cock you desire! . . . Do you feel it, you hussy? Tell me, tell me, do you feel it piercing you? . . .

MADAME DE SAINT-ANGE. Oh, drive it down to the bottom of my bowels! . . . Oh, sweet ecstasy! How vast is your realm!

DOLMANCÉ. Never have I fucked an ass like that! It's worthy of Ganymede himself! Go to it, Eugénie! With your help, Augustin will now fuck an ass!

EUGÉNIE. Here it is, it's all yours. (To AUGUSTIN.) Look, gorgeous angel! Do you see the hole you have to perforate?

AUGUSTIN. I sure do! . . . Damn it! There's space inside! . . . At least it'll fit better than yours, Mademoiselle. So kiss me a little to make it slide in more easily.

EUGÉNIE (embraces him). I'll kiss you as much as you like— you're so sweet! . . . But do push! . . . How quickly the head of your dick is engulfed! . . . Ah! I don't think the rest will keep us waiting for long. . . .

DOLMANCÉ. Shove, shove, oh, dick! . . . Rip me to shreds if you must! . . . Hey, do you see my ass? The way it stretches? . . . Ah, God in heaven! What a club! . . . I've never received anything like it! . . . How many inches to go, Eugénie?

EUGÉNIE. Barely two!

DOLMANCÉ. So I've got eleven up my ass! . . . What sheer bliss! . . . It's killing me, I can't stand it any longer! . . . C'mon, Chevalier, are you ready?

CHEVALIER. Grab hold and tell me what you think.

DOLMANCÉ. Here, my children, let me bring you together! . . . I'll help this heavenly incest as best I can. (*He slips the* CHEVALIER'S *cock into his sister's pussy.*)

MADAME DE SAINT-ANGE. Ah! My friends! I'm getting fucked coming and going! . . . Damn it! What divine pleasure! . . . No, there's nothing like it in the whole world! . . . Ah, fucking! How I pity the woman who hasn't tasted it. . . . Jerk me, Dolmancé, jerk me! Let your violent movements force me upon my brother's sword! And you, Eugénie! Gaze at me! Watch me in my vices, learn by my example, savor my vices, relish them, delight in them. Look, my love! See everything I perpetrate at once: scandal, seduction, bad role model, incest, adultery, sodomy! . . . Oh, Lucifer! Lone and single god of my soul! Inspire me more! Offer my heart new deviations, and you will see me plunge into them!

DOLMANCÉ. Voluptuous creature! How you stimulate my gism, how your words and the extreme fervor of your ass hasten my orgasm! I'm all set to shoot! . . . Eugénie, excite my fucker's valor, press his flanks, spread his ass cheeks. You now know how to reanimate wavering desires. . . . Your sheer closeness energizes the cock that's fucking me! . . . I can feel it—its thrusts are more intense! . . . You slut! I must yield to you what I'd never have wanted to owe except to my ass! . . . Chevalier, you're ablaze. I can feel it. . . . Wait for me! . . . Wait for me! . . . Oh, my friends! Let's all come at the same time! That's the only happiness in life! . . .

MADAME DE SAINT-ANGE. Oh, fuck, fuck! Shoot whenever you like! . . . I can't hold out any longer! God almighty—whom I don't give a damn about! . . . Sacred bugger of God!

I'm coming! . . . Inundate me, my friends! . . . Inundate your whore! . . . Spurt the tides of your foamy gism to the very bottom of my flaming soul! My soul exists purely to receive your sperm! . . . Ah! . . . Ah! . . . Ah! . . . Fucker! . . . Fucker! . . . What an incredible excess of bliss! . . . I'm dying! . . . Eugénie, let me kiss you, let me eat you, let me devour your gism while I lose mine! . . . (AUGUSTIN, DOLMANCÉ, and CHEVALIER shoot in chorus. The fear of monotony prevents us from repeating the expressions that are all alike in such instants.)

DOLMANCÉ. That was one of the finest orgasms I've ever had in my life. (Pointing to AUGUSTIN.) That bugger filled me with gism! . . . But I gave you tit for tat, Madame! . . .

MADAME DE SAINT-ANGE. Ah! Don't tell me about it. I'm inundated.

EUGÉNIE. You can't say the same thing about me! (She throws herself playfully into MADAME's arms.) You say you've sinned a lot, my darling. Well, goodness knows I've never committed a single sin! But if I live on air, I needn't worry about indigestion!

MADAME DE SAINT-ANGE (laughing her head off). The funny creature!

DOLMANCÉ. She's enchanting! . . . Come here, my little girl, so I can whip you. (He slaps her butt.) Kiss me, your turn will come soon.

MADAME DE SAINT-ANGE. In the future, my brother, we must deal purely with her. Have a look, she's your prey. Examine this charming virginity, in next to no time it will be all yours.

EUGÉNIE. Oh, not in front! That would be too painful! But in back you can do it all you like, as Dolmancé just showed me.

MADAME DE SAINT-ANGE. What a naïve and delicious girl! She asks you precisely for what is so difficult to obtain from others!

EUGÉNIE. Oh, I'm not saying it without a bit of remorse. For you haven't reassured me that it's not the enormous crime that I've always heard it is—especially when it's man to man, as it now was with Dolmancé and Augustin. Let's see, Monsieur, let's see how your philosophy explains this brand of offense. It's dreadful, isn't it?

DOLMANCÉ. You must start, Eugénie, with the assumption that there is nothing dreadful about deviation, because everything inspired by deviation is equally inspired by nature. Focus on the most extraordinary actions, the most bizarre, those that seem to most blatantly defy all laws, all earthly institutions (for I'm not speaking about heaven). Well, Eugénie, none of these exploits is the least bit dreadful, nor can a single one of them not be demonstrated in nature. It is certain, lovely Eugénie, that the feat you are speaking about is the same one referred to by such a peculiar fable in the insipid romance of the Holy Scripture, a tedious compilation assembled by an ignorant Jew during the Babylonian Captivity. However, it is utterly wrong and unfeasible to claim that these towns or market villages were burned to ashes as punishment for their deviations. You see, Sodom and Gomorrah were perched on the craters of several ancient volcanoes, and they perished like those Italian towns that were devoured by the lava of Mount Vesuvius. So much for the entire miracle. And yet this thoroughly simple event was the basis for barbarously devising the fiery execution inflicted on those miserable Europeans who have submitted to this natural fantasy.

EUGÉNIE. Oh! Natural! . . .

DOLMANCÉ. Yes, natural, I declare. After all, Nature doesn't have two voices, of which one voice has the daily chore of condemning what is inspired by the other voice. It's quite certain that the people infatuated with this mania receive their impressions entirely through the voice of nature. People who want to proscribe or condemn such desires claim that they harm the populace. How limited are these imbeciles who never have anything on their minds but the idea of propagation and who never see anything but crime in whatever deviates from that concept! Is there any evidence that nature has such a huge need for this population increase as those morons try to make us believe? Is it quite certain that we offend nature every time we diverge from this path of dim-witted procreation?

To convince us of its course and its laws, let's examine it for a moment. If nature only created and never destroyed, I could share the opinion of those boring sophists: I could then agree that the most sublime actions would be to work incessantly toward procreation, and the refusal to do so would necessarily constitute a crime. Yet doesn't the slightest glance at nature's operations verify that destruction is as crucial to nature's plans as creation? Doesn't it verify that the two of them are so thoroughly interlinked and interlocked that neither can possibly proceed without the other, that nothing can be born, nothing can be regenerated without destruction? Hence, destruction is as much a law of nature as creation.

Given this principle, how can I insult nature by refusing to procreate? If my rejection is presumably wicked, it would, no doubt, become infinitely smaller than the act of destroying, which, however, is a natural law, as I have just demonstrated. If, on the one hand, I admit that nature imbues me with a destructive leaning, and if, on the other hand, I know that destruction is even indispensable for nature and that, in destroying, I move within the framework of nature's goals, where, I ask you, do I commit a crime? But—the idiots and populators, who are one and the same, will object—this productive semen is placed in our loins for no other purpose than propagation. Hence, deviating from that function is an offense.

First of all, I have just proved the opposite since this loss doesn't even equal a destruction, and since destruction per se, which weighs far more heavily than mere loss, is not a crime.

Second, it's wrong to say that nature wants this spermatic liquid to be entirely and absolutely destined for procreation. If this were so, nature would prevent this ejaculation from occurring in any other circumstances, as we know to be the case from experience. After all, we shoot our gism when we like and where we like. Furthermore, nature would inhibit these losses of semen from taking place without coitus, as happens both in our dreams and in our memories. Indeed, nature would hoard such a precious liquid and never allow it to shoot except into the vessel of propagation. Nature would assuredly not want this ecstasy it rewards us with to be felt just as keenly as when we divert our homage. It would not be reasonable to suppose that nature agrees to give us pleasure at the very moment when we overwhelm nature with our flagrant insults.

Let's go further and assume that women were born solely to

breed, which would certainly be true if such reproduction were
so dear to nature. Now given a woman's longest possible life,
would there be all in all only seven years in which she could
pass life on to her counterpart? What's that? Why, nature is
simply ravenous to procreate! Anything that doesn't aim at this
goal offends nature! And of its hundred years, the sex destined
to reproduce can do so in only seven years! Nature wants only
procreation, and the semen that nature lends a man for this
purpose shoots as often as the man desires! The man finds the
same delight in that outpouring as in a more useful expedient,
and never the slightest disadvantage! . . .

Let's stop it, my friends, let's stop believing these absurdities!
They make common sense shudder! Ah! Far from insulting nature, the sodomite and the lesbian, quite the contrary, serve nature by stubbornly rejecting any union that results purely in
offspring which are tedious for nature. This propagation—let's
not deceive ourselves—has never been a natural law; at most,
as I've said, it's a toleration. Now really! What does nature care
if the human race is extinguished or annihilated on this planet?
Nature laughs at our arrogant conviction that everything
would end if that calamity were to occur! But nature would not
even notice it! Does anybody actually imagine that there have
been no races that died out? Buffon counts several, and nature,
mute about such precious losses, didn't perceive a thing! The
entire human species could be snuffed out, and the air would
be no less pure, the constellations no less radiant, the rhythm of
the universe no less exact!

Yet how moronic would it be to believe that our species is so
crucial to the world that anyone who didn't work for its propagation or who interfered with its propagation would necessarily be a criminal! Let's stop blinding ourselves to this point,
and may the example of nations more reasonable than ours
serve to convince us of our errors! There's not a single corner of
the earth where this alleged crime of sodomy did not have its
temples and its adherents! The Greeks, who turned it into a
virtue, as it were, erected a statue to sodomy, Venus Callipygos;
while Rome went in search of Athenian laws and imported this
divine pleasure.

What progress didn't sodomy make under the Caesars! Under the aegis of the Roman eagles, sodomy spread from one end of the world to the other. With the collapse of the Roman empire, sodomy took refuge near the pope's triple crown, it was a haven for the arts in Italy, and it reached us when we grew civilized. When we discover a hemisphere, we find sodomy. Captain Cook dove into a new world, where sodomy holds sway. Had our balloons landed on the moon, they would have found the same thing. A delicious joy, the child of nature and pleasure, you must occur wherever men are to be found, and wherever you will be known, they will put up statues to you! Oh, my friends! Can there be anything sillier than imagining that a man is a monster worthy of death because he prefers coming up an ass to coming in a cunt, because a young man with whom he enjoys two pleasures, as both lover and mistress, strikes him as preferable to a girl, who promises him only one way of coming! He is a villain, a scoundrel for playing the role of a sex that isn't his. So then why did nature make him susceptible to this pleasure?

Let's examine his body parts. You'll find that they are totally different from those of men who haven't inherited that taste. His buttocks are whiter, plumper, more dimpled, and not a single hair darkens the altar of pleasure, whereby the interior, lined with a more delicate, more sensitive, more sensual membrane, is certainly of the same composition as the inside of a vagina. This man's character likewise differs from that of other men: it is more pliable, more flexible. It includes nearly all the vices and all the virtues of a female. You will even recognize her weaknesses. They will all have the manias of women and some even their characteristics. In making them similar to women, could nature have possibly been so angry at these men for enjoying female tastes? Isn't it obvious that this class of men differs from other classes, and that nature created such men in order to reduce the birth rate? After all, too vast a spread of reproduction would undoubtedly harm nature.

Ah, my dear Eugénie! If you only knew how delicious it feels to have a big cock fill your butt, to shove it in all the way to the balls and ardently thump it back and forth, to pull it out all the way to the foreskin and then thrust it back down to the hair! No! There is no bliss in the entire world that equals this delight! It is the bliss of heroes, the bliss of philosophers, and it would be the bliss of gods if these divine ecstasies themselves weren't the only gods that we should worship on earth!

(However, since we can look forward to a much more extensive discussion of these subjects later on, we have limited ourselves to the barest analysis.)

EUGÉNIE (*very animated*). Oh, my friends! Fuck my ass! . . . Here are my buns! . . . I'm offering them to you! . . . Fuck me, I'm coming! . . . (*Uttering those words, she collapses in the arms of* MADAME DE SAINT-ANGE, *who hugs and kisses her and who presents the girl's raised loins to* DOLMANCÉ.)

MADAME DE SAINT-ANGE. Divine mentor, can you resist that presentation? Doesn't this sublime derriere tempt you in the least? Watch it gape, watch it open!

DOLMANCÉ. Please forgive me, beautiful Eugénie. If you like, it won't be I who snuffs the fire that I kindle. Dear child, in my eyes you have the great drawback of being a female. I was willing to forget my entire bias in order to pluck your first fruits. Be glad that this is as far as I'll go. The Chevalier will take care of that task. His sister, armed with this dildo, will pound and pound away at her brother's ass. At the same time, she will present her gorgeous bottom to Augustin, who will fuck it while I fuck Augustin's ass. You see, I won't hide the fact that this handsome boy's ass has been enticing me for an hour now, and I absolutely want to pay him his just desserts.

EUGÉNIE. I accept the change. But honestly, Dolmancé, the frankness of your declaration doesn't make it any the less impolite.

DOLMANCÉ. A thousand pardons, Mademoiselle! But we buggers pride ourselves purely on frankness and exactness in our principles.

MADAME DE SAINT-ANGE. Still, their reputation for frankness is not applicable to those who, like yourselves, are accustomed to taking people only from behind.

DOLMANCÉ. You believe that we are a bit treacherous—indeed, a bit false? Well, Madame, I've demonstrated to you that such characteristics are indispensable in society. We are doomed to live with people who are bent on hiding themselves from our view, on disguising their vices, on showing us only the virtues that they don't possess. Hence it's extremely dangerous for us to reveal only frankness to them. For it's clear that we'd be handing them all the advantages that they refuse to give us, and the dishonesty would be apparent. Hypocrisy and dissimulation are modes of behavior that society has forced upon us, and we have to yield. Madame, allow me to use myself as an example for a moment. In all the world, there is assuredly no person more corrupt than I. But my contemporaries haven't an inkling. Ask them what they think of me, and they'll tell you that I'm a decent man—whereas there is no crime in which I haven't enjoyed my supreme bliss.

MADAME DE SAINT-ANGE. Oh, you're not going to persuade me that you've committed atrocities.

DOLMANCÉ. Atrocities. . . . Why, Madame, I've perpetrated horrors.

MADAME DE SAINT-ANGE. Well, yes! You're like the man who says to his confessor: "The details don't matter, Monsieur. Rest assured that I've done everything but theft and murder!"

DOLMANCÉ. Yes, Madame. I'll say the same thing, though with no exceptions.

MADAME DE SAINT-ANGE. What, you libertine? You've indulged in . . . ?

DOLMANCÉ. In everything, Madame, everything! Is there anything a man with my temperament and my principles won't do?

MADAME DE SAINT-ANGE. Ah! Let's fuck! Let's fuck! . . . With all this talk I can't hold out any longer! We'll resume our dialogue later on, Dolmancé. To lend more faith to your confessions, I need to hear them with a fresh mind. Whenever you get a hard-on, you love to recite horrors, and perhaps you're passing off as truth the licentious marvels of your inflamed imagination. (*They get into their positions.*)

DOLMANCÉ. Wait, Chevalier, wait. I'm going to insert it myself. But first I have to ask beautiful Eugénie to forgive me and allow me to get her going by whipping her. (*He whips her.*)

EUGÉNIE. I've already advised you that this ceremony is

superfluous. . . . Tell me openly that it satisfies your lust! But
don't, I beg you, pretend that you're doing it for my sake.

DOLMANCÉ (*still whipping her*). Ah! You'll be changing your
tune presently! . . . You don't know the powerful effect of this
prelude. . . . C'mon, c'mon, little vixen, you're to receive a
thorough flogging!

EUGÉNIE. Oh God! He's so forceful! . . . My ass cheeks are
blazing! . . . Why, you're hurting me—really! . . .

MADAME DE SAINT-ANGE. I'll get even with him, darling, I'll
give him tit for tat! (*She whips* DOLMANCÉ.)

DOLMANCÉ. Oh! With all my heart! I ask Eugénie for only
one favor: to let me whip her as hard as I desire to get whipped
myself. You can see me acting according to natural law! But
wait! Let's arrange the tableau. Eugénie should climb on your
loins, Madame, and cling to your neck the way a child clings to
its mother's back. I'll now have two asses under my hands, and
I'll thrash them together! The Chevalier and Augustin will pay
me back by lashing both my buttocks at once. . . . Yes, that's
right! . . . There we are! . . . What bliss! . . .

MADAME DE SAINT-ANGE. Don't spare that little slut, I beg
you! And since I'm not asking you for any favor, I don't want
you to do her any favor whatsoever!

EUGÉNIE. Ow! Ow! Ow! I honestly think I'm bleeding!

MADAME DE SAINT-ANGE. The blood will embellish your ass
cheeks by coloring them. . . . Courage, my angel, courage. Remember that pain is always what leads to pleasure.

EUGÉNIE. I just can't anymore.

DOLMANCÉ. (*Pauses for a moment to contemplate his handiwork, then resumes.*) Another sixty, Eugénie. Yes, yes, sixty
more on each ass! . . . Oh, you sluts! How much you'll love to
fuck now! (*The arrangement comes apart.*)

MADAME DE SAINT-ANGE (*examining* EUGÉNIE'S *buttocks*).
Oh, the poor thing! Her derriere is covered with blood! . . .
You bastard, how you love to kiss the marks of your cruelty!

DOLMANCÉ (*shooting*). Yes, I won't hide it! And my kisses
would be more ardent if the traces were crueler!

EUGÉNIE. Oh, you monster!

DOLMANCÉ. I agree!

CHEVALIER. At least he's truthful.

DOLMANCÉ. C'mon, Chevalier! Sodomize her!

CHEVALIER. Hold her loins and three bangs will get me in!

EUGÉNIE. Oh goodness! Your dick is bigger than Dolmancé's! . . . Chevalier, you're tearing me apart! Be careful, I beg you! . . .

CHEVALIER. That's impossible, my angel! I have to reach my goal! . . . After all, my mentor is watching me closely! So I've got to be worthy of his lessons.

DOLMANCÉ. It's in! . . . I love to see the hair of a cock rubbing against the sides of an anus! C'mon, Madame! Fuck your brother's ass! . . . Augustin's cock is quite ready to slide in, and as for me, I promise not to spare your fucker! . . . Ah! Good! The rosary seems to be formed. Now we want to think only of coming!

MADAME DE SAINT-ANGE. Just observe the little tramp as she wiggles and wriggles!

EUGÉNIE. Is it my fault? I'm dying of ecstasy! . . . That flogging. . . . That immense dick. . . . And that amiable Chevalier, who is still banging me! . . . My dear, my dear! I can't anymore! . . .

MADAME DE SAINT-ANGE. Good God! Neither can I! I'm coming! . . .

DOLMANCÉ. A little togetherness, my friends! If you can grant me just two more minutes, I'll swiftly catch up with you, and we can all come simultaneously.

CHEVALIER. There's no time! My gism is squirting into beautiful Eugénie's ass. . . . I'm dying! . . . Oh, sacred name of God! What ecstasies! . . .

DOLMANCÉ. I'm following you, my friends, I'm, following you! . . . The gism is likewise blinding me! . . .

AUGUSTIN. And me too! . . . Me too! . . .

MADAME DE SAINT-ANGE. What a spectacle! . . . That bugger has filled my ass! . . .

CHEVALIER. To the bidet, ladies, to the bidet!

MADAME DE SAINT-ANGE. No! I really like it! I love feeling the gism in my ass! I never give it up if I have some!

EUGÉNIE. Honestly, I can't anymore! . . . Tell me, my friends, whether a woman must always accept an offer to fuck her in this manner?

MADAME DE SAINT-ANGE. Always, my darling, always. She must go even further. Since this kind of fucking is delicious, she must always require it of whomever she's using. But if she's dependent on the person she's amusing herself with, and if she hopes to obtain his favors, his presents, or his gratitude, she must act scarce, she must play hard to get. In such an instant, no man with this taste will not be ruined by a woman adept enough to reject his desire purely in order to fan its flames even more. She gets anything she wants so long as she has the skill to grant for a single purpose that which is demanded of her.

DOLMANCÉ. Well, my little angel, are you converted? Have you stopped believing that sodomy is a crime?

EUGÉNIE. And what if it were a crime, who cares? Haven't you demonstrated that crimes are invalid? Now there are very few actions that I regard as crimes.

DOLMANCÉ. Nothing on earth, dear girl, is a crime. Doesn't even the most monstrous deed have an aspect that's advantageous for us?

EUGÉNIE. Who can doubt it?

DOLMANCÉ. Well, from then on, that action is no longer a crime. In order for that which, by turning useful, became a crime by being harmful, we would have to prove that the creature being harmed is more precious to nature than the creature being served. However, since all individuals are equal in the eyes of nature, this predilection is impossible. Hence, the action that serves one person by harming another is profoundly uninteresting to nature.

EUGÉNIE. But what if an action hurt a huge majority of people while providing us with just a smidgen of pleasure, wouldn't it be dreadful to perform that action?

DOLMANCÉ. Not more dreadful, because there is no comparison between what others feel and what we undergo. The strongest dose of pain in others must assuredly be of no concern for us, and the slightest titillation of pleasure felt by us will touch us personally. So whatever the price, we must prefer this slight and delicious titillation to the immense quantity of other people's sufferings, which must never cause us distress. On the other hand, a singularity of our organs—a bizarre inclination—can make the torment of our neighbors agreeable, which often happens. In that case, who can doubt that we must indisputably prefer the torment that amuses us, to the absence of pain, which signifies a privation for us?

The source of all our moral errors is the ludicrous acceptance of that bond of brotherhood invented by the Christians in their century of distress and misfortune. If you're compelled to beg other people for sympathy, it makes sense to claim that all men are brothers. Once you acknowledge that assumption, how can you refuse to help a person? However, there is no way we can agree. Aren't we all born alone? Indeed, don't we come into the world as enemies of each other in a state of perpetual and reciprocal warfare? Now given that supposition, I ask you: Is it possible that the virtues demanded by these so-called bonds of brotherhood are truly inherent in nature? If nature's voice instilled those virtues in man, he would experience them at his very birth. Pity, charity, and humanity would then be natural virtues that we couldn't resist and that would render this primitive state of savage man the utter contrary of what we see.

EUGÉNIE. But if, as you say, nature bears men alone, making them mutually independent, then you must at least agree that their needs, by drawing them closer together, were sure to knot some bonds between them. So I hope that at the very least, you respect the ties of love, friendship, gratitude, and blood relationships.

DOLMANCÉ. Actually, I don't respect them any more than others. But fine, we'll examine them. Let me glance at each in turn, Eugénie.

Would you, for instance, say that in my need to get married, either to prolong my clan or to increase my fortune, I must establish indissoluble or sacred bonds between myself and the woman to whom I get attached? Wouldn't it, I ask you, be absurd to make such a statement? So long as the act of coitus lasts, I may, no doubt, need that person in order to participate. But once the need is satisfied, what, I ask you, remains between her and me? And what concrete obligation will fetter the results

of that coitus to her or to me? Those last ties were the fruits of
the terror endured by the parents, the fear of being abandoned
in their old age, and, with the anything but selfless care with
which they treated us in our childhood, they wish to purchase
the same attention in their final years. Let's stop being duped by
all those things! We owe nothing to our parents! . . . Nothing
at all, Eugénie! And since they worked far less for us than for
themselves, we are permitted to despise them and even get rid
of them if we are irritated by their conduct. We should love
them only if they treat us decently. Nor must their tenderness
be one degree higher than what we feel for our other friends,
because a birthright establishes nothing, institutes nothing. By
scrutinizing it with wisdom and reflection, we will find nothing
but reasons to abhor these people who have thought purely
about their own pleasures and who have often given us an unhappy and unhealthy existence.

You speak to me about the bonds of love, Eugénie! I hope you
never get to know them! Ah! For the happiness I wish you, I
pray that such a sentiment never approaches your heart! What
is love? It strikes me that we can define it only as the effect
wrought upon us by the qualities of a beautiful entity. These effects transport us, they inflame us. If we can possess that entity,
we are satisfied. If we cannot possibly have it, we despair.

But what is the basis of this sentiment? Desire. What is the
sequel of this sentiment? Madness. So then let's stick to the motive and defend ourselves against the effects. The motive is to
possess the person. Fine! Let's try to succeed, but wisely. Let's
enjoy the person as soon as we have him. And let's find solace
in the opposite case. A thousand similar persons, and often far
better ones, will comfort us for that loss. All men resemble each
other, as do all women. There is absolutely no love that resists
the effects of sound reflection. Oh, how gullible is this intoxication, which, absorbing the results of our senses, places us in
such a condition that we no longer see, no longer exist except
by means of this insanely worshipped person! Is that really living? Isn't it voluntarily relinquishing all the delights of life? Isn't
it preferable to remain in a burning fever that engrosses and devours us, leaving us no other happiness than the metaphysical

joys that so closely resemble the effects of madness? If we were
to love that sacred person forever, if we were certain we would
never abandon it, that would, no doubt, be foolish, but at least
excusable. Yet does that ever happen? Are there many examples of these eternal bonds that are never dissolved? A few joy-
ful months, which soon restore the person to his appropriate
site, make us blush at the thought of the incense we have
burned on his altars, and we often don't even comprehend
what we saw in him in the first place.

Oh, lustful girls, give us your bodies as often as you can!
Fuck, entertain—that's all that counts! But be sure to flee love!
Only one's own body is good, said Buffon, the naturalist, and
that wasn't the only thing he pondered as a good philosopher. I
repeat: enjoy, but don't fall in love! Nor should you make any
effort to be loved. Your goals aren't sighs, dirges, stolen
glances, *billets doux*. You must aim at fucking, at multiplying
and frequently changing your fuckers—above all, at fighting
anybody who tries to capture you. By tying yourself to him, this
constant love will prevent you from submitting to another—a
cruel egotism that would soon prove fatal to your pleasures.
Women aren't meant for one man; nature has created them for
many. Ignoring nature's holy voice, a woman should yield to
any man who desires her. Always hookers, never lovers, fleeing
love, adoring pleasure, women will find nothing but roses on
the path of life; and they will lavishly scatter nothing but flowers along the way! Ask, Eugénie, ask the charming woman who
wants to take charge of your education—ask her what you
should do with a man after you come. (*Softly so AUGUSTIN
can't hear.*) Ask her if she'd take even a single step to keep Augustin here after he's filled her day with bliss. If he were re-
moved, she'd take another, she'd give Augustin no further
thought, and, soon weary of the new man, she'd immolate him
herself within two months if new delights were spawned by
that sacrifice.

MADAME DE SAINT-ANGE. My dear Eugénie can be quite assured that Dolmancé is explaining my heart, indeed the hearts
of all women, as if we'd exposed our innermost thoughts to him.

DOLMANCÉ. The last part of my analysis refers to the bonds

of friendship and the bonds of gratitude. Let's respect the bonds of friendship for all I care, so long as they're useful for us. We ought to keep our friends so long as they serve us, and we ought to drop them once we've nothing more to gain from them. We should never like a person for his own sake. Doing so is dishonest. Nature never inspires other feelings, other sentiments than the ones that are good for something. Nothing is as egotistical as nature. So we must likewise be egotistical if we are to submit to nature's laws.

As for gratitude, Eugénie, it's probably the weakest of all bonds. Do people do us favors for our own sakes? Don't believe it at all, my dear. The true motives are pride, ostentation. Isn't it humiliating to thus become the plaything of other people's self-love? Isn't it even more degrading to be obliged to someone? No burden is heavier than a good turn. There is simply no way out. One must repay it or suffer disgrace. Proud souls behave poorly under the load of a good deed. It weighs down on them so brutally that the only sentiment they can express is hatred for the benefactor. Now what, in your opinion, are the bonds that compensate for the isolation in which nature placed us when it created us? Where are the bonds that must establish relations between human beings? On what basis should we love those bonds, cherish them, prefer them to ourselves? Why should we provide comfort for their misery? Where in our souls is the cradle of our lovely and useless virtues of charity, humanity, and beneficence, as indicated in the absurd scriptures of a few moronic religions? Preached by beggars or imposters, these religions had to necessarily recommend whatever supported or tolerated them.

Well, Eugénie, do you still believe there is something holy about relations between human beings? Can you conceive of any reasons for not preferring ourselves to others?

EUGÉNIE. My heart has always belonged to these teachings, which are too pleasant to be rejected by my mind.

MADAME DE SAINT-ANGE. They are part of nature, Eugénie. This is proved by the sole endorsement that you give them. How could what you feel be the fruit of corruption since it blossomed first in your own bosom?

EUGÉNIE. But if all the delusions you advocate are natural, why do human laws oppose them?

DOLMANCÉ. Because laws are made not for the individual but for the generality. This places them in perpetual contradiction with self-interest, which always contradicts general interest. Although laws are good for society, they are very bad for the individuals making up society. While they favor or protect the individual, they also impede or detain three-quarters of his life. Thus the wise man, who scorns them, nevertheless tolerates them, just as he endures serpents and vipers, which, although injuring or poisoning, can be helpful in the medical field. The wise man protects himself against laws just as he shields himself against those venomous beasts. He will seek refuge from them through caution and secrecy—measures that offer no difficulty to a wise and prudent man. I do hope that the fantasy of several crimes inflames your soul, Eugénie, and you may rest assured that you can commit them in peace, between your friend and me.

EUGÉNIE. Ah, that fantasy is already in my heart!

MADAME DE SAINT-ANGE. What caprice is agitating you, Eugénie? You can confide in us.

EUGÉNIE (excited). I'd need a victim.

MADAME DE SAINT-ANGE. And of what sex should your victim be?

EUGÉNIE. Mine!

DOLMANCÉ. Well, Madame, are you content with your pupil? Is her progress fast enough?

EUGÉNIE (still excited). A victim, darling, a victim! . . . Oh, God! That would make me the happiest girl on earth! . . .

MADAME DE SAINT-ANGE. And what would you do to your victim?

EUGÉNIE. Everything, everything! Everything that would make her the most wretched of creatures! Oh, Madame! My friend! Take pity on me! I can't hold out any longer!

DOLMANCÉ. Damn it! What an imagination! . . . Come on, Eugénie, you're delicious! Let me shower you with thousands and thousands of kisses! (He takes her in his arms again.) Look, Madame, look! Watch this lusty creature! She comes from her mind without being touched! . . . I absolutely have to fuck her up the ass again!

EUGÉNIE. Can I get what I want after that?

DOLMANCÉ. Yes, you lunatic! . . . Yes, you have our guarantee.

EUGÉNIE. Oh, my friend! Here's my butt! Do whatever you like with it!

DOLMANCÉ. Wait till I arrange this enjoyment a bit more lecherously. (*Everyone follows his directions.*) Augustin, stretch out on the edge of the bed and let Eugénie lie in your arms. While I sodomize her, I'll jerk her clitoris with the superb head of Augustin's cock. And he will hold back his semen by taking care not to come. The dear Chevalier, without saying a word, has been jerking very gently while listening to us. He will now be so kind as to stretch out over Eugénie's shoulders and expose his gorgeous ass cheeks to my kisses, so that I'll jerk him down below. With my dick inside a butt, I'll squeeze a cock in each hand. And as for you, my lady: after being your husband, I want you to be my husband. Put on your most gigantic dildo. (*MADAME DE SAINT-ANGE opens a small chest filled with dildos, and our hero selects the most fearful one.*) Good! According to the data, this dildo is fourteen inches long and ten inches around. Hang it around your loins, Madame, and pound on it dreadfully!

MADAME DE SAINT-ANGE. Honestly, Dolmancé, you're crazy! I'd cripple you!

DOLMANCÉ. Don't worry about a thing. Push, my angel, penetrate! I won't fuck your dear Eugénie's ass until your enormous member is way inside my butt! It's in! It's in! God damn it! . . . Ah, I'm in seventh heaven! . . . Don't pity me, my beauty! . . . I tell you—I'm going to fuck your ass without preparing it! . . . Ah, God damn it! The gorgeous derriere! . . .

EUGÉNIE. Oh, Dolmancé, my friend, you're ripping me to shreds! . . . At least prepare the route.

DOLMANCÉ. God damn it, I won't! We lose half the pleasure with such stupid attentions! Remember our principles, Eugénie! I work for my own self! My beautiful angel, you may be a victim for a moment, but then you'll be a tormenter! . . . Ah, God damn it! He's entering!

EUGÉNIE. You're killing me! . . .

DOLMANCÉ. Oh, damn it to hell! I'm touching bottom! . . .

EUGÉNIE. Ah, do whatever you like! He's inside me! . . . I feel nothing but delight! . . .

DOLMANCÉ. How I love to shake this huge dick against a virginal clitoris! . . . As for you, Chevalier, expose your gorgeous ass. . . . Am I jerking you well, you libertine? . . . And you, Madame, fuck me, fuck your slut! . . . Yes, I'm your slut, and that's what I want to be! . . . Eugénie, come, my angel, yes, come! . . . Despite himself, Augustin fills me with gism. I've received the Chevalier's juice, and mine joins in! . . . I won't resist any further! . . . Eugénie, wiggle your butt so that your anus presses my dick! I'm going to shoot the burning gism to the end of my entrails. Ah, fucking bugger of God! I'm dying! (*He withdraws; the arrangement breaks up.*) Here, Madame! Here you are! Your little libertine is still full of come. The entrance to your cunt is flooded. Jerk it! Her clitoris is soaked in gism! Shake it hard! It's one of the greatest pleasures imaginable.

EUGÉNIE (*palpitating*). Oh, my darling Madame! What pleasures you bring me! . . . Ah, dear love, I'm all ablaze with lust! (*The arrangement recurs.*)

DOLMANCÉ. Chevalier, since you'll be deflowering this lovely child, help your sister, so that Eugénie will faint in your arms. And present your ass cheeks to me in that position. I'm going to fuck your butt while Augustin fucks mine! (*They all position themselves.*)

CHEVALIER. Am I lying correctly?

DOLMANCÉ. Raise your ass just a wee bit higher, my love! . . . There! That's right! . . . With no preparation. Chevalier . . .

CHEVALIER. Goodness! Whatever you like! Can I feel anything but pleasure in the bosom of this delicious girl? (*He kisses her and jerks her while gently slipping a finger into her cunt, as* MADAME DE SAINT-ANGE *tickles* EUGÉNIE'S *clitoris.*)

DOLMANCÉ. As for me, dear boy, rest assured that I've gotten a lot more from you than I had from Eugénie. There's a vast difference between a boy's ass and a girl's! . . . Do fuck my ass, Augustin! What are you waiting for?

AUGUSTIN. Oh, my, Monsieur! It's on account of it ran out too close to the thing of this pretty turtledove, and you want me to get it hard again for your ass, which really ain't so beautiful! No sir!

DOLMANCÉ. Imbecile! But why lament? That's nature. Each person prays to his own saint! C'mon! C'mon! Get it in, Augustin, you lover of truth. And when you have a bit more experience under your belt, you'll tell me whether asses aren't better than cunts. . . . Eugénie, please respond to the Chevalier's efforts; you're focusing purely on yourself. You are right to do so, libertine! But you should jerk him for the sake of your own joys since he's going to deflower you.

EUGÉNIE. Well, I've been jerking him, kissing him, losing my mind! . . . Oh! Oh! Oh! My friends, I can't anymore! . . . Take pity on my condition! . . . I'm dying, I'm coming! . . . God damn it! I'm beside myself! . . .

DOLMANCÉ. As for me, I'm going to behave! . . . I only wanted to get me going again in that stunning ass! The gism that was kindled here—I'm saving it for Madame de Saint-Ange. There's nothing I enjoy more than starting something in one ass and finishing it in another! Very good, Chevalier! You're doing fine! . . . Shall we devirginize? . . .

EUGÉNIE. Oh, heavens! No! I don't want it from him! I'd die! Your cock is smaller, Dolmancé. Let me owe this procedure to you, I beg you!

DOLMANCÉ. That's impossible, my angel. I've never fucked a cunt in all my life! You will permit me not to start at my age. The fruit of your virginity belongs to the Chevalier. He alone here is worthy of picking it. Let's not rob him of his rights.

MADAME DE SAINT-ANGE. Rejecting a virgin . . . so fresh, so lovely as this one. For I challenge anybody to say that my Eugénie is not the most beautiful girl in Paris! Oh, Monsieur! . . . Monsieur! . . . Honestly, you're sticking a bit too closely to your principles!

DOLMANCÉ. Not as closely as I should, Madame, for I've loads of colleagues who certainly wouldn't fuck you up the ass. . . . I've done it and I'll do it again. So I don't drive my cult to fanaticism, as you suspect, Madame.

MADAME DE SAINT-ANGE. Then let's get going, Chevalier! But do be careful. Look at the narrow strait that you wish to enter: Is there any proportion between the content and the container?

EUGÉNIE. Oh, I'm dying! It's inevitable! . . . But my ardent desire to get fucked enables me to try anything and fear nothing. . . . C'mon, my darling, penetrate me, I'm abandoning myself to you.

CHEVALIER (*clutching his stiff member*). Yes! Fuck! I've got to penetrate! My sister and Dolmancé—each of you grab a leg! . . . Ah, damn it! What an enterprise! . . . And she has to endure it even if she's sliced and torn apart!

EUGÉNIE. Gently, gently, I can't stand it! (*She yells, tears roll down her cheeks.*) Help me, my dear friend! . . . (*She struggles.*) No, I don't want it to enter me! . . . If you persist, I'll scream bloody murder! . . .

CHEVALIER. Scream as much as you like, you little slut! I tell you, it has to enter even if you kick the bucket a thousand times.

EUGÉNIE. How barbaric!

DOLMANCÉ. Ah! Fuck! Is a man tactful when he gets a hard-on?

CHEVALIER. Hey! My dick's inside! . . . It's inside, damn it! . . . Fuck! To hell with her virginity! . . . Watch her blood flow!

EUGÉNIE. Go on, tiger! . . . Go on! Tear me to shreds now if you like! I don't give a damn! . . . Kiss me, my executioner, kiss me! . . . I adore you! . . . Ah! It's all right once that dick is inside me! All pains are forgotten! . . . I pity the girls who'd be intimidated by such an attack! . . . What great pleasures they'd reject for a very minor hurt! . . . Push, push, Chevalier! I'm coming! Let your gism moisten the wounds you've covered me with! . . . Shove your cock down to the very bottom of my womb! . . . Ah! Pain gives way to pleasure! . . . I'm ready to faint! . . . (*The* CHEVALIER *shoots. While the* CHEVALIER's *been fucking* EUGÉNIE, DOLMANCÉ *has been jerking the* CHEVALIER's *ass and his balls, and* MADAME DE SAINT-ANGE *has been tickling* EUGÉNIE's *clitoris. The arrangement breaks up.*)

DOLMANCÉ. Since all routes are open, I'd advise the little slut to get fucked immediately by Augustin.

EUGÉNIE. By Augustin! . . . A cock that huge! . . . Ah, time's a-wasting! . . . While I'm still bleeding! . . . Do you want to kill me? . . .

MADAME DE SAINT-ANGE. My dear love, kiss me! . . . I pity you. . . . But the verdict has been pronounced. There is no appeal, my darling, you have to submit!

AUGUSTIN. Ah! Damn it! I'm ready! In order to drill this little girl, I'd walk here all the way from Rome, by God.

CHEVALIER (*grabbing* AUGUSTIN's *gigantic cock*). Here, Eugénie. Look at this hard-on! . . . Isn't it worthy of replacing me! . . .

EUGÉNIE. Ah, just heavens! What a sentence! . . . Oh, you want to kill me, that's clear! . . .

AUGUSTIN (*grabbing* EUGÉNIE). Oh, no, Mam'selle. It never kills anyone!

DOLMANCÉ. One moment, beautiful boy, one moment! . . . She has to present me with her ass while you fuck her! . . . Yes, that's it! Come closer, Madame de Saint-Ange. I promised to fuck your butt, and I'll keep my word! . . . But lie there in such a way that I can fuck Eugénie and leave enough space to whip her! Meanwhile, the Chevalier should whip me! (*They all get into their positions.*)

EUGÉNIE. Ah! Fuck! He's tearing me apart! . . . Be gentle, you big clod! . . . Ah, the bugger! He's shoving it in! . . . He's in! . . . He's hit rock bottom! . . . I'm dying! . . . Oh, Dolmancé, how hard you whip! . . . The flames are being kindled on both sides! You're setting my ass cheeks on fire!

DOLMANCÉ (*lashing with all his strength*). You'll get more . . . more, you little vixen! . . . You'll come all the more deliciously! How hard you're jerking her, Saint-Ange. . . . How sweetly this light finger must sweeten the sufferings that Augustin and I are inflicting on her! . . . But your anus is tightening! . . . I see it, Madame, we're all going to come together! . . . Ah, how heavenly I feel between the brother and the sister!

MADAME DE SAINT-ANGE (*to* DOLMANCÉ.) Fuck, my star, fuck! . . . I don't believe I've ever known such pleasure!

CHEVALIER. Dolmancé, let's change places. Pass quickly from my sister's ass to Eugénie's ass and show her the pleasures of being lucky Pierre. I'll ass-fuck my sister, while she pays back on your buttocks the strokes of the rod that's made Eugénie's buttocks bleed.

DOLMANCÉ (*changing places*). I accept. . . . Here we are, my friend. Can any change be swifter than this one?

EUGÉNIE. What! Both of them on me, damn it! . . . I don't know what to watch out for! . . . I already had enough with this clod! . . . Ah, how much juice will this double delight cost me! . . . My juice is already running! . . . Without this sensual ejaculation, I think I'd be dead! What's that, my darling? You're imitating me? Oh, let's hear the little slut curse! . . . Dolmancé, come! . . . Do come, my love! . . . This big peasant is flooding me! He's spurting to the bottom of my guts! . . . Ah! My fuckers! Both of you at once, damn it! . . . My friends, receive my juice! It merges with yours! . . . I'm wiped out! . . . (*They leave their positions.*) Well, my dear, are you satisfied with your pupil? . . . Am I enough of a whore now? . . . Why, you've put me in a state . . . an agitation! . . . I'm so intoxicated that if I had to, I'd get fucked in the middle of the street! . . .

DOLMANCÉ. How beautiful she looks!

EUGÉNIE. I hate you—you rejected me!

DOLMANCÉ. Could I act against my principles?

EUGÉNIE. Fine, I forgive you. And I must respect standards that lead to debaucheries. How can I fail to adopt them if I want to live only in crime? Let's sit down and chat a bit. I'm at the end of my tether. Continue instructing me, Dolmancé, and tell me something to console me for the excesses I've plunged into. Get rid of my remorse! Encourage me!

MADAME DE SAINT-ANGE. Fair enough! Some theory should succeed practice. That will make a perfect pupil.

DOLMANCÉ. Very well, Eugénie! What do you wish to be told about?

EUGÉNIE. I'd like to know whether a government truly needs a set of morals, whether they can really influence the essence of a nation.

DOLMANCÉ. Oh, God! When I went out this morning, I

bought a pamphlet at the Palais-Royal, and if you believe the title, this pamphlet would necessarily answer Eugénie's question. It's hot off the press.

MADAME DE SAINT-ANGE. Let's see. (*She reads.*) "Frenchmen, Some More Effort if You Wish to Become Republicans." Goodness, what a peculiar title! It's so suspenseful! Chevalier, you've got a beautiful voice. Why don't you read us the text!

DOLMANCÉ. If I'm not mistaken, this answers Eugénie's question perfectly.

EUGÉNIE. It certainly seems to.

MADAME DE SAINT-ANGE. Go out, Augustin, this isn't meant for your ears. But don't get too far away. We'll ring for you when we need you.

CHEVALIER. I'm starting.

FRENCHMEN, SOME MORE EFFORT IF YOU WISH TO BECOME REPUBLICANS

Religion

I am going to present you with some grand ideas. They will be listened to, they will be pondered. You may not like all of these ideas, but at least a few will please you. I will have contributed in some way to the progress of the Enlightenment, and that will be enough for me. I won't deny that I find it painful to watch the sluggishness with which we try to obtain our goal. I am worried because I sense that we are about to miss it again. Does anyone really believe that our goal is reached once we are given laws? Let's not delude ourselves. What good are laws without a religion? We need a religion, one that's adjusted to the character of a republican, a religion so sharply distant from that of Rome that we can never return to the religion of Rome. In this century, we are furthermore convinced that religion must be based on morality and not morality on religion. Hence we require a religion that is faithful to morals, that is virtually their further development, their necessary consequence, and that, in uplifting the soul, can perpetually keep it on the acme of that precious freedom which is now its unique idol.

Now I ask you whether we can presume that the religion of a slave of Titus, the religion of a common Judean mountebank, can be appropriate to a free and warlike nation that has just been regenerating itself. No, my compatriots, no! You do not believe that! If, to his misfortune, the Frenchman were buried deeper in the darkness of Christianity, the results would be twofold. On the one hand, we would suffer the arrogance, the tyranny, and the despotism of the priests—the vices constantly reappearing in that impure horde. On the other hand, we would endure the despair, the platitudes, and the narrow-mindedness of the dogmas and mysteries of that unworthy and uncanny religion that dulls the pride of the republican soul. In so doing, it would instantly be led back to the yoke that its energy has just broken.

Let's not forget that this puerile creed was one of the best weapons in the hands of our tyrants. One of its earliest dogmas was to "render unto Caesar what is Caesar's." Yet we dethroned Caesar and we don't want to render anything unto him. Frenchmen, it is no use imagining that the spirit of a sworn-in clergy must no longer be the spirit of a refractory clergy; there are state vices that can never be corrected. In less than a decade, your priests, by means of the Christian religion, its superstitions and its prejudices, would regain their grip on souls—despite their oaths and despite their poverty. They would chain you back to kings, because this royal power has always buttressed clerical power, and your republican edifice would collapse for lack of a foundation.

Oh, you, who are clutching the sickle, give the tree of superstition its final stroke. Do not be content with hacking off the branches. Tear out by its very roots a plant with such noxious effects. Be perfectly convinced that your system of liberty and equality interferes too blatantly with the priests at Christ's altar. There is not even a single one who would either sincerely adopt it or fail to shake it when he succeeded in reclaiming some of his might over consciences. Where is the priest who, in comparing the state he is reduced to with the state he once enjoyed, will not do anything in his power to recover both the

confidence and the authority he was deprived of? And how many
feeble and cowardly beings would soon again become the slaves
of that ambitious and tonsured cleric! Why can't we assume
that earlier disasters can be reborn? In the infancy of the Christian Church, weren't the priests what they are today? You can
see how far they have come; but who brought them here?
Weren't those the means furnished by religion? Now if you do
not defend that religion absolutely, then those who preach it,
having the same means, will soon arrive at the same goal.

So wipe out forever anything that could destroy your work
some day. Remember that since the fruits of your labors are
reserved for your posterity, it is a matter of your duty, your integrity, to avoid leaving your progeny any of those dangerous
germs that would plunge them back into the chaos that it took
such efforts to escape. Our prejudices are already dissipating,
people are already recanting the absurdities of Catholicism.
The nation has already abolished the temples, it has toppled
the idols. It agrees that marriage is nothing but an act of civil
law. The shattered confessionals serve in public forums. The
so-called faithful, deserting the apostolic banquets, are leaving
the flour gods to the mice.

Frenchmen, do not stop! All Europe, with one hand already
on her blindfold, is awaiting your efforts to tear the blindfold
from her eyes. Hurry! Holy Rome is intent on weakening your
strength in every way; do not allow Rome enough time to make
a few more proselytes. Strike Rome relentlessly on its arrogant
and tottering head, so that in less than two months, the Tree of
Liberty, overshadowing the ruins of the Holy See, will focus the
weight of its victorious branches on covering all those despicable Christian idols that were insolently elevated on the ashes of
a Cato or a Brutus.

Frenchmen, I repeat! Europe is waiting for you to deliver her
from both scepter and incense. Remember that you cannot possibly liberate her from royal tyranny without simultaneously shattering the restraint inflicted by religious superstition: the bonds
of royal tyranny are too intricately involved with the bonds of
religion. By letting one of those forces survive, you will soon slide
back under the dominion that you neglected to eliminate in the

first place. A republican must kneel no more in front of an imaginary being or a vile imposter; his only gods must now be Courage and Liberty. Rome vanished once Christianity was preached there, and France is doomed if it still reveres Christianity.

Scrutinize the absurd dogmas, the terrifying mysteries, the monstrous ceremonies, the impossible morality of this disgusting religion and you will see whether it can be worthy of a republic. Do you honestly believe that I would let myself be dominated by the opinions of a man whom I had just seen at the feet of that idiotic priest Jesus? No! Absolutely not! That man will remain vile forever; in accordance with the depravity of his views, he will cling forever to the atrocities of the Ancien Régime. If a man was able to surrender to the stupidities of such a wishy-washy religion that we were foolish enough to admit, then he cannot dictate laws to me or contribute to my enlightenment; I now see him purely as a slave to prejudice and superstition.

To convince us of this truth, let us glance at the few individuals who have remained loyal to the nonsensical faith of our fathers. We shall see if they are not irreconcilable enemies of the present system; we shall see if they do not contain the entire membership of that so justly despised caste of royalists and aristocrats. If the slave of a crowned brigand wishes to kneel at the feet of a clay idol, let him do so; such an object was made for his muddy soul. The man who can serve kings must worship gods! But we Frenchmen, we, my compatriots, must we still humbly crawl under such contemptible restraints? Better to die a thousand times than submit anew!

Since we believe a faith is necessary, let us imitate the religion of the Romans: the actions, the passions, the heroes—those were the respectable objects of their worship. Such idols elevated the soul, they electrified it! They did even more: they communicated the virtues of the respected being. The worshipper of Minerva wanted to be prudent. Courage filled the heart of the man who was seen at the feet of Mars. Not a single god of these great men was lacking in energy; as for the fire that inflamed them, they carried it to the soul of the man who venerated them. And, since a man could hope to be worshipped himself eventually, he aspired to being at least as great as the ideal per se.

Yet what, on the contrary, do we find in the ineffectual deities of Christianity? What, I ask you, does this moronic religion offer us? If we inspect it thoroughly, we will find that the impieties cramming it derive partly from the ferocity and innocence of the Jews and partly from the indifference and confusion of the Gentiles. Instead of appropriating what might be good from the nations of Antiquity, the Christians seemed to have shaped their religion as a fusion of the vices they encountered everywhere.

Does the tepid imposter of Nazareth encourage you to engender several grand ideas? Does his filthy and disgusting mother, that unchaste Mary, inspire any virtues in you? And among the saints adorning his Elysium, do you find any model of grandeur, or heroism, or virtue? No, this stupid faith arouses no grand ideas; no artist can employ its attributes in the monuments he raises. In Rome itself, most of the ornaments and embellishments of the Papal Palace derive from paganism; and as long as the world exists, paganism alone will excite the vitality of great men.

Now will pure deism contain more motives for grandeur and sublimity? Will the adoption of a chimera, giving our souls that degree of energy essential to republican virtues, encourage man to cherish them or practice them? Not by a long shot! We have abandoned that phantom, and at present atheism is the sole philosophy of all rational minds. With increasing enlightenment, we have felt that, since movement is inherent in matter, the agent necessary for inspiring motion is an illusory being; and we have also grasped that, since every existing thing must be intrinsically in motion, a prime mover is superfluous.

We have felt that this chimerical god, prudently invented by the earliest legislators, simply constituted, in their hands, one more way of enchaining us; and since they alone reserved the right to make this phantom speak, they managed quite well to let it say only whatever supported the ridiculous laws with which they strove to enslave us. Lycurgus, Numa, Moses, Jesus Christ, Muhammad—all these big scoundrels, all these big despots of our ideas knew how to bond their concocted divinities with their immense ambitions. Certain of captivating nations with the sanction of their gods, these villains, as we know, took care either to question their deities at an appropriate moment or to have them answer only whatever they believed could serve their purpose.

Today let us scorn both the sham god preached by the imposters and all the religious hair-splitting that derives from his ludicrous adoption; we cannot entertain free men with this child's rattle. The total annihilation of divine worship should comprise an indispensable part of our principles, which we are spreading throughout Europe. We should not be content with shattering scepters, we must smash idols forever. There has never been more than one step from superstition to royalism.

Survey the histories of all nations. You will never see them exchange their form of government for a monarchy, given their gradation by superstition; you will always see kings supporting religion, and religion supporting kings. We know the story of the steward and the cook: "Pass me the pepper, and I'll pass you the butter." Wretched humans, are you doomed to resemble forever the master of these two scoundrels?

Such is the case, no doubt, since one of the primary articles of a royal coronation has always been the maintenance of the dominant religion as one of the political fundaments that could best support a throne. However, since the throne has, fortunately, been toppled for all time, we should not be afraid to likewise destroy its buttresses.

Yes, citizens, you have understood that religion and freedom are incompatible with each other. Never will a free man bow to the gods of Christianity; never will its dogmas, never will its rites, never its mysteries, never its morals be suitable for a republican. Some more effort: since you are aiming to destroy all prejudices, let not one survive, for it takes only one to resurrect all of them. How more certain of their return should we be, if the one prejudice we allow to survive is definitely the cradle of all the others!

Let us stop believing that religion can be useful to man. Instead, let us have good laws, and we can then do without religion. But, it is claimed, people need religion; it entertains them, it helps control them. All well and good! In that case, give us a religion that is suitable for free men. Give us back the pagan gods. We will gladly worship Jupiter, Hercules, or Pallas Athena, but we want nothing more of the fabled creator of a universe that moves itself; nothing more of a god who, although without spatial extension, nevertheless fills everything; no more of a god who, although omnipotent, never carries out what he desires; no more of a being who, although sovereignly good, creates nothing but malcontents; a being who loves order, but in whose government everything is in disorder. No, we want nothing more of a god who upsets the system of nature, who is the father of confusion, who moves men at the very instant that man commits horrors. Such a god makes us shudder with indignation, and we relegate him forever to the oblivion from which the infamous Robespierre wanted him to emerge.

All religions concur in exalting the deep-seated wisdom and power of a divinity, but once its conduct is exposed, we find nothing but imprudence, weakness, and folly. God, we are told, created the world for himself, but so far he has failed to have the world honored appropriately. God created us to worship him, and we spend our days mocking him! What a wretched god he is!

Frenchmen, let us replace this unworthy phantom with the imposing simulacra that made Rome the mistress of the universe; let us treat all Christian idols as we treated those of our kings. We have placed the attributes of freedom back on the foundations that used to support tyrants; now let us also rebuild the effigies of great men on the pedestals of those scoundrels worshipped by Christianity. (We are dealing here purely with those whose reputations were established long ago.)

We should also stop dreading the effects of atheism on our rustic population; didn't the peasants feel the necessity of destroying the Catholic creed, which so deeply contradicted the true principles of liberty? Didn't they fearlessly and painlessly watch the overthrow of their altars and their presbyteries? Ah! Believe me, they will likewise renounce their laughable god. The statues of Mars, Minerva, and Liberty will be set up in the most conspicuous points of their habitations; a festivity will be celebrated annually, and the citizen's crown will be awarded to the citizen who has done the most for his country. At the entrance to a solitary forest, Venus, Hymen, and Amor, their statues erected in a rural temple, will receive the tributes of lovers; there, by the hands of the Graces, beauty will crown constancy.

Love alone will not be worthy of this crown, it must be earned: heroism, talents, humanity, spiritual grandeur, outstanding citizenship—those are the qualities that the lover must lay at the feet of his beloved; and these qualities counterpoise those of birth and wealth that used to be demanded by a mindless arrogance. This religion will permit at least a few virtues to blossom, while the other religion, that we used to be weak enough to profess publicly, will generate nothing but crime. This new religion will bond with the freedom we serve; it will animate it, maintain it, and set it ablaze—contrary to theism, which, in both essence and nature, is the most mortal enemy of the freedom we serve.

Did it cost even a drop of blood when the pagan idols were destroyed during the Byzantine Empire? The revolution, prepared by the stupidity of a nation that has reverted to slavery, took place without the slightest obstacle. How can we fear that the work of philosophy is more arduous than that of despotism? It is the priests alone who still hold this nation captive at the feet of its chimerical god, this nation that you so greatly fear to enlighten; get the priests away from that god, and the veil will drop by itself. Be convinced that this nation is far wiser than you imagine, and that, released from the fetters of tyranny, it will soon be free of the shackles of superstition. You are afraid of the people if these reins drop? Preposterous! Ah, believe me, citizens! The man who is not restrained by the concrete sword of laws will not be hindered by the abstract fright of the tortures of hell, which he has ridiculed since childhood. Your theism has, in a word, caused many heinous crimes, but never prevented a single one.

If it is true that passions blind us, that they cover our eyes with a cloud that disguises the dangers surrounding the passions, how can we assume that these dangers, which lurk as far away as the punishments threatened by your god—that these dangers can dissipate this cloud? After all, the latter cannot be dissolved even by the sword of the laws, which always hangs ominously over the passions. If it is thus proved that the additional restraints inflicted by the idea of a god are superfluous, if furthermore it is demonstrated that this god is dangerous in his other effects, then I ask you: What use is he, and what motives can we rely on for prolonging his existence? Will I be told that we are still not mature enough to consolidate our revolution so strikingly? Ah, my fellow citizens! The road we have traveled after 1789 has been far more arduous than the road still lying ahead of us, and in regard to what I now propose, we do not need to affect public opinion anywhere as deeply as we have tormented it in every way since the storming of the Bastille. Believe me, a nation that was wise enough, courageous enough to conduct an insolent monarch from the pinnacle of his grandeurs to the feet of the scaffold; a nation that, within a few short years, has managed to vanquish so many prejudices, managed to shatter so many ridiculous controls—this nation possesses enough wisdom and courage to sacrifice for the good of the cause, for the prosperity of the republic, to immolate a phantom far more illusory than any king could ever be.

Frenchmen, you will strike the first blows; your national education will take care of the rest! But get to work quickly, let this task be one of your top priorities; and, above all, you must found it on the essential morality that is so greatly neglected in religious upbringing. Replace the deific stupidities with which you exhaust the young organs of your children, substitute outstanding social principles. Instead of memorizing worthless prayers that they will be proud to forget by the age of sixteen, they should be instructed about their duties within society. Teach them to cherish virtues that you barely spoke about in the past, and that suffice for their personal happiness without your pious stories; let them realize that this happiness consists of making others as fortunate as we ourselves wish to be. If, however, you graft these verities on Christian fantasies, as you once did in your madness, then the instant your pupils recognize the futility of the foundation, they will raze the edifice; and they will become scoundrels only because they believe that the religion they have rejected prohibits them from being scoundrels.

However, by being convinced that virtue is obligatory solely when their own happiness depends on it, they will be decent out of selfishness; and this law, which rules all mankind, is still the most reliable power. So you must, with the greatest care, avoid mixing any religious fable whatsoever into the national education. Never lose sight of the fact that we are trying to shape free men and not vile worshippers of some god or other. Let a simple philosopher teach these new pupils about the incomprehensible sublimities of nature; let him prove to these pupils that the often highly dangerous conviction of the existence of a god has never served their happiness, and that they would never be happier by admitting, as the cause of what they do not grasp, something they grasp even less. The philosopher must teach these pupils that it is far less essential to understand nature than to enjoy and respect its laws; that these laws are both wise and simple; that they are written in all human hearts, and that one need merely question a heart in order to appreciate its impulses. If pupils absolutely insist that you talk to them about a creator, tell them that, since things have always been what they still are, with never any start and never any finish, it therefore becomes both ineffectual and unfeasible for men to go back to an imaginary origin that would explain nothing and advance nowhere. Tell the pupils that it is impossible for humans to have correct ideas about a being that does not act upon any of our senses.

All our ideas are representations of the objects that affect our senses; then what can be represented by the idea of God, which is obviously an idea without an object? Isn't such an idea, you will add, as impossible as effects without causes? Isn't an idea without a prototype anything but a chimera? Some Doctors of the Church, you will continue, assure us that the notion of God is innate, and that a man already has this notion in his mother's womb. But that is wrong, you will add; every principle is a judgment, every judgment is the result of an experience, and an experience can be gained only through the exercise of the senses. And it thereby follows that religious principles are obviously based on nothing and are not innate at all. How, you will go on, could anyone persuade rational beings that the hardest thing to grasp was the most essential thing for them? They were terrified; and when you are terrified, you are no longer rational. Above all, they were told to distrust their reasoning; and when the brains are muddled, you believe everything and examine nothing. Fear and ignorance, you will continue, are the two mainstays of any and all religions. Man's incertitude in regard to his God is precisely the motive that attaches him to his religion. Man is frightened in the dark, both physically and mentally; fear becomes habitual in him and changes into need; he would believe he was lacking something if he had nothing to hope for or be afraid of.

Let us now return to the usefulness of morality. In regard to this great subject, give your pupils far more examples than lessons, far more proofs than books, and you will make them good citizens; you will make them fine warriors, fine fathers, fine husbands. You will make them far more attached to the liberty of their country than any idea of servitude that could occur to them, any religious dread that could baffle their minds. True patriotism will then burst out in all souls; it will rule with all its strength and in all its purity, because it will be the sole dominant emotion, and because no alien idea will weaken its energy. Hence your second generation is safe, and your work, which it consolidates, will become the law of the universe. But what if, through fear or cowardice, this advice is not followed, what if the foundation of the edifice, the bases that we thought destroyed actually survive—what will happen? We will rebuild on that same foundation, and there we will put the same colossuses, with the cruel difference that this time we will cement them in place so forcefully that neither your generation nor the subsequent ones will manage to topple them.

Let nobody doubt that religions are the cradles of despotism. The first of all despots was a priest; the first king and the first emperor of Rome, Numa and Augustus, both allied themselves with the priesthood; Constantine and Clovis were abbots rather than sovereigns; Heliogabalus was the priest of the sun. In all times, in all centuries, despotism and religion have been so thoroughly interconnected that, as is easily demonstrated, in destroying one you undermine the other, for the profound reason that each will help the other to gain power. However, I do not propose massacres or expulsions; all those horrors are too far from my soul for me to dare consider them for even a minute. No! Do not murder and do not expel. These atrocities are the handiwork of kings or of the villains who ape them; if you behave as they do, you will not force anyone to despise the people who commit such brutalities. Let us inflict violence only on idols;

those who serve them should only be ridiculed. The sarcasm of Julian the Apostate damaged the Christian religion more than all of Nero's tortures. Yes! Let us destroy forever any idea of God and let us make soldiers of priests—indeed, some are already soldiers—let us hold fast to this noble republican vocation, but they are never again to talk about their chimerical being or its concocted religion—the single object of our loathing.

The first of these blessed charlatans to talk about God or religion will be condemned to being jeered at, scoffed at, covered with mud at all crossroads of the major French towns. If that scoundrel breaks that same law a second time, he will be locked away in an eternal prison. Let the most insulting blasphemies, the most atheistic writings be fully authorized, so that we may completely extirpate those horrifying toys of our childhoods from human hearts and memories. Let us hold a contest to find at last the text most capable of enlightening Europeans about such a major subject; and let a substantial prize be established by the Nation as recompense for the man who, having said and proved everything about this theme, will leave his compatriots only a sickle to shatter all these phantoms and a straightforward heart to detest them.

In six months everything will be finished: your infamous God will have dissolved into nothingness—and without stopping to be just, to be eager for the esteem of other people, without stopping to fear the sword of the law and to be a decent man; because we will have felt that the true friend of the Nation must never be led by chimeras—unlike the slaves of kings. In short, neither the frivolous hope of a better world nor the fear of greater evils sent by nature may conduct a republican, whose sole guide is virtue—conduct him as the sole constraint of remorse.

Morals

After demonstrating that theism is unsuitable for a republican government, I find it crucial to prove that French morals are likewise inappropriate. This commentary is all the more essential because the laws to be promulgated are based on morals.

Frenchmen, you are too enlightened not to sense that a new form of government will require new morals; a citizen of a free state cannot possibly behave like the slave of a despotic king. These differences in their interests, in their duties, in their interrelations will essentially determine a completely dissimilar conduct in the world. A throng of minor errors, of minor social offenses was regarded as onerous under the reigns of kings, who had to demand all the more that they needed to impose barriers in order to make themselves respectable or unapproachable in regard to their subjects; but now these throngs are becoming null. In a republican state, under a government without kings or religion, other offenses, known as regicide or sacrilege, must likewise be wiped out. Citizens, remember: in granting freedom of conscience and freedom of the press, you must also allow freedom of action, with few exceptions. And aside from what directly shakes the foundations of government, you will have infinitely fewer crimes to punish; for in a society based on liberty and equality, there are, at bottom, very few criminal acts. If things are thoroughly examined and investigated, then nothing is criminal but what the law rejects; for nature, dictating both vices and virtues, takes charge of our mental and physical constitution, or, to put it more philosophically, our need for vices and virtues; and what nature inspires would become a very uncertain measure for precisely regulating what is good and what is evil.

However, to more clearly expound my ideas about such a crucial subject, we are going to classify the different human actions that have until now been labeled criminal, and then we are going to evaluate them according to the actual duties of a republican.

In all times, the duties of man have been considered in terms of the three following and different aspects:

1. Duties toward the Supreme Being as imposed by conscience and credulity.
2. Duties that man must fulfill toward his brothers.
3. Finally, duties relating only to himself.

Necessary for us is the certainty that no god has dealt with us, that we are natural creatures like plants and animals, that we exist because it was impossible for us not to exist. As we can see, this certitude, at one swoop, extinguishes the first type of these duties: I mean those for which we falsely believe we are responsible toward the divinity; together with them, all the religious offenses will vanish, all the offenses known under the vague and unclear names of *impiety, sacrilege, blasphemy, atheism,* and so forth. In short, they are all those whom Athens punished so unjustly in Alcibiades, and France so unjustly in the unfortunate La Barre.

If there is anything absurd in the world, it is the fact that men, who know their god and his possible demands purely on the basis of their own restricted notions, nevertheless wish to decide on the nature of what contents or angers this ludicrous phantom of their imagination. I therefore ask that we not limit ourselves to letting all religions exist equally side by side; instead, I desire the freedom to scorn or mock all religions; the people who gather in some temple to invoke the Eternal in their fashion should be seen as stage actors, whom everyone is permitted to laugh at. If you do not view the religions in these terms, they will reclaim their serious character, and then their importance; indeed, they will soon protect opinions; and once again we squabble about religions rather than for religions.

Every nation claims that its religion is the best, and to bolster its claim, a nation relies on an infinity of not only internal but also mostly external contradictions. In our profound ignorance, which of these religions can truly please God, assuming there is a god? If we are wise, we must either protect all religions equally or likewise proscribe them all; now proscription is assuredly the best approach, since we have the moral certainty that all religions are mummeries, none of which can please a god who does not exist.

The equality destroyed by preference or the protection accorded one of them will soon disappear from the government, and the reconstructed *theocracy* will soon give birth to the *aristocracy.* I cannot reiterate it often enough: no more gods, Frenchmen, no more gods, if you do not want their catastrophic dominion to quickly plunge you back into the horrors of despotism; but you will destroy them purely by deriding them; all the dangers in their wake will promptly resurface in throngs if you fight them listlessly and take them too seriously. Do not topple their idols in anger; pulverize them while playing, and public opinion will tumble of its own accord.

This suffices, I hope, to demonstrate that we should not pass any antireligious law; for the man who offends a chimera offends nothing. It would be utterly inconsistent to punish men who outrage or disparage a religion whose priority over other religions is not clearly proved; it would necessarily mean adopting a bias and therefore disturbing the scales of equality, the first law of your new form of government.

Let us pass to the second type of human duties, those that tie man to his fellow men; this type is undoubtedly the most widespread.

Christian morality, too vague about interhuman relations, sets up doctrines so full of sophisms that we cannot possibly accept them; for when we desire to establish principles, we must take care not to provide sophisms as their foundations. This absurd morality tells us to love our neighbors as ourselves. Nothing would assuredly be more sublime if it were possible for deceit to bear the traits of beauty. It is not a matter of loving your neighbors as yourselves, since this contradicts all the laws of nature, and since its mere inspiration must direct all the actions of our lives; it is simply a question of loving our neighbors as brothers, as friends whom nature gives us, and with whom we must live all the better in a republican state, in which the disappearance of social classes must necessarily tighten the bonds.

Hence, humanity, fraternity, and charity should prescribe our mutual duties, and we should fill them individually with the simple degree of energy that nature has given us on this point. By the same token, we should avoid scolding and, above all, avoid punishing those men who, colder or moodier, will fail to experience in these nevertheless so poignant bonds all the delights that others encounter in them. For, as we will concur, it would be a palpable absurdity to impose universal laws in this context; this procedure would be as ridiculous as that of an army general who would make each of his soldiers wear a uniform cut according to the same measurements. It is dreadfully unjust to demand

that men with unequal characters must submit to equal laws—
something that fits one person will by no means fit another.

I do agree that we cannot pass as many laws as there are men,
but laws may be so mild, so few in number, that all men, no
matter what their characters, can easily comply. I would also
require that this tiny number of laws should be structured in
such a way as to adjust readily to all those different characters;
leave it up to the man who would apply those laws to punish
more or less severely, with respect for the individual who had
to be struck. As it has been demonstrated, there are some
virtues that certain men could not possibly practice, just as
there are remedies that could not suit particular temperaments.
So it would be the pinnacle of your injustice to inflict the law
upon a man who could not possibly submit to the law! Would
not the iniquity that you thereby committed be the same as
forcing a blind man to discern colors?

As we can see, these supreme principles make it necessary to
promulgate mild laws and, above all, to wipe out forever the
atrocity of capital punishment; because the law that assaults a
human life is unjust, impracticable, and inadmissible. It is not,
as I am about to explain, that there is no infinity of cases in
which human beings, without offending nature (and that is
what I will prove), had received, from this mother of all men,
the complete freedom to lay hands on one another. The law,
however, cannot possibly obtain the same privilege, because,
unfeeling in and of itself, the law cannot be accessible to the
human passions that legitimize the cruel act of murder. Nature
gives man the impulses that can make him excuse such a misdeed; while the law, on the contrary, forever opposing and not
receiving anything from nature, cannot be authorized to perform the same excesses: Since the law does not have the same
motives, it cannot possibly have the same rights. Those are
some of the subtle and philosophical distinctions that escape
many people, because very few people reflect; however, those
distinctions will be welcomed by the educated people whom I
address, and I hope they will influence the new Statute Book
that is being prepared for us.

The second reason for wiping out the death penalty is that it has never prevented any crime, since it is committed daily at the foot of the scaffold. We must, in short, eliminate this punishment, because there is no worse calculation than killing a man for having killed another. The obvious result of this action is that instead of our having one less person we suddenly have two less people, a reckoning plausible only to executioners and imbeciles. Be that as it may, the offenses we can inflict on our brothers boil down to four principle transgressions: slander; theft; the offenses that, caused by impurity, can disagreeably assault others; and murder.

Are all these actions, which are regarded as capital offenses in a monarchy, equally serious in a republican state? That is what we will analyze with the torch of philosophy, for this is the only light in which such an examination must occur. Do not accuse me of being a dangerous innovator; do not tell me that, as these writings might do, it is risky to blunt the remorse in the souls of evildoers; do not say to me that I would be imposing the greatest damage because, supposedly, the mildness of my morality strengthens the criminal proclivities of those same evildoers. I expressly testify here that I do not have one of those perverse views; I am revealing the ideas that have been identified with me since the Age of Reason and that have been opposed for so many centuries by the infamous despotism of the tyrants. Too bad for them if those grand ideas were corruptive, too bad for them if those men can grasp only evil in philosophical opinions, which they would allow to be corrupt! Who knows if they might not be corrupted by reading Charron and Seneca? It is not those easily corrupted men to whom I am speaking; rather, I am addressing only people who are capable of understanding me and who will read me without danger.

To be perfectly frank, I confess that I have never felt there was anything wrong with slander, especially in a form of government like ours, in which all men, more interlinked and more mutually attached, obviously have a greater interest in getting to know each other. Now, one of two things may happen: slander may strike either a truly perverse man or a virtuous being. We agree that in the former case it scarcely matters whether a slightly nastier thing is said about a man who is already well known for his great wickedness; perhaps the wickedness that does not even exist may shed light on what does exist, and thus the evildoer is better known.

Let us assume that Hanover is afflicted by unhealthy weather, but that, if I expose myself to the inclemency of the climate, I will run no further risk than suffering a bout of fever. Should I then be angry at the person who, to prevent my going there, would tell me that people were dying upon their arrival in Hanover? Absolutely not! For in scaring me with a major evil, that man prevented me from enduring a minor evil.

Can slander, on the other hand, strike a virtuous man? He should not be alarmed! Instead, he ought to show himself in public, and all of the slanderer's venom will soon fall back on the slanderer. For such victims, slander is merely a kind of purifying poll from which they emerge all the more brilliantly. There is even a gain for all the virtues of the republic; since this virtuous and sensitive man, stung by the injustice he has endured, will apply himself to doing better, he will want to overcome that slander, from which he felt secure, and his noble deeds will simply acquire one more degree of moral perfection.

Thus, in the first case, the slanderer will have produced a lot of good effects by having the vices of a dangerous man seem greater; in the second case, the slanderer will have achieved excellent results by making virtue offer itself to us quite fully. Well, now I ask you: In what circumstance should a slanderer be feared, especially in a state in which it is so essential to know evil people and to increase the power of good people? We should avoid pronouncing any judgment against slander; instead, we must consider slander under the double aspect of a beacon and an incentive, and in any case something highly useful. The legislator, all of whose ideas must be as vast as his labor, should never test the effects of the offense that strikes only an individual; rather, it is his effects on the masses that we must examine. And when he thereby observes the results of slander, I challenge him to find anything worth penalizing; I challenge him to catch even the slightest glimmer of justice in a law that makes slander punishable. On the contrary, by favoring or rewarding it, he becomes a man of utmost justice and integrity.

The second of the moral offenses that we intend to examine is theft.

If we scrutinize Antiquity, we notice that theft was permitted and recompensed in all the Greek republics; Sparta and Laconia supported it openly; a few other states regarded it as a military virtue; it is certain that theft maintains strength, courage, dexterity—in short, all virtues that are useful to a republican regime, hence to our regime. I will, impartially now, ask whether theft, which equalizes wealth, can be so wicked in a state that aims at equality. Not at all! For if theft maintains equality on the one hand, it inspires you, on the other hand, to safeguard your property more carefully. There was even a state that punished not the thief but his victim in order to teach him to look after his assets more warily. This leads us to more comprehensive reflections.

God forbid that I plan to attack or destroy the oath to respect private property—an oath that has just been sworn by the nation—but will I be allowed to express a few thoughts about the injustice of that oath? What is the goal of an oath sworn by all the members of a nation? Is not its point to sustain a perfect equality among all citizens, to submit them all equally to the law that shields all private property? Now I ask you: Is there true justice in a law that commands a man who has nothing to respect a man who has everything? What are the essential elements of the social contract? Does the social contract not imply yielding a bit of your freedom and your property in order to ensure and preserve whatever you keep of both?

All laws have those foundations; they are the reasons for the penalties inflicted on the man who abuses his freedom. They even authorize the imposition of taxes; this means that a citizen does not protest when they are exacted from him, because he knows that, by giving something, he conserves what remains for him. But once again, by what right should the man who has nothing bow to a contract that protects only the man who has everything? If you perform an act of equity by preserving, through your oath, the rich man's property, then are you not being unjust by demanding this oath from the "preserver" who has nothing? What benefit does the preserver derive from your oath? And why do you want him to promise something that is advantageous purely to the man who differs from him so widely by his riches? There is assuredly nothing more unjust. An oath must have an equal effect on all the people who swear it; nor can it possibly subjugate the man who is uninterested in maintaining it because it would not constitute the pact of a free nation. It would be the strong man's weapon over the weak man's weapon, whereby the latter would revolt endlessly against the former. Now that is what occurs in the oath to respect private property, an oath just demanded by the nation; the rich man alone fetters the poor man to the oath, the rich man alone benefits from the oath, which the poor man swears without giving it a second thought; indeed, he fails to see that through this oath, which is extorted from his credulity, he is committing himself to doing something that cannot be done for him.

Convinced, as you should be, by that barbaric inequality, do not aggravate your injustice by punishing the man who has nothing, by penalizing him for daring to filch something from the man who has everything. Your inequitable oath grants the pauper this right more than ever. By forcing him to perjure himself through this oath, which is absurd for him, you legitimize all the crimes he commits because of that perjury; it is not your job to punish something that you have caused. Nor need I say more about the dreadful brutality in punishing thieves. Imitate the wise law of the state I have just described; punish the man who is negligent enough to be robbed, but do not visit any kind of penalty upon the thief. You must realize that your oath empowers him to carry out this action, and that, by submitting, he has simply followed the first and the wisest of nature's drives: namely, to preserve one's own existence, no matter what this self-preservation may cost others.

The offenses we have to examine in the second type of a man's duties toward his fellow men consist of the actions that can be triggered by sexual perversion; among them we can especially point out the transgressions that shatter the rights of our fellow men: prostitution, adultery, incest, rape, and sodomy. We certainly should not doubt for even a moment that all so-called moral crimes—that is, all the above-cited actions—are morally indifferent in a state with only the following task: to decide which means whatsoever to use for maintaining the form that is essential and necessary for that state. That is the sole morality of a republican constitution.

But since that state is forever assaulted by the surrounding despots, one could not reasonably imagine that its methods of self-preservation can be "moral means," for it will survive purely through warfare, and nothing is less moral than a war. Now I wonder: How can one manage to demonstrate that, in a state made immoral by its obligations, it is essential for individuals to be moral? I say, furthermore, it is good that individuals are immoral. The Greek legislators perfectly understood the importance and necessity of corrupting the citizens so that their moral dissolution would influence the dissolution that would be useful for the wheels of government. The result was the insurrection that is always indispensable in a state that, thoroughly happy like the republican government, is bound to arouse the hatred and jealousy of all the surrounding states.

Insurrection, those wise legislators felt, is by no means a moral condition, yet it must remain the permanent condition of a republic. It would therefore be both absurd and dangerous to require that the people maintaining the perpetual immoral agitation of the state machinery must themselves be highly moral. After all, a man's moral condition is one of peace and tranquillity, whereas his immoral condition is one of perpetual motion, bringing him close to the necessary insurrection, in which the republican must constantly adhere to the form of government he belongs to.

Let us now go into detail, starting with an analysis of modesty, the cowardly urge that contradicts the impure passions. If nature meant humans to be modest, it would not, assuredly, let them be born naked. An endless number of populations, less corrupted by civilization than we, go about naked and feel no shame. There is no doubt that the sole reasons for the custom of wearing clothes were the inclemency of the climate and the coquetry of women; for women sensed they would soon lose all the fruits of desire if they anticipated them instead of letting them grow. They assumed that, since nature had not created them without defects, they would be far more certain of having all methods of pleasing by disguising those faults with ornaments. Thus, modesty, far from being a virtue, was simply one of the first outgrowths of corruption, one of the first modes of female coquettishness. Lycurgus and Solon, clearly seeing that modesty keeps a citizen in the immoral condition essential to the republican laws, compelled girls to appear nude in the theater. Supposedly, these legislators, by dulling the male passion for a naked girl, aimed at intensifying the passion that men sometimes feel for their own sex. These sages presented things they wanted men to feel disgust for, and they concealed things they believed suitable for arousing the sweetest desires. In all cases, were they not working toward the aim we have just mentioned? They sensed, as we can see, the need for immorality in republican customs.

In any event, Rome soon imitated the Greek custom of having naked girls in the theater; participants in the games of Flora danced nude; the majority of pagan mysteries were celebrated thusly; furthermore, nudity was even touted as a virtue among some populaces.

At any rate, modesty spawns lecherous proclivities, and the results make up the alleged crimes we are analyzing, the first being prostitution.

Now that we have recognized a huge throng of religious errors that held us in their fetters, and now that we have overcome so many prejudices that alienated us from nature, we listen only to the voice of nature. Indeed, we are convinced that, if there are such things as crimes, they actually consist of defying the tendencies inspired in us by nature; and since lechery is a consequence of these tendencies, the issue is not so much to snuff out this passion within us as to regulate the means of satisfying it in peace. For that reason we must focus our efforts on creating order in this realm and making certain of all the necessary security. As a result, the citizen, instinctually driven to objects of lechery, can, with those objects, submit to everything his passions inflict on him, but he must never be impeded by anything; for no human passion is more needful of the entire measure of freedom than this one.

At certain points in the city, we should establish various sites that are healthy, enormous, appropriately furnished, and safe in all respects. There, all sexes, all ages, all creatures will be offered to the whims of the libertines, who come there for a good time; utter subordination will be the rule of the presented individuals, and the slightest refusal will be promptly and arbitrarily punished by the rejected libertine. I must further explain this and gauge it according to republican customs; I promised to apply the same logic everywhere, and I will keep my word.

If, as I have just said, no passion needs the entire measure of freedom more than this passion, then no passion, doubtlessly, is as despotic—that is where man likes to be in control, to be obeyed, to be surrounded by slaves who are required to satisfy him. If a man is not given the secret possibility of exhaling the dose of tyranny that nature has put at the bottom of his heart, then he will be forced to take out his frustration on the beings that surround him, and he will imperil the state. If you wish to avoid this danger, you must allow the free development of those authoritarian urges, which, notwithstanding, torment him endlessly. Content with having exercised his bit of sovereignty in a harem of pages or sultanas, whom your care and his money make accessible to him, he will emerge satisfied; nor will he feel any need to alarm a government that so obligingly makes all methods of gratifying his concupiscence available to him.

But should you proceed otherwise, you will place the ridiculous shackles of public lechery on these beings—the shackles invented long ago by ministerial tyranny and by the lubricity of our Sardanapalus. Man, soon embittered against your government, soon jealous of the despotism he sees you exercise all alone, will shake off the yoke you inflict on him, and, weary of your manner of ruling, will change it, as he has just done. As we know, the infamous and notorious Sartine, lieutenant-general of the French police, composed techniques of lechery for Louis XV: three times a week, Sartine had Madame Dubarry read to the king, delving into all the intimate and embellished details of everything occurring in the wicked haunts of Paris. This brand of libertinage practiced by the French Nero cost the state three million!

See how the Greek legislators, convinced of the correctness of these ideas, treated debauchery in Sparta and Athens; far from prohibiting it, they intoxicated the citizen with it, and no type of lubricity was excluded. Socrates, whom the Oracle declared the wisest philosopher on earth, passed indiscriminately from the arms of Aphasia to those of Alcibiades. And yet he remained no less the glory of Greece. I will go even further, and however contrary my notions to our present-day customs, my object is to prove that we must change our customs hastily if we wish to preserve the form of government we have adopted; I will therefore try to persuade you that the prostitution of women who are known to be decent is no more dangerous than the prostitution of men. Not only should we let these women participate in the perversions at the houses I demand; we should also create special houses for them, places where they can satisfy themselves with all sexes, gratify their whims and the needs of their temperaments, which, indeed, are far more ardent than our own.

First of all, by what right do you demand that a woman should be excepted from the blind submission that nature prescribes for her in male caprices? And then, by what other right do you demand that she should surrender to a continence that is impossible for her body and absolutely hopeless for her honor?

I am going to treat these two issues separately.

In the first place, it is indisputable that, in the natural condition in which women are born, they enjoy the advantages of all other female animals and, like them and with no exception, they belong to all males. Such, no doubt, were the first natural laws and the sole institutions of the first human gatherings. Self-interest, egoism, and love corrupted these initially so simple and so natural views; men believed they were enriching themselves by taking a wife along with her family's wealth. These satisfied the first two feelings of the ones I have just indicated. More often, however, a man kidnapped a wife and attached himself to her emotionally; that was the second reason—in any case, the result was injustice.

No act of possession can ever be perpetrated on a free being; it is as unjust to own a wife monogamously as it is to own slaves. All men are born free, all are equal before the law; we must never lose sight of these principles. Hence, no sex is granted the legitimate right to seize the other sex exclusively, and never can any sex or any class possess the other arbitrarily. In the purity of natural laws, a woman cannot reject a man's advances by claiming she loves another; this turns into a reason for exclusion, and no man can be excluded from possessing a woman the instant it becomes clear that she resolutely belongs to all men. The act of possession can be exercised only on an animal or an immobile object, but never on an individual that resembles us; and all the bonds that can secure a woman to a man, whatever those fetters may be, are both unjust and chimerical.

If it is therefore incontestable that nature has given us the right to express our desires for all women without exception, it is equally incontestable that we have the right to force them all to submit to us; and not exclusively—for that would contradict what I have said above—but for the moment.

Do not say that I am contradicting myself, and that, after establishing that we have no right to attach a woman to ourselves, I am destroying those principles by now saying that we have the right to force her. Let me repeat: the issue at hand is sensual pleasure and not property. I have no right to own the wellspring that I encounter on my road, but I do have certain rights to enjoy it; I have the right to profit from the limpid water that it offers my thirst. By the same token, I have no legal right to the property belonging to this woman or that, but I do have the undeniable right to enjoy her, and I do have the right to force her if she rejects me for whatever reason.

Indeed, we even have the right to pass laws that compel a woman to yield to the ardor of the man who desires her, whereby violence itself, as a result of such a right, can be used legally by us. And did not nature prove we had this right when it provided us with the necessary force to make women submit to our desires?

In vain must women defend themselves by citing their modesty or their attachments to other men; these far-fetched excuses are null and void; we have already seen that modesty is an artificial and contemptible sentiment. Love, which can be called the "folly of the soul," no longer legitimizes fidelity; in satisfying only two individuals, the beloved and the lover, love cannot serve the happiness of others; yet it is for universal happiness and not for an egoistical and privileged happiness that we have been given women. Hence, all men have an equal right to enjoy all women; and so there is no man who, according to natural laws, can inflict a single and personal right on a woman. The law that forces them to be prostituted as often as we like in the pleasure houses I have discussed, this law that punishes them if they flout it, is quite equitable, and there is no legitimate or justifiable reason to attack it.

A man who wants to enjoy any girl or any woman, if the laws you promulgate are fair, can summon her to one of those houses; and there, safeguarded by the matrons of this temple of Venus, she will be delivered to him. With both humility and submission, she will satisfy all the caprices that occur to him and delight him, no matter how bizarre or abnormal they may be; for there is no sexual quirk that cannot be found in nature or accepted by nature. All we need do is fix the age; still, I maintain that we cannot do so without disturbing the freedom of the man who desires a girl of such and such an age. The man who wishes to eat the fruit of a tree can, assuredly, pick the fruit whether it be green or ripe, following the inspiration of his taste.

But, you will object, there is an age in which a man's sexuality can damage a girl's health. Well, this consideration is worthless. Once you grant me the right of ownership of a pleasure, this right is independent of the effects produced by this pleasure; as of this moment, it no longer matters whether this enjoyment be useful or harmful to the chosen female. Have I not already proved that it is fully legal to restrict a woman's will in this problem, and that, once she arouses a man's desire, she must submit to his enjoyment, irrespective of her egoistic feelings? The same is true of her health. As soon as her consideration destroys or weakens the pleasure of the man, who desires her and has the right to appropriate her, age becomes a moot point. In no wise does our examination cover the emotions of the female, condemned by law and by nature to fulfill the male's desires, for an instant. Our sole issue is whatever benefits the man. We are redressing the balance.

Yes, we will redress the balance; no doubt, we owe that to our women, whom we have so cruelly subjugated, and to whom we must incontestably make amends. And that will form the answer to the second question that I have posed.

If we admit, as we have just done, that all women must surrender to our pleasures, then we can, assuredly, allow them to amply satisfy their own desires; in that case, our laws must favor their ardent temperaments. It is absurd to place both their honor and their virtue in the antinatural force with which they resist the drives they have received far more profusely than we. This injustice in our customs is all the more flagrant in that we consent both to enfeeble women by seducing them and then to punish them by making them yield to all our efforts to provoke their downfalls. The utter nonsense of our customs is, I think, engraved in that inequitable atrocity; and this mere exposure should let us feel our tremendous need to exchange them for purer customs.

Having received far more aggressive penchants than men for lecherous pleasures, women, I therefore say, could submit to their leanings as often as they might wish; for they would be absolutely liberated from all bonds of marriage and all false prejudices of modesty, thereby completely restoring the natural condition. I want the laws to permit women to have as many men as they care to; I want the enjoyments of all sexes and all body parts to be allowed for women as they are for men; and on the special condition that women could surrender to all men who would desire them, they would have the freedom of equally enjoying all men whom women would believe worthy of satisfying them.

What, I ask, are the dangers of this freedom? Fatherless children? Well, what does that matter in a republic where no individual can have any mother but the fatherland, where whoever is born is a child of the fatherland? Ah! Rather, the fatherland would be loved all the more by citizens who are familiar with no other form of government, who realize, from birth, that they can only expect anything of the republic! Do not imagine that you are making good republicans of children whom you isolate in their families and who should belong totally to the republic. By giving only some individuals the measure of fondness that they should feel for all their brothers, they will inevitably adopt the often perilous biases of those individuals; their views and thoughts will focus on their narrow milieus, on their particular structures, and all the virtues of a statesman will be totally impossible for them. Ultimately, they give their hearts entirely to the people who bore them, and their hearts no longer contain any love for the fatherland, which must allow them to live, which brings them up and educates them—as if those second benefits were not more crucial than the first benefits!

Now, there may be the greatest drawback in leaving children in their families and nourishing special interests that are often very different from those of the fatherland; it may indeed be highly advantageous to divide them from their parents. And are they not naturally separated from their families by the methods I propose? For in thoroughly destroying all the bonds of matrimony, they enjoy the fruits of female pleasure and produce only those progeny who are not allowed to know their fathers. As a result, they no longer have the possibility of belonging to only one family, instead, as they should, being purely children of the fatherland.

Thus, some pleasure houses will be designed for female lechery, and, like those for male delights, they will be under government protection. Individuals of both sexes will be supplied with all the people they could desire, and the more these women visit these houses, the more they will be esteemed. There is nothing so barbarous and so ludicrous as making a woman's honor and virtue depend on her challenging desires that she has received from nature, and that also ceaselessly excite the people who are brutal enough to condemn them.

Babylonian women did not wait seven years to bring their virginity to the temple of Venus. A girl's first stirring of concupiscence is the moment when nature decides that the girl must prostitute herself; and, with no other sort of consideration, she must yield when her nature speaks. If she resists, she disobeys the laws of nature.

Thus, in her most tender age, a girl with severed paternal bonds has nothing to save for marriage (which is totally abolished by the wise laws that I desire); transcending the prejudice that once enchained her sex, she will manage to submit to anything dictating her temperament in the pleasure houses. She will be

welcomed respectfully and satisfied profusely. Next, upon returning to good society, she can speak as publicly about her
pleasures in those houses as she now speaks about a ball or a
stroll. You charming sex, you will be free; like men, you will
enjoy all the delights that nature has made your obligations; you
will not have to be constrained in any pleasure. Must the more
divine section of humanity be clapped in irons by the less divine
section? Ah, smash those chains—nature wants you to smash
them! You should have no other limits than your leanings, no
other laws than your cravings, no other morals than nature;
stop languishing in those barbaric prejudices that caused your
charms to fade and imprisoned the godly surges of your hearts.

Women do not realize how greatly embellished they are by lust.
Compare two women fairly equal in age and beauty, whereby
one is a celibate and the other a libertine: you will see how much
fresher and grander the second woman looks. Any violence inflicted on nature drains more than the abuse of pleasure; and
we all know that childbirth beautifies a woman. You charming
sex, you are as free as we men, and a lifetime of the combats of
Venus is as open to you as it is to us. You should no longer fear
nonsensical reproaches; pedantry and superstition are abolished; you will never again be caught blushing because of your
enchanting escapades; our esteem for you, with your wreaths
of myrtles and roses, will increase all the more the deeper you
plunge into your debauchery.

What we have just said ought actually to exempt us from examining adultery, but let us glance at it anyway, however void
it may be in light of the laws I have described. How ridiculous
it was to criminalize it in our ancient institutions! If there was
anything absurd in this world, it was quite without doubt the
eternal validity of conjugal bonds! One need only, I think, inspect or experience the full load of these bonds to stop viewing
as a crime the action that lightened the burden. Since nature, as
we have just said, has endowed women with a more fiery temperament, a more reflective sensitivity than individuals of the
male sex, the yoke of lifelong marriage has weighed more heavily on the female. Sensitive as you women are, and inflamed by
the fires of love, you can now be indemnified without fear; you

must convince yourselves that there can be nothing wrong about following natural impulses, that nature has created you not for a lone man but for pleasing all men indiscriminately. Let nothing hinder you. Imitate the Greek republicans; their legislators never meant to criminalize adultery, and nearly all of them accepted female lechery. In *Utopia*, Thomas More proves that it is advantageous for a woman to indulge in debauchery, and the ideas of this great man were not always dreams. Thomas More also wanted engaged couples to see each other naked before their nuptials. How many marriages would be foiled if that law were practiced! You must admit that the opposite truly means buying a pig in a poke!

Among the Tartars, the more a woman prostituted herself, the more she was honored; she publicly wore the marks of her immodesty on her neck, and women not decorated in this fashion were not esteemed. In the Asian kingdom of Pégu, the families themselves hand over their wives and daughters to visiting strangers; they rent them out for so much a day like horses and carriages! Finally, countless volumes would not suffice to demonstrate that lechery has never been regarded as a crime among all the wise nations in the world. All philosophers know that lechery was criminalized only thanks to the Christian imposters. The priests had their reasons for outlawing depravity: this urgent recommendation, by reserving for themselves the knowledge and the absolution of these secret vices, gave the priests an incredible power over women and opened for them the possibilities of endless iniquity. We know that they benefited from this privilege and that they would be abusing it today if their credit had not been destroyed for good.

Is incest more dangerous? No, not at all! It loosens family ties and therefore strengthens the citizens' love for their country; indeed, incest is dictated for us by the supreme natural laws; we treat it cordially, and the enjoyment we gain from the people belonging to us always seems more delightful than any other pleasure. The earliest social institutions fostered incest; it is found in the origins of societies; it is consecrated in all religions; it has been favored by all laws. If we crisscross the universe, we will find incest established everywhere. The natives of the Pepper Coast and Rio Gabon prostitute their wives to their own children; in the kingdom of Judah, the eldest son has to marry his father's wife; the inhabitants of Chile sleep indiscriminately with their sisters and their daughters, and they often wed both mother and daughter.

In short, I venture to assure you that incest must be legal for any regime based on brotherhood. How can a reasonable person be so absurd as to believe that the pleasure of his mother, his sister, or his daughter could ever be criminalized? I ask you: Is it not an abominable prejudice that turns a man into a wrongdoer, who, for his own delight, simply prefers a being who, because of his natural feeling, is closer than any other?

One could just as readily state that we are prohibited from loving too intensely the individuals whom nature enjoins us to love most, so that the more nature intensifies our feelings for that person, the more nature simultaneously distances itself from that person! These contradictions are nonsensical; they can be believed or adopted only by people brutalized by superstition. Since the community of women that I will create must necessarily involve incest, there is little left to say about an alleged offense whose nullity is too clearly demonstrated for us to dwell on it any further.

Let us instead turn to rape. Now at first glance, rape, of all the deviations of libertinage, seems to be the kind whose injury is the most firmly ascertained in regard to the outrage it appears to inflict. Yet it is definite that rape, an uncommon action that is so hard to prove, does less injustice to your neighbor than theft, because theft invades the property that the rapist is content merely to damage. And besides, what should we retort to the rapist who claims that the harm he has done is quite second-rate, since he has merely placed the abused victim a bit earlier in the condition in which love or marriage would have soon brought the victim anyway?

But sodomy, that supposed crime which drew the heavenly fires over Sodom and Gomorrah, two cities devoted to sodomy— is it not a monstrous deviation that cannot be punished too harshly? It is no doubt quite painful for us to have to reproach our ancestors for the judicial murders they committed in this context. Can you possibly be so barbaric as to condemn a miserable individual to death for the sole crime of not having the same leanings as you? We shudder to think that less than forty years have passed since the absurdity of the legislators was still at that point. Console yourselves, citizens! Such nonsense will not come again. The wisdom of our lawmakers is our guarantee. Today we are fully enlightened about this weakness of a few men, and so we know that such an error cannot be a crime; in regard to the juice flowing in our loins, nature would not have given it so much significance that we should be angry about the route we let this liquid flow.

What is the sole crime that can exist here? Assuredly it is not the process of inserting the penis into such or such a crevice of the body, unless you wish to maintain that the body parts are not equal in value, and that some are pure and some dirty. But since it is impossible to contend such absurdities, the only crime alleged here can subsist in the loss of semen. Now I ask you: Is it likely that this semen is so precious in the eyes of nature that any possible loss thereof can be deemed a crime? Would nature keep allowing such daily squandering if that were so? And would nature not be authorizing that waste if it were to pleasure a pregnant woman in dreams? Can we possibly imagine that nature could give us the prospect of a crime that would outrage nature? Can we possibly allow nature to let men destroy it and thereby become stronger than nature?

What a shocking gulf of absurdity we plunge into when, in order to reflect, we abandon the help offered by the torch of reason! Let us therefore be assured of the following: it is just as easy to enjoy a woman in one way or another; it absolutely makes no difference whether you enjoy a girl or a boy; and when it is certain that we cannot have any other natural leanings, nature is too clever and too consistent ever to place within us something that could offend it. The penchant for sodomy is the result of our physical structure, to which we contribute nothing. Children in the earliest age reveal this leaning and never get rid of it. Sometimes it is the fruit of satiety, but does that make it any less natural? However we view it, sodomy is a product of nature, and in any event, whatever it inspires must be respected by men.

Let us posit that an exact census might prove that sodomy is infinitely more fascinating than the other preference; that the resulting pleasures are far livelier; and that the advocates of sodomy therefore number a thousand times more than its enemies. Would it then be possible to conclude that, far from outraging nature, this vice would serve the views of nature, which is much less interested in having progeny than we are foolish enough to believe?

Now, in crisscrossing the universe, how many peoples have we seen despising women! Some men use women purely to create the necessary babies to replace them. Men's habits of living together in republics will always make sodomy more frequent, but it is certainly not dangerous. Would the Greek legislators have introduced it into their republic if they had assumed that? Quite the opposite; they deemed it crucial for a warrior nation. Plutarch enthusiastically discusses a battalion of lovers and beloveds; they alone defended Greece's freedom for a long time. This vice reigned supreme in the association of brothers-in-arms; it cemented them, and it included the greatest men. When America was discovered, it was populated by men with this taste. In Louisiana, among the Illinois, some male Indians dressed as females prostituted themselves like courtesans. The Black Africans of Benguela keep men openly. And today, nearly all Algerian seraglios are filled entirely with young boys. In Thebes, pederasty, the love of boys, was not just tolerated, it was required. And indeed, Socrates prescribed it in order to mellow the conduct of young men.

We know to what extent sodomy flourished in Rome: there were public sites where young boys in female attire prostituted themselves as did young girls in male attire. Martial, Catullus, Tibullus, Horace, and Virgil wrote to men as if to their mistresses, and finally Plutarch writes (in *Moral Works*) that women should not in any way participate in male love.

The Amasians on the island of Crete used to kidnap young boys among the most singular ceremonies. If a man loved a boy, he would tell the latter's parents on which day he, the abductor, planned to capture the boy. If the boy did not care for the kidnapper, he would put up resistance, but if the boy did

like the kidnapper, he would accompany him; and once the seducer had used the boy, he would return him to the boy's parents. For in this passion as in the passion for women, you
always have too much once you have enough. Strabo informs
us that on this same island, harems were not filled with boys;
rather, they were prostituted publicly.

If you want an ultimate authority to attest how useful this
vice is in a republic, just listen to Jerome the Peripatetic. The
love of boys, he tells us, spread throughout Greece because it
provided strength and courage and served to expel the tyrants;
conspiracies formed among lovers, and they submitted to torture rather than name their accomplices. Patriotism thus sacrificed everything to the prosperity of the state. Citizens were
certain that these relationships solidified the republic; they de-
claimed against women, and it was a weakness reserved for
despotism to attach oneself to females.

Pederasty was always the vice of warrior nations. Caesar
teaches us that the Gauls were extraordinarily devoted to the
love of boys. By separating the sexes, the wars sustaining the
republics propagated this vice, and since one realized the so
useful consequences for the state, pederasty was soon hallowed
by religion. It is well known that the Romans sanctified the loves
of Jupiter and Ganymede. Sextus Empiricus assures us that this
kind of love was required among the Persians. Lastly, the jealous and derided women offered the same service to their men
as they obtained from young boys. A few men tried it, but then,
finding illusion impossible, they resorted to their former habits.

The Turks, who were dedicated to this depravity, which
Muhammad consecrates in his Koran, declare nevertheless that
a very young virgin girl can quite easily replace a boy; and seldom do their girls become women before undergoing this trial.
Pope Sixtus the Fifth and Sanchez allowed this perversion;
indeed, Sanchez even attempted to bear out that it was useful
for propagation, and that a baby conceived after such a digres-
sion was infinitely better constituted. In the end, the women
made amends to one another. This vagary has, no doubt, no
more disadvantages than the other, because its outcome is
merely its refusal to generate, and because the methods used by

the sponsors of propagation are too powerful for their adversaries ever to harm them.

The Greeks likewise supported this female perversion for reasons of state. Since the women sufficed for each other, their communications with men were less frequent, and they did not at all injure the affairs of the republic. Lucian describes for us the progress effectuated by that license, and it is not without interest that we find it in Sappho.

In short, there is no danger in any of these manias. Let us even assume that the women went so far, carried themselves so far, as to caress monsters and animals, which is taught by the examples of several peoples. In that case, there would be nothing the least bit detrimental in any of these follies, because moral corruption, which is often very useful in a regime, can never impair a regime; and we must expect our legislators to be wise enough and prudent enough. If so, they will not issue a law suppressing the weaknesses that, deriving solely from the individual constitution, would never produce more guilt in those weaknesses than in the individual whom nature has created and tarnished.

All that remains now is the investigation of murder in the second category of a man's crimes against his neighbor, and we will then pass on to his duties toward himself. Of all the offenses that a man can inflict on his neighbor, murder is, indisputably, the cruelest, since it deprives him of the only good that he has received from nature, the only good whose loss is irreparable. Nevertheless, a few questions crop up, aside from the injustice perpetrated on the murderer's victim:

1. Is this misdeed truly criminal, given the laws of nature?
2. Is it criminal relative to the laws of politics?
3. Is it harmful to society?
4. How is it to be considered in a republican state?
5. Finally, must murder be repressed by murder?

We will investigate all these questions independently. The subject is essential enough for us to dwell upon it briefly; perhaps we can even find slightly exaggerated versions of our own ideas. What difference does that make? Have we not won the right to express everything? Allow us to reveal great truths to human beings; they expect them from us. It is time for error to disappear; its blindfold must fall next to the blindfolds of kings. Is murder a crime in the eyes of nature? That is the first question we ask.

We will most likely humiliate man's pride by lowering him to the level of all other natural products, but philosophy does not flatter minor human vanities. Always eager to pursue truth, man divides it from the stupid prejudices of self-love, holds it fast, develops it, and boldly displays it to the astonished world.

What is man, and how does he differ from all the other plants, from all the other animals in nature? There is no difference whatsoever. Placed on this planet by chance like them, he was born like them; he propagates like them, grows and perishes like them, he becomes old like them and plunges like them into nothingness after completing the term that nature assigns to every animal species by virtue of its physical structure. If the correspondences are so precise that it becomes fully impossible for the philosopher's examining eye to perceive any dissemblance, then it is an equally major or minor evil to kill an animal or a human being, and the distinction is to be found purely in the prejudices of our pride; however, nothing is so wretchedly absurd as the prejudices of our pride.

Let us nonetheless delve further. We cannot deny that it boils down to the same thing whether you destroy a man or a beast. Is not the destruction of any living creature decidedly an evil, which is what the Pythagoreans believed, and which the inhabitants along the Ganges still believe today? Before answering, let us first remind our readers that we are studying this matter only in reference to nature; we shall discuss it next in regard to mankind.

Now I ask you: If living creatures do not cost nature the slightest pain or the slightest concern, what value can they have for nature? A worker estimates the merit of his work purely according to the labor he puts into it, the time he spends creating it. So does man cost nature anything? And assuming this is true, does man cost nature more effort than a monkey or an elephant? I will go further: What are the primal materials of nature? What are the beings that come into the world composed of? Do not the three elements forming them derive primordially from the destruction of other bodies? If all individual beings lived forever, would it not be impossible for nature to create new beings? If eternal lives are impossible for nature, their destruction becomes a natural law. Now, if destruction is so useful for nature that it absolutely cannot do without it, and if nature cannot create life without drawing on the raw materials of destruction prepared for by death, then the concept of total annihilation that we associate with death will no longer be real. There will no longer be an established obliteration. What we call the end of an animal's life will no longer be an actual end, it will be a simple transmutation based on perpetual motion, which is the true essence of matter, and which all modern philosophers accept as one of the supreme laws of matter. Hence, death, according to these irrefutable principles, is nothing but a change of form, an imperceptible passage from one existence to another—and thus we have what Pythagoras named "metempsychosis."

Once these truths are allowed, I wonder if we could ever label destruction a crime. With the goal of preserving your nonsensical prejudices, do you dare to tell me that transmutation is destruction? Absolutely not! You would have to prove it means a moment of inaction in matter, an instant of repose. But you would never ascertain that moment. Small animals take shape the instant a large animal draws its final breath, and the lives of these small creatures are simply among the necessary effects determined by the momentary sleep of the large creature. Would you therefore venture to say that nature likes one more than the other? Proof would be impossible; you would have to show that the long or square form is more helpful, more agreeable to nature than the oblong or triangular form; you would have to show that in regard to nature's sublime plans, a good-for-nothing fattening up in lethargy and indolence is more useful than other animals. The idler would have to confirm that the horse, whose service is vital, or the cow, whose body is so precious that every part of it is used, is more valuable. You would have to declare that the venomous serpent is more necessary than the faithful dog.

Now, since all of these systems are untenable, we must absolutely concur that we cannot possibly wipe out the works of nature. After all, the only thing we do by surrendering to destruction is to operate a variation in the forms, a variation that cannot snuff life; and it therefore transcends human strength to verify that any crime can exist in the so-called destruction of a creature, whatever its age, whatever its sex, whatever its species. Conducted further by our series of consequences, which spawn one another, we must finally agree that, far from harming nature, the action you commit, in varying the shapes of nature's differing works, is advantageous for nature. That is because this action furnishes the raw materials of its reconstructions, whose work will become impracticable if you do not annihilate it.

"So what! Let it go!" is the response. Assuredly, we must let it go. But it is those impulses that man follows when he commits homicide. It is nature that drives him, and the man who destroys his fellowman is, so far as nature is concerned, the same as a plague or a famine. Everything comes from nature's hands, and nature uses any and all possible methods to obtain, at an earlier moment, the unconditionally required raw materials of destruction.

We must deign for an instant to illuminate our souls with the sacred torch of philosophy. What other voice besides the voice of nature suggests personal hatred, vengeance, warfare—in short, all those motives for incessant murders? Now if nature advises us to perpetrate all those misdeeds, it must need them. How, then, can we, accordingly, feel guilty toward nature if we are simply following nature's plans?

However, those statements are more than enough to convince every enlightened reader that a murder can never outrage nature.

Is murder a crime in politics? Let us, on the contrary, dare to avow that murder is, alas, one of the greatest political incentives. Was it not through a number of murders that Rome became the mistress of the world? Is France not free today because of murders? We need not, of course, bother to point out that we do not mean murders in wars or atrocities committed by rebels and destructive elements; such men, doomed to public execration, need only be summoned to arouse general horror and indignation forever. Which body of human knowledge requires the support of murder more than the science that

tries only to deceive and whose only aim is the expansion of
one nation at the cost of another? Are wars, the sole fruits of
this barbaric politics, anything but the means by which this
politics nourishes itself, strengthens itself, sustains itself? And
what is war if not the science of destruction? What a strange
human blindness that publicly teaches the art of killing, that rewards the man who does the best job of it, and that punishes
the man who gets rid of his enemy for a special reason! Is it not
time we corrected these inhuman errors?

Finally, is murder a crime against society? What rational human being could ever imagine that? Ah! Who cares if this huge
society has one member more or one less? Would its laws, its
mores, its customs be vitiated thereby? Has the death of an individual ever affected the general masses? And after the loss of
the greatest battle, nay, after the extinction of half the world,
indeed, the entire world, would the tiny number of survivors
experience the slightest material difficulty? Alas, no! And much
less the whole of nature; hence the stupid pride of man, who
believes that everything is for his benefit. After the complete destruction of the human species, a man would be totally amazed
upon seeing that nothing changes in nature, and that the
courses of the stars remain as steady as ever. But let us get on.

How should murder be viewed in a republican warrior state?

It would certainly be extremely dangerous to condemn or
punish murder. Republican pride asks for a little ferocity; if a
republican grows soft, if he loses his energy, he will soon be
subjugated. A very singular reflection presents itself here, but
since it is valid though daring, I will offer it now:

A nation just starting to govern itself as a republic will up-
hold itself purely through virtue, because, in order to achieve
something major, we must always begin with something minor.
On the other hand, an old and corrupt nation, which will,
courageously, shake off its monarchic yoke and adopt a republican government, must sustain itself purely through numerous
crimes, for it is already steeped in crime. And if it wished to
pass from crime to virtue—that is, from violence to gentleness—
it would plunge into an inertia that would definitely spell its
doom. What would become of the tree that you transplanted

from a rich terrain to a dry and sandy wasteland? All intellectual ideas are so deeply subordinated to nature's physical constitution that the comparisons furnished by agriculture can never lead us morally astray.

The most independent men, the ones closest to nature, the savages kill daily and impunitively. In Sparta, in Lacedaemon, the inhabitants hunted down helots just as Frenchmen pursue partridges. The freest nations are those that welcome murder. In Mindanao (one of the Philippines), the man who wants to kill is elevated to the rank of hero; he is instantly decorated with a turban. Among the Caraguos, you have to kill seven men before obtaining the honor of this headgear; the inhabitants of Borneo believe that all their victims of murder will serve them when they are no longer here. The Spanish votaries even swore to Saint James of Galicia that they would kill twelve Americans a day. In the Asian kingdom of Tangut, they choose a strong and vigorous young man, who is allowed, on certain days of the year, to murder anyone he encounters. And is there a more murderous nation than the Jews? We see them commit murder in all its forms, on all the pages of their history.

From time to time, the Chinese emperor and the mandarins take measures to spark the nation to rebel; in this way, the ruler and his underlings obtain the right to perpetrate a horrible carnage. If this effeminate and emasculated nation gets rid of the yoke of its tyrants, it will, in turn, slaughter them far more appropriately; and murder, still legitimate and necessary, will merely change victims—it was the happiness of some, and it will be the felicity of others.

An infinite number of nations tolerate public murders. They are fully permitted in Genoa, Venice, Naples, and throughout Albania. In Kachao, the capital of Tonkin, on the banks of the San Domingo, the murderers, in a familiar and recognizable costume, will follow your orders and, under your very eyes, they will cut the throat of whomever you designate. In India, the men take opium as an incentive to kill; when they then dash out into the street, they massacre everybody they run into. Furthermore, British travelers have also unearthed this mania in Batavia.

Which nation was both larger and crueler than Rome, and

which nation preserved its splendor and its freedom longer than Rome? The spectacle of its gladiators upheld Rome, which became a warrior nation because of its habit of making a game out of murder. Some fourteen or fifteen hundred victims daily filled the circus arena; and women, more truculent than men, went so far as to insist that the dying should fall gracefully and retain good form even under the convulsions of death. The Romans then passed on to the pleasure of watching dwarfs cut their own throats. And when the Christian faith, infecting the earth, convinced men that suicide and murder were wrong, tyrants promptly fettered this nation, and the heroes of the world soon became the playthings of tyrants.

Everywhere, then, people rightfully believed that a murderer—a man, that is, who choked back his sensibilities so deeply that he could kill his fellowman and brave public or private vengeance—everywhere, I tell you, people believed that such a man was bound to be very dangerous and, consequently, very useful to a military or republican government.

Let us traverse even more ferocious nations, who were satisfied only by immolating children, and very often their own children; indeed, we will see these universally adopted actions sometimes being made into laws. A number of savage tribes slaughter their progeny at birth. The mothers who lived on the banks of the Orinoco River likewise killed their newborn daughters, persuaded as they were that life meant only unhappiness for girls; after all, they were doomed to marry those savages, who could not stand females, and who sacrificed their infants the moment they saw the light of day. In Taprobane and in the kingdom of Sopit, all deformed babies were offered up by their own parents. In Madagascar, the children born on certain days of the week were exposed to wild beasts by their mothers. In the Greek republics, all newborns were meticulously examined, and if they were not found capable of eventually defending the republic, they were promptly immolated. Back then, no one believed that it was necessary to build richly furnished mansions in order to preserve those vile dregs of human nature.

It is to be hoped that France will abolish these extremely superfluous expenditures; every individual who is born without the qualities needed to be valuable some day to the republic has no right to live. And the best we can do is to end his life the very instant he receives it.

Until the transfer of the seat of government, all Romans who did not wish to nourish their children threw them into the garbage dump. The ancient legislators had no scruples about handing over their babies to die, and never did any of their penal codes repress the rights that a father believed he always had over his family.

Aristotle recommended abortion. And those ancient republicans, permeated with ardor and enthusiasm for their country, were unacquainted with the individual commiseration that we find in modern nations. Those citizens loved their children less, and they loved their country more.

Every morning, throughout all Chinese towns, we find an incredible number of abandoned children in the streets; at daybreak, a garbage cart picks them up and carries them to a pit. Frequently, a midwife takes care of it herself, by promptly drowning them in basins of boiling water or hurling them into a river. In Peking, they are put into small reed baskets; these are then discarded in canals, which are cleaned daily. The celebrated traveler Jean-Baptiste Duhalde estimates that more than thirty thousand children's corpses are fished out every day.

It cannot be denied that it is extremely crucial and politically essential to erect a barrier against population growth in a republic, while, for opposite reasons, such growth is encouraged in a monarchy. After all, a tyrant is rich only because of the number of his slaves, so that he certainly needs men. However, we cannot doubt that overpopulation is a real vice in a republican regime. Still, we should not kill in order to reduce the populace, as we were told to do by our modern decemvir. We must simply not leave it the means to increase the population beyond the limits prescribed by its felicity. Guard against overmultiplying a populace in which each member is sovereign, and make very certain that revolutions are never the consequences of overpopulation.

You may allow your warriors the right to destroy men for the glory of the state; if so, then for the preservation of that state, you must accord each individual, as often as he likes, the privilege of getting rid of children whom he cannot nourish or who are utterly useless to the state; for this individual can do so without infuriating nature. Let him also, at his own risk and peril, eliminate all the enemies who might harm him; because the results of these actions, which, in and of themselves, are absolutely insignificant, will be to keep your population within moderate limits and never large enough to overthrow your government. Tell your monarchists that no regime is vast because of its huge populace; this regime will always be poor if the populace exceeds its own means of survival; and it will always flourish if, contained within just borders, it can market its surplus. Do you not prune a tree if it has too many branches, and do you not trim the branches in order to preserve the trunk?

Every system that deviates from these principles is a folly, and its blunders would soon occasion the total collapse of the edifice that we have just erected so painstakingly. But if we wish to reduce the population, we should not destroy a man who is already fully grown—it is unjust to shorten the life of an already well-shaped individual. But, I say, it is not unjust to prevent the birth of a being who is sure to be worthless. The human species must be purified right in the cradle; if you foresee that someone is bound to be useless, you should cut that embryo out of the womb of society. Those are the only rational methods for diminishing a populace whose magnitude, as we have just proved, is its greatest mistake.

It is time we summed up.

Should murder be stopped by murder? Never! We shall not punish the murderer by any means other than those inflicted by the revenge of his friends or the victim's family. "I pardon you," King Louis XV said to Charolais, who had just killed a man for fun. "But I will also pardon the man who kills you." All the bases of the law against murder are to be found in that sublime remark.

Salic law penalized murder with a simple fine, which, however, was easily evaded by the culprit. So in a rule issued in Cologne, Childebert, king of Austrasia, inflicted the death penalty not on the killer but on the man who eluded the fine. Ripuarian law likewise castigated murder with a fine that was proportionate to the status of the victim. If the dead man was a priest, the fine was exorbitant: a lead tunic was fitted for the killer, who had to offer his weight in gold; if he failed to achieve the same weight as the tunic, the culprit and his family became the slaves of the Church.

In short, murder is a horror, though a horror that is often necessary, never criminal, and indeed essential in a republican state. I have shown examples in the entire universe. But is murder a misdeed that can be atoned for by capital punishment? The man who solves the following dilemma has answered this question adequately: Is murder a crime or is it not? If it is not a crime, why pass laws against it? And if it is a crime, with what moronic and barbaric inconsistency will you punish such a crime?

We now have to speak about a man's duties toward himself. A philosopher recognizes such duties insofar as he thereby gains pleasure or self-preservation; hence, it is useless to recommend his practice of these duties, and even more useless to inflict punishments for ignoring them.

The sole offense that a man can commit against these duties is suicide. I won't bother proving the stupidity of the people who regard suicide as a crime. If you have any doubts, let me refer you to Rousseau's famous letter (Letter XXI in Part Three of *The New Heloise*). Nearly all ancient states authorized suicide in politics and in religion. When an Athenian was about to kill himself, he would go to the Areopagus, the Supreme Tribunal, where he exposed his reasons for committing suicide and then stabbed himself. Indeed, all the Greek republics tolerated suicide; it was covered by the legislators. A man even killed himself in public, turning his death into an ostentatious spectacle. The Roman republic encouraged suicide; the so famous sacrifices for their nation were nothing but suicides. When Rome was conquered by the Gauls, the most illustrious senators took their own lives; by acting in the same spirit, we appropriate the same virtues.

During the French campaign of 1792, a soldier killed himself out of grief that he could not follow his comrades into the battle of Jemmapes. Incessantly placed on the lofty rank of these proud republicans, we will soon surpass their virtues: the form of government makes the man. A so lengthy tradition of despotism had totally enervated our courage and depraved our customs. But we are experiencing a rebirth. We are going to see what sublime deeds the French genius and the French character are capable of when a Frenchman is free. And this freedom, which has already claimed so many victims, must be sustained, even at the price of our lives and our fortunes. Let us not feel remorse for a single death so long as we reach our goal. The volunteers all dedicated their lives, may their blood not have been spilled in vain. And we must practice unity . . . unity, or we shall lose the fruits of our struggles. Let us construct excellent laws upon the foundations of our victories; our earliest legislators were still the slaves of the despot whom we overthrew at last, and they gave us only laws worthy of that tyrant, whom they still showered with flattery. Let us redo their work from scratch, and let us remember that we are finally laboring for republicans and for enlightened people, and let our laws be as mild as the people they govern.

In presenting, as I have just done, the nullity and indifference of an endless suite of actions that our forebears, seduced by a false religion, regarded as criminal, I can reduce our efforts to a very tiny number of things. Let us pass few but good laws. It is not a matter of multiplying restraints; rather, we must give indestructible value to the laws we apply. The sole aims of the laws we promulgate are: the happiness and tranquillity of the citizens and the welfare of the republic. But, Frenchmen, I hope that after you drive the enemy from your soil, I would not care to see the ardor of propagating your principles to go any farther; it is exclusively with fire and sword that you can carry your principles to the four corners of the world.

Prior to fulfilling these resolutions, bear in mind the wretched outcome of the Crusades. Believe me! When the foe is on the other side of the Rhine, protect your borders and stay at home! Animate your commerce, expand your factories, and seek new outlets for your manufactured goods. Let your arts blossom again, encourage agriculture, which is so crucial in your kind of regime, a regime whose goal is to nourish everyone without needing anyone. Let the thrones of Europe crumble on their own: your case in point, your prosperity will soon topple them without your interference.

If you are invincible on the inside and exemplary for all other nations thanks to your administration and your good laws, no government on earth will not struggle to emulate you, no other government will not be honored to be your ally. But if, for the hollow distinction of bringing your principles far away, you abandon your concern of your own felicity, the tyranny that merely lies dormant will be reborn. Internal dissensions will tear you to shreds, you will use up your finances and your purchases—and all that simply to kiss again the chains imposed on you by despots who will have subjugated you during your absence. Everything you desire can be found at home without your needing to leave home; once other nations see how happy you are, they will run to happiness along the same road that you have traced. And please recall that it was the infamous Dumouriez who proposed a foreign war.

EUGÉNIE (to DOLMANCÉ). Now that's what I call a very smart pamphlet. And it's so deeply reflective of your basic ideas, at least many of them, that I am tempted to regard you as the author.

DOLMANCÉ. I quite certainly agree with some of these views; and the things I've told you, which have proved my concurrence, make this essay seem almost like a repetition—

EUGÉNIE (interrupting). I didn't notice. Intelligent things cannot be stated often enough. However, I find some of these principles a bit dangerous.

DOLMANCÉ. Only pity and charity are dangerous in this world. Goodness is never anything but a frailty, and the ingratitude and impertinence of the weak always force decent people to repent those attributes. If a good observer tries to catalog all the dangers of pity and compares them with the dangers of an unflagging solidity, he will see that the dangers of pity carry the day. But we are getting too far afield, Eugénie. For the sake of your education, let us sum up the sole counsel that we can draw from everything that has just been said: never listen to your heart, my child. It is the worst guide that we have received from nature. Close it off with utmost care against the fallacious appeal of misfortune. You do far better to turn down the person who is truly meant to interest you than to risk giving something to a scoundrel, a villain, an intriguer. One has quite meaningless consequences, the other is very disadvantageous.

CHEVALIER. Please allow me, I beg you, to return critically to Dolmancé's principles and to refute them if I can. Ah, you cruel man! How different would those principles be were you deprived of your immense fortune, which enables you to satisfy your passions relentlessly. If only you could spend a few years languishing in that crushing desolation in which your ferocious mind dares to compose errors for the miserable! Cast a glance of pity on them, and do not snuff out the feelings of your soul to the point of hardening it forever to the tattering shrieks of need! When your body, exhausted from lust, rests drowsily on featherbeds, take a look at their bodies; they are stooped from the labor that keeps you alive. See how difficult it is for them to collect even a wisp of straw for protection against the coolness of the ground; like animals, they have only the cold surface to stretch out on. Look at them when, in the forest, they fight the wolves for the bitter root of a parched soil, while you are surrounded by succulent dishes with which twenty disciples of Comus arouse your sensuality every day. When games, grace, and laughter conduct the most bewitching creatures of the Temple of Cythera to your impure bed, watch this desolate man lying next to his cheerless wife. Satisfied by the joys he has gathered in the womb of tears, he cannot even suspect the existence of other delights. Look at him when you refuse him everything, when you swim in surplus. Look at him, I tell you, when he doggedly lacks even the barest necessities of life; glance at his hopeless family. Watch his trembling spouse tenderly divide her time between the cares that she owes her languishing husband and the cares that nature orders for the progeny of the spouse's love. Observe her being robbed of the chance to fulfill any of these duties so holy to her sensitive soul. Listen, if you can without shuddering, listen when she begs you for the superfluousness that your cruelty has rebuffed!

You barbarian! Are they not human beings like you? And since they resemble you, why must you enjoy while they suffer?

Eugénie, Eugénie, never throttle the sacred voice of nature in your soul. In spite of yourself, nature's voice will lead you to benevolence when you know how to separate its voice from the fire of the passions, the flames that absorb it. Let us leave the religious tenets aside for now: I concur. But let us not abandon the virtues aroused in us by our sensibilities. Only by practicing them will we ever relish the sweetest and most delectable joys of the soul. All your mental deviations will be redeemed by a good work that will quench within you the remorse generated by your misconduct. And forming a sacred asylum in the depths of your conscience, a haven where you sometimes fall back upon your own thoughts, you will find consolation for the debauchery to which your blunders have led you.

My sister, I am young, I am impious, I am a libertine; I am capable of all the dissolutions of the mind. But my heart remains, and it is pure. And, my friends, it is with my heart that I comfort myself for all the eccentricities of my age.

DOLMANCÉ. Yes, Chevalier, you are young, and you prove it by everything you say. You lack experience. We'll converse again when you have matured through experience. By then, my friend, you will not speak so kindly of other people, for you will have gotten to know them. It was their ingratitude that desiccated my heart, their duplicity that destroyed, within you, those fatal virtues for which I may have been born as you were. Now if some people's vices allow other people's virtues to become dangerous, are we not doing youth a good turn by stifling it early on? What are you telling me about remorse, my friend? Can remorse exist in the heart of a man for whom nothing is a crime? Do you smother remorse through your principles when you fear its goads? Will you manage to repent a misdeed of indifference that you have thoroughly penetrated? Once you no longer believe in wickedness, what evil can you repent?

CHEVALIER. Remorse doesn't come from the mind, it is purely the fruit of the heart. And never have the sophisms of the mind snuffed out the stirrings of the soul.

DOLMANCÉ. However, the heart deceives, for it is never anything but the expression of miscalculations of the mind. Let the mind mature and the heart will soon give in. False definitions always lead us astray whenever we try to think rationally. I, for one, don't know what the heart is; I merely apply that term to the foibles of the mind. A single torch burns in me: When I am strong and healthy, my torch never goes off the track. Am I old, cowardly, or a hypochondriac? My torch swindles me. I then call myself sensitive, whereas I'm basically feeble or timid.

Once again, Eugénie: do not be taken in by this treacherous sensitivity. You may rest assured that it is purely a weakness of the soul. We cry only because we fear such a weakness, and that's why kings are tyrants. You should therefore reject and detest the Chevalier's perfidious advice; by telling you to open your heart to all the imaginary ills of misfortune, he is trying to present you with a throng of torments that, since they aren't your torments, would soon tear you apart in pure futility. Ah, you must believe me, Eugénie! You must believe that the pleasures spawned by apathy are richly equal to the pleasures offered by sensitivity. The latter can strike the heart in only one point, while apathy tickles it and devastates it all over. In sum: Can the permitted delights therefore be compared to the joys in which the far more prickly enticements fuse with the inestimable charms, shattering the social barriers and bringing down all laws?

EUGÉNIE. You win, Dolmancé, you have triumphed! The Chevalier's words have merely grazed my soul, while your words seduce it and sweep it away! Ah, believe me, Chevalier, if you want to convince a woman, you should appeal more to the passions than to the virtues.

MADAME DE SAINT-ANGE (to the CHEVALIER). Yes, my friend. Fuck the hell out of me, but don't sermonize. You won't convert us, and you might disturb the lessons that aim to imbue the mind and the soul of this enchanting girl.

EUGÉNIE. Disturb? Oh, no, no! Your work is complete. What morons call corruption is too deeply rooted in me ever to allow any hope of reversal, and your principles are too solidly anchored in my heart ever to be destroyed by the Chevalier's sophisms.

DOLMANCÉ. She's right. Let's stop talking about that, Chevalier. You would have to eat humble pie, and all we want to do is help you to enjoy.

CHEVALIER. Fine! We are here for a very different goal, I know, than the one I wanted to reach. That's fine with me. Let's head straight for that goal. I will save my morality for others, who are less intoxicated and therefore more capable of listening to it.

MADAME DE SAINT-ANGE. Yes, my brother, yes, yes! Don't give us anything but your gism. We can skip your morality, it is too mild for roués like us.

EUGÉNIE. Dolmancé, I'm truly scared that the cruelty you so fervently advocate may slightly influence your pleasures. I believe I've already noticed that you display a harshness when you come. I probably also feel leanings toward this vice. To untangle my thoughts about all this, please tell me how you view the person who serves your delights?

DOLMANCÉ. I view him as an absolute nullity, my dear; whether or not he shares my lust, whether or not he experiences satisfaction, apathy, or even pain; provided I'm happy—everything else is of no consequence whatsoever.

EUGÉNIE. It's even better if the person suffers, right?

DOLMANCÉ. Assuredly a lot better. I've already told you: the more active repercussion of pain on us determines, far more swiftly and far more energetically, the direction the animal drives must take for turning into sensual delight. Open the African seraglios, the Asian seraglios, the south European seraglios, and check what happens when the owners of these famous harems have an erection; see whether the owners care about giving pleasure to the creatures who serve them. The owners command, they are obeyed; they enjoy, nobody dares to oppose them; once they are satisfied, the pleasure-servers move away. Some owners would treat it as disrespect for the server to share the gratification and they would punish them for their boldness. The king of Achem in Sumatra pitilessly chops off the head of any woman who has dared to forget herself to the point of enjoyment in his presence; and he very often decapitates her himself. This despot, one of the most bizarre in Asia, is guarded exclusively by women; he gives them orders purely by way of signs. The cruelest death is the punishment for the woman who fails to understand him, and the tortures are committed either by him or in his company.

All this, my dear Eugénie, rests fully on the principles that I have laid out for you. What do we desire in joy? We desire that everybody surrounding us concern himself only with us, think only about us, care only about us. If the people serving our pleasure reach orgasm, they are obviously occupied more with themselves than with us, thereby interfering with our bliss. There is no man who doesn't wish to be a despot when he has an erection—evidently he feels less pleasure if others seem to have as much pleasure as he. At this moment, out of a quite natural stirring of pride, he would like to be the only person in the world capable of feeling what he experiences. The thought of seeing another person come like him leads to an equality that troubles the ineffable lures experienced by *despotism*.

The poverty of the French language compels us to use words that our happy regime quite rightly disapproves of today. We hope that our enlightened readers will understand and not confuse the absurd political despotism with the intensely pleasurable despotism of the passions of libertinage. Incidentally, it is wrong to claim that we gain pleasure by giving it to other people. That would mean serving them, and the man with an erection is far from desiring to be useful to someone else. On the contrary, by adding pain, he experiences all the charms tasted by a vigorous individual who is utilizing his strength. That man dominates—he is a *tyrant*. And what a difference for vanity! Let's not believe that vanity is not involved here.

The act of orgasm is a passion that, I agree, subjugates all other passions, yet also unites them. The pleasure of ruling at that instant is so powerful in nature that we recognize it even in animals. Check to see whether enslaved creatures procreate as much as free creatures. The dromedary goes even further; he refuses to procreate unless he believes he is alone. When you try to surprise him and consequently show him who's boss, he will promptly separate from his companion and flee. If nature didn't mean for man to be superior, then it would not have taken the creatures given to him for this instant and created them weaker than man. The debility to which nature has doomed women proves incontestably that it intends for man, who delights more than ever in his power, to exercise it with all the violence he prefers. Indeed, he can even torture the woman to death if he so wishes.

Wouldn't pleasure at its high point be a sort of rage, if this mother of the human race didn't intend a woman in coitus to be treated as if she were in the throes of fury? Where is the well-constituted man—in short, the man who, endowed with robust organs and reaching orgasm, would not care to torment the object of his pleasure in one way or the other? I fully realize that an endless number of morons, who never become aware of their own feelings, will barely grasp the philosophical system that I am establishing—but who cares about those imbeciles!? It's not they I'm speaking to! I leave those shallow worshippers of women at the feet of their insolent ladyloves, where they can wait for the sigh that will make them happy. They are the lowest slaves of the sex that they should dominate, and I abandon them to the vile pleasures of wearing chains with which nature gives them the right to trample others!

Let those animals vegetate in degrading baseness; it's no use preaching to them. However, they shouldn't denigrate what they cannot understand. May they finally recognize that people who wish to found their principles on such things can do so only on the following basis: the enthusiasm of a vigorous soul and of a boundless imagination. And that is what we are doing, Madame. You and I, Madame, will always be the only persons who deserve to be listened to, the only persons who are made to prescribe laws and give lessons! . . .

Fuck! I'm getting a hard-on! Please call back Augustin. (*MADAME rings, AUGUSTIN enters.*) It's incredible how deeply haunted I've been by that handsome boy's superb ass while I've been talking! All my thoughts seem to be involuntarily directed at his ass! . . . Show me that masterpiece, Augustin! . . . Let me kiss it and caress it for a quarter hour! . . . Come, beautiful lover, come. Make me worthy of lighting the fires of Sodom in your stunning butt! It's got the most astounding ass cheeks, the whitest! I would like Eugénie to kneel down and suck his cock during that time! In this position, she'd expose her derriere to the Chevalier, who'd fuck her up the ass, while Madame de Saint-Ange, mounted on Augustin, would present her buttocks for me to kiss. If she'd lean slightly forward, she could, I believe, do a fine job of whipping the Chevalier with a handful of rods;

nor would this stimulating ceremony cause me to spare our trainee. (*The positions are taken.*) Yes, that's it, my friends. Everything for the best! Honestly, it's a pleasure arranging tableaux for you; no artist in the world can do as good a job executing them! . . . This rascal has the tightest ass! . . . I can barely squeeze into it! . . . Would you be so kind, Madame, as to allow me to bite and pinch your gorgeous buttocks while I'm fucking?

MADAME DE SAINT-ANGE. As much as you like, my friend. But I warn you, I'll get even with you! I swear that for every infliction I will fart in your mouth!

DOLMANCÉ. Ah! God damn it! What a threat! That means I have to make sure I offend you! (*He bites her.*) Let's see if you keep your word! (*He receives a fart.*) Ah! Fuck! Delicious! Delicious! . . . (*He slaps her behind and instantly receives another fart.*) Oh, that's divine, my angel! Save some farts for when I come! . . . And you can be certain that when you climax, I'll treat you with all the cruelty . . . all the barbarity. . . . Fuck! . . . I can't hold back! . . . I'm coming! . . . (*He bites her, slaps her, while she keeps farting.*) Look at how I treat you, you hussy! . . . How I master you! . . . Take that and take that! . . . And may the final insult strike the very idol I've sacrificed to! (*He bites her asshole, the tableau breaks up.*) And what have the rest of you been doing, my friends?

EUGÉNIE (*releasing the gism from her ass and her mouth*). Alas, my master! . . . You can see how well your pupils have served you! My behind and my mouth are full of semen, I'm disgorging nothing but semen all over!

DOLMANCÉ (*vividly*). Wait, I want you to fill my mouth with the gism that the Chevalier shot up your ass!

EUGÉNIE (*taking the necessary position*). What delight!

DOLMANCÉ. Ah! There's nothing so good as the gism from the depths of a gorgeous ass! . . . It's sheer ambrosia! (*He swallows the come.*) You can see how greatly I value it! (*He returns to AUGUSTIN's ass and kisses it.*) Ladies, I'm going to ask your permission to spend an instant with this young man in an adjacent room.

MADAME DE SAINT-ANGE. Can't you stay here and do everything you like with him?

DOLMANCÉ (*in a soft, mysterious tone*). No! There are certain things that absolutely require a veil.

EUGÉNIE. Ah! Goodness! At least tell us about them.

MADAME DE SAINT-ANGE. Otherwise I won't let you go!

DOLMANCÉ. You really wish to know?

EUGÉNIE. Absolutely!

DOLMANCÉ (*dragging* AUGUSTIN *along*). Well, ladies, I'm going to—but honestly, it mustn't be articulated!

MADAME DE SAINT-ANGE. Is there any infamy in the world that we aren't worthy of hearing and carrying out?

CHEVALIER. Fine, my sister! I'll tell you! (*He speaks softly to the two women.*)

EUGÉNIE (*with a repugnant expression*).You're right, it's disgusting.

MADAME DE SAINT-ANGE. Oh, I suspected it.

DOLMANCÉ. You can see that I couldn't tell you this fantasy. And you will now admit that one has to be alone and in the dark in order to surrender to such turpitude.

EUGÉNIE. Do you want me to join you? I'll jerk you off while you have your fun with Augustin.

DOLMANCÉ. No, no. It's an affair of honor, it has to take place between men. A female would only be in the way. . . . We'll be back in a moment or two, my ladies. (*He leaves, dragging* AUGUSTIN *along.*)

Sixth Dialogue

MADAME DE SAINT-ANGE, EUGÉNIE,
THE CHEVALIER

MADAME DE SAINT-ANGE. Honestly, my brother. Your friend is quite the libertine.

CHEVALIER. So I didn't deceive you by depicting him as that.

EUGÉNIE. I'm convinced that he doesn't have his equal in all the world. . . . Oh, my dear, he's charming! Let's see a lot of him, I beg you.

MADAME DE SAINT-ANGE. Someone's knocking. . . . Who can that be? . . . I'm not receiving anybody. . . . It must be very urgent. . . . Please go and see who it is, Chevalier.

CHEVALIER. A letter brought by Lafleur. He withdrew very fast. He said he remembered your orders, but the matter struck him as both urgent and crucial.

MADAME DE SAINT-ANGE. Ah! Ah! What can this be? It's from your father, Eugénie!

EUGÉNIE. My father! . . . Ah! We're doomed! . . .

MADAME DE SAINT-ANGE. Let's read it before it dampens our spirits. (*She reads.*)

"Would you believe, my beautiful lady, that my unbearable wife is so alarmed about my daughter's sojourn with you that she has just gone out to bring her back? She's imagining all sorts of things . . . which, even assuming they were true, are actually quite simple. I ask you to punish my spouse rigorously for this impertinence. I corrected her yesterday for a similar insolence, but the lesson wasn't harsh enough. Please do me a favor and pull the wool over her eyes thoroughly, and believe me: no matter how far you drive the girl's instruction, I won't complain. . . . This slut has been my burden for such a long time . . . that in reality. . . . You understand? Whatever you do is fine so far as I'm concerned. That's all I can say. She will arrive shortly after my letter, so be on your guard. Adieu. I wish I could join you. I beg you: don't send Eugénie back to me unless she's well instructed. I'm willing to let you gather the first harvest, but rest assured that you will also have worked a bit for me."

Well, Eugénie, do you see that there's nothing much to be scared of? However, we must admit that your mother is quite an impudent little woman.

EUGÉNIE. The whore! Ah, my darling, since my papa has given us carte blanche, we must, I beg you, receive this slut as she deserves.

MADAME DE SAINT-ANGE. Kiss me, my dearest. How relieved I am to catch you in this disposition! . . . Go and set your mind at rest. I guarantee that we will not spare her. You wanted a victim, Eugénie? Here you have a victim provided by both fate and nature.

EUGÉNIE. We'll have fun, my darling, we'll have fun, I swear it!

MADAME DE SAINT-ANGE. Ah! How I long to know how Dolmancé will take this news!

DOLMANCÉ (*returning with* AUGUSTIN). In the best way possible, my ladies. I wasn't far enough away not to hear you. I know everything. . . . Madame de Mistival is coming at precisely the right moment. . . . You will be resolute, I hope, about following her husband's suggestions?

EUGÉNIE (*to* DOLMANCÉ). Follow them? . . . We will outdo them, my friend! . . . Ah! May the earth collapse beneath me if you see me weaken, no matter what horrors you inflict upon this whore! . . . Dear friend, please take charge and direct all this!

DOLMANCÉ. Just give Madame and me free rein. As for the rest of you, obey! That's all we ask of you! . . . Ah! The insolent creature! I've never encountered the likes of her!

MADAME DE SAINT-ANGE. How awkward she is! Well? Should we prepare to receive her a bit more decently?

DOLMANCÉ. Quite the opposite! The moment she enters, nothing must prevent her from being certain about the way we pass the time with her daughter! We must all together present a scene of total mayhem!

MADAME DE SAINT-ANGE. I hear noise. It's her! Come on, Eugénie, courage! Remember our principles! . . . Ah! God damn it! What a delicious sight! . . .

Seventh and Final Dialogue

MADAME DE SAINT-ANGE, EUGÉNIE, THE CHEVALIER,
AUGUSTIN, MADAME DE MISTIVAL DOLMANCÉ

MADAME DE MISTIVAL (*to MADAME DE SAINT-ANGE*). Please forgive me, Madame, for coming here without warning you. But I've been told that my daughter's here, and since her age does not allow her to go unchaperoned, I beg you, Madame, to please return her to me and not to disapprove of my action.

MADAME DE SAINT-ANGE. Your action is utterly rude, Madame! You make it sound as if your daughter were in wicked hands!

MADAME DE MISTIVAL. Goodness, Madame. To judge by the state I find her in—her, you, and your other guests, Madame—I believe it is not so wrong of me to judge that she is in very wicked hands indeed.

DOLMANCÉ. Your entrance is impertinent, Madame, and without knowing the exact degree of your exact relationship with Madame de Saint-Ange, I will not conceal the fact that in her place I would have already had you defenestrated!

MADAME DE MISTIVAL. What do you mean "defenestrated"? Listen, Monsieur, a woman like me is not thrown out of a window! I don't know who you are, but it is easy to judge your morals by the words you speak and by the state you're in. Eugénie, follow me.

EUGÉNIE. Please forgive me, Madame, but I cannot accept that honor.

MADAME DE MISTIVAL. What? My daughter resists me?

DOLMANCÉ. Why, as you can see, Madame, she even disobeys you very severely! Believe me, you shouldn't put up with that. Should I get hold of some rods to punish this rebellious child?

EUGÉNIE. I'm quite afraid that once the rods were brought, they'd serve Madame rather than me!

MADAME DE MISTIVAL. The impertinent creature!

DOLMANCÉ (*approaching* MADAME DE MISTIVAL). Gently, my dear. No invectives allowed here! We all protect Eugénie, and you might repent your outbursts.

MADAME DE MISTIVAL. What? My daughter disobeys me, and I can't make her feel the rights she has over me?

DOLMANCÉ. And what, if you please, are those rights, Madame? Do you really suppose they are legitimate? When Monsieur de Mistival, or whoever else, filled your vagina with the fuck drops that made Eugénie blossom, did you intend for her to do so? Not at all, correct? Then how can you now demand her gratitude for discharging your gism when you were fucking your hideous cunt? You must learn, Madame, that nothing is more illusory than the paternal or maternal sentiments for children, and the children's sentiments for their progenitors. There is no basis, no foundation for such feelings, which may be customary here but are detested elsewhere. Indeed, there are countries where parents kill their offspring, and there are other countries where children slit the throats of the people who gave them life.

If, on the other hand, the stirrings of mutual love were natural, then the power of blood would no longer be chimerical, and, without being seen, without knowing one another, parents would recognize and adore their sons. Then, in the midst of the largest assembly, a son, for his part, would identify his unknown father, fly into his arms, and worship him. But what do we find instead? We find mutual and inveterate hatred; children who can't stand the sight of their fathers even before attaining the age of reason; fathers who keep their children away because they could never endure their presence to begin with! Hence, these alleged feelings are absurd, illusory. Self-interest alone devised them, custom has prescribed them, habit has kept them alive; but nature has never imprinted them in our hearts.

Let's check whether animals know those feelings. Absolutely not! Yet it is always they we must consult should we care to acquaint ourselves with nature. Oh, fathers! Stay calm about the supposed injustices that your passions or your interests lead you to inflict upon these creatures, which are null for you, and which a few drops of your semen have given the light of day. You owe those creatures nothing. You are in the world for your sake and not theirs. You'd be quite foolish to bother with them. Be concerned only with yourself; you must live only for yourself. And, you children! Since you are far more untrammeled—if that's possible—from the filial piety based on a genuine chimera, you must realize that you owe nothing further to the individuals whose blood has given you life. Love, pity, gratitude—none is their due. The people who produced you haven't a single claim to such a feeling. They worked purely for themselves; so let them manage as best they can. However, the biggest dupery of all would be to serve them or help them, which you do not owe them in any way. No law imposes it, and if you happen to imagine discerning its voice—whether in the inspirations of custom or in the inspirations of the moral effects of character—you should remorsefully throttle these nonsensical emotions . . . these localized feelings, the fruits of climate-bound mores that nature reproves and that reason has always disavowed!

MADAME DE MISTIVAL. Come now! My concerns about her, the education I've provided her with! . . .

DOLMANCÉ. Oh, as for concerns, they are never anything but the fruits of custom or pride. Since you've never done more for Eugénie than is prescribed by the conventions of the country you live in, she certainly owes you nothing. As for her education, it must have been wretched, for we've been obliged to refashion all the principles that you've inculcated in her. Not a single one of your principles contributes to her happiness, not a single one isn't absurd or nonsensical.

You spoke to her about God as if there were such a being; about virtue as if it were crucial; about religions as if they were all anything but the results of the hypocrisy of the strongest person and the stupidity of the weakest. And you talked about Jesus Christ as if that rogue were anything but a rascal and a scoundrel!

You told her that fucking was a sin, whereas it is actually the greatest joy in life. You wanted to teach her mores as if a girl's happiness weren't the product of debauchery and immorality, as if the happiest of all women weren't incontestably the one who wallows most in filth and libertinage, the one who best defies all prejudices, and who gives less of a damn about her reputation!

Ah! Get over your delusion, Madame, get over it! You've done nothing for your daughter, you haven't fulfilled a single obligation dictated by nature: hence, Eugénie owes you nothing but hate!

MADAME DE MISTIVAL. Heavens above! My Eugénie is doomed—that's obvious! . . . Eugénie, my dear Eugénie! Listen one last time to the supplications of the woman who brought you into the world! These are not orders, my child, these are prayers! It's all too true, alas, that you're among monsters here! Tear yourself away from this dangerous company and follow me—I beg you on bended knees! (*She kneels before her daughter.*)

DOLMANCÉ. Ah, fine! A tearful scene! Come on, Eugénie, soften your heart!

EUGÉNIE (*half naked, we recall*). Just look, my dear little Mama! I'm offering you my buttocks! . . . There they are, on the very same level as your mouth! Kiss them, my darling, suck them! That's all that Eugénie can do for you. . . . Remember, Dolmancé: I will always show myself worthy of being your pupil!

MADAME DE MISTIVAL (*horrified as she pushes EUGÉNIE away*). Ah, you monster! Go away! I renounce you forever as my daughter!

EUGÉNIE. You can even add your curse if you like, dearest— to make things even more poignant, and you will find me equally self-possessed.

DOLMANCÉ. Oh, gently, gently, Madame. You've insulted someone here. You've just shoved Eugénie a bit too harshly in our eyes! I told you that she was under our aegis. Your crime must be punished. Be so kind as to strip naked and receive the kind of punishment that is merited by your brutality.

MADAME DE MISTIVAL. Strip naked? . . .

DOLMANCÉ. Augustin, act as a ladies' maid to Madame, since she is resisting.

(*AUGUSTIN gets to work brutally; she defends herself.*)

MADAME DE MISTIVAL (*to MADAME DE SAINT-ANGE*). Oh, heavens! Where am I? Madame, just look at what you are allowing them to do to me in your own home? Do you imagine I won't lodge a complaint?

MADAME DE SAINT-ANGE. It's not certain that you'll be able to!

MADAME DE MISTIVAL. Oh, good Lord! They're going to kill me!

DOLMANCÉ. Why not?

MADAME DE SAINT-ANGE. One moment, gentlemen! Before showing you the body of this charming beauty, let me warn you about the state you'll find it in. Eugénie has just whispered to me that yesterday her father whipped the hell out of her mother because of some minor flaws in the housekeeping. . . . And Eugénie assures me that you will find buttocks that look like mottled taffetas.

DOLMANCÉ (*when* MADAME DE MISTIVAL *is naked*). Ah! By God! It's true! I've never seen a more thoroughly mistreated ass. . . . Damn it all! . . . And her front is no different from her back! . . . What a gorgeous butt! (*He kisses it and touches it.*)

MADAME DE MISTIVAL. Leave me alone, leave me alone, or I'll yell for help!

MADAME DE SAINT-ANGE (*approaching her and grabbing her arms*). Listen, slut, I'm going to teach you some manners! . . . You are a victim sent here by your husband! You must suffer your fate! Nothing can save you! . . . What will it be? I don't know! Perhaps you'll be hanged, broken on the wheel, torn with pincers, burned alive. The choice of your torture depends on your daughter; she will issue the verdict. But you will suffer, you slut! Oh, no! You won't be immolated until you endure an infinity of torments! As for your yelling, I warn you: it's useless! An ox can be slaughtered in this room, and no one will hear its bellows from the outside! Your horses and your servants are gone. Once again, my beauty, your husband authorizes us to do what we will do! The step you take is merely a trap set by your own stupidity. And you couldn't find a better trap!

DOLMANCÉ. I do hope that Madame is perfectly tranquil now.

EUGÉNIE. Warning her like this is what is known as being so accommodating!

DOLMANCÉ (*feels her up and keeps spanking her ass*). Honestly, Madame, one sees that you have a good friend in Madame de Saint-Ange. . . . Where else can you find such frankness? . . . She speaks so truthfully! . . . Eugénie, come and place your ass next to your mother's ass. . . . I want to compare them! (*EUGÉNIE obeys.*) Goodness! Your ass is beautiful, my dear! But damn it, your mother's ass isn't half bad! . . . I want to enjoy myself for a moment and fuck both butts! . . . Augustin, restrain Madame de Mistival.

MADAME DE MISTIVAL. God Almighty! What an outrage!

DOLMANCÉ (*staying his course and starting by fucking the mother's ass*). Oh, come on! There is nothing, absolutely nothing that could be easier. . . . Look, you barely felt it! Ah, it's so obvious that your husband has often taken this route! . . . Now it's your turn, Eugénie. . . . What a difference! . . . Fine, I'm satisfied! . . . I just wanted to maul you a little so as to get me going! . . . A little order now. . . . First of all, ladies, you, Madame de Saint-Ange, and you, Eugénie: be so kind as to arm yourselves with a dildo so that you may punch this respectable lady alternately and fearfully in either her pussy or her ass! The Chevalier, Augustin, and myself will agitate our own limbs and relay one another precisely! I'll commence. And as you can imagine, their asses will once again receive my homage. While each ass is enjoying itself, it will determine the precise torture, but it will do so gradually so as not to wipe her out with one fell swoop!

Augustin, please fuck me and get me over the obligation to sodomize this old pig. Eugénie, let me kiss your gorgeous ass while I fuck your mother's ass. And you, Madame, bring your ass closer to me so I can work it over, socratize it! . . . One has to be surrounded by asses when one fucks an ass.

EUGÉNIE. What are you going to do to that slut, my dear? What will you condemn her to as you lose your sperm?

DOLMANCÉ (*still whipping*). The most natural thing in the world! I'm going to depilate her and pinch her thighs till they bleed.

MADAME DE MISTIVAL (*getting pinched*). Oh! The monster! The scoundrel! He's crippling me! . . . Heavenly justice! . . .

DOLMANCÉ. Don't implore heaven, my friend! It will turn a deaf ear to you, as it does to all men! That mighty heaven has never bothered about a single ass!

MADAME DE MISTIVAL. You're hurting me horribly!

DOLMANCÉ. Incredible effects of the oddities of the human mind! . . . You suffer, my dear, you weep, and I discharge! . . . Ah, you damn slut! I'd strangle you if I didn't wish the others to have their pleasure! It's your turn, Madame de Saint-Ange. (*MADAME DE SAINT-ANGE fucks her ass and her pussy with the dildo. She punches her several times. The CHEVALIER is next; he likewise goes the same routes, and slaps her during his orgasm. Now it's AUGUSTIN's turn; he does the same and completes his work by snapping her fingers and rapping her nose. During these various assaults, DOLMANCÉ's rod has entered all the asses, inciting them by talking to them.*) Come on, beautiful Eugénie, fuck your mother; first in her cunt!

EUGÉNIE. Come on, lovely Mom, come on! Let me serve as your husband! It's a bit larger than your spouse's, isn't it, my dear? No matter, it will get in! . . . Aw, you shriek, Mother, you shriek, when your daughter fucks you! . . . And you, Dolmancé, you fuck me up the ass! I'm committing both incest, adultery, and sodomy, and all that from a girl who only got devirginized today! . . . How much progress, my friends! How swiftly I'm taking the thorny road of vice! . . . Oh, I'm doomed! . . . I believe you are coming, my sweet Mother? . . . Dolmancé, look at her eyes! Isn't she definitely coming? . . . Ah, slut! I'll teach you to be a libertine! . . . Come on, you slut, come on! . . . (*She squeezes her mother's breasts together so hard that the blood recedes.*) Ah, fuck, Dolmancé, fuck! I'm dying! (*While coming, EUGÉNIE pounds her mother's breasts and ribs ten or twelve times.*)

MADAME DE MISTIVAL (*losing consciousness*). Pity me, I beg you! . . . I'm sick, I'm fainting! . . . (*MADAME DE SAINT-ANGE tries to help her, but DOLMANCÉ steps in the way.*)

DOLMANCÉ. No, no! Leave her in her fainting spell; there's nothing more lubricious to see than an unconscious woman. We'll whip her to bring her to again. . . . Eugénie, stretch out on the victim's body. . . . Now I'll determine how firm you really are. Chevalier, fuck her on the bosom of her unconscious mother, while she jerks off Augustin and me with both hands.

CHEVALIER. Honestly, Dolmancé, what you're making us do is horrible! It's an outrage both to nature, to heaven, and to the most sacred laws of humanity!

DOLMANCÉ. Nothing is more entertaining than the solid outbursts of the Chevalier's virtue! Where the devil does he find the slightest outrage to nature, to heaven, and to humanity in what we are doing? My friend, it is nature from which the roués draw their principles, which we translate into actions! I've already told you a thousand times that nature requires both vices and virtues for perfectly maintaining its equilibrium, and that it, each in turn, inspires the motions that are necessary for nature. We therefore do no evil in following these motions no matter what they may be. As for heaven, my dear Chevalier, please stop fearing its curse. A single mover governs the universe, and that mover is nature. The miracles, or rather the physical effects of this mother of the human race, interpreted variously by men, have been deified by men in a thousand different shapes, each more extraordinary than the next. Swindlers or schemers, abusing the credulity of their fellow men, have propagated their ludicrous reveries. And that is what the Chevalier calls heaven, that is what he fears to outrage! . . .

The laws of humanity, he adds, are violated by the twaddle we indulge in! Remember once and for all, you simple and cowardly man, that what fools call humanity is merely a weakness born of fear and egoism. This chimerical virtue, which subjugates only feeble men, is unknown to those whose character is formed by courage, stoicism, and enlightenment. So act, Chevalier! Act without fear! We'll pulverize this slut so meticulously that there won't be even a soupçon of a crime. Crimes are impossible for man. By inculcating the irresistible desire to commit crimes, nature has prudently enough kept them away from any actions that might disturb the laws of nature. Go for it, my friend! Rest assured that everything else is absolutely permitted, and that nature has not been crazy enough to give us the power to thwart its plans or upset its actions. If, as merely the blind instruments of its inspirations, nature ordered us to set the universe ablaze, the sole crime would be to resist! And all the scoundrels on earth are purely the agents of nature's caprices. . . .

Come on, Eugénie! Lie down! . . . But what's this? She's turning pale! . . .

EUGÉNIE (*stretching out on her mother*). I? Turn pale? You're about to witness the very opposite! (*She stretches out;* MADAME

DE MISTIVAL *is still unconscious. When the* CHEVALIER *comes, the group disbands.*)

DOLMANCÉ. What? The bitch still hasn't come to!? Rods! Rods! . . . Augustin, go to the garden, quickly, and pick a handful of thorns for me! (*While waiting, he slaps and smacks* MADAME DE MISTIVAL.) Oh, my goodness, I'm scared she might be dead! Nothing is helping!

EUGÉNIE (*irritated*). Dead! Dead! Huh? Now I'll have to wear mourning this summer after ordering so many lovely gowns!

MADAME DE SAINT-ANGE (*laughing her head off*). Ah! The little monster!

DOLMANCÉ (*after taking the thorns from* AUGUSTIN, *who has just come in*). Let's see the effect of this last remedy. Eugénie, suck my dick while I do my best to give you back a mother, and Augustin will return to me each blow that I carry out. Chevalier, I wouldn't mind at all if you fucked your sister up the ass! Place yourself in such a way that I can kiss your ass cheeks during the process.

CHEVALIER. We have to obey, for we have no means of persuading this rogue that everything he makes us do is horrifying! (*The tableau is formed; and the more* MADAME DE MISTIVAL *is whipped, the more she recovers her senses.*)

DOLMANCÉ. Well, well! Do you see the effect of my remedy? I did tell you that it was certain.

MADAME DE MISTIVAL (*opening her eyes*). Oh, my heavens! Why have you summoned me back from the depths of graves? Why have you brought me back to the horrors of life?

DOLMANCÉ (*still whipping*). Truly, my little mother, not everything has been said as yet. Don't you have to hear your sentence? . . . Mustn't it be carried out? . . . Come on, let's gather around the victim, who should kneel at the center of the circle and listen, trembling, to the judgment. Begin, Madame de Saint-Ange. (*The following judgments are felled while the participants remain in action.*)

MADAME DE SAINT-ANGE. I sentence her to be hanged!

CHEVALIER. To be chopped up into eighty thousand pieces as is done by the Chinese!

AUGUSTIN. And I find that we're quits with her if she's broken on the wheel!

EUGÉNIE. My lovely little mother will be larded with sulfur wicks, and I'll take care of kindling each one! (*The arrangement dissolves.*)

DOLMANCÉ (*keeping cool*). Well, my friends, in my quality as your instructor, I mitigate the judgment. But the difference between my sentence and yours is that yours is merely the result of a scathing mystification, whereas mine will be carried out! I've got a servant down there with one of the most gorgeous members to be found in nature. Unfortunately, it distills a poisonous virus and it is devoured by the most horrible syphilis ever seen on earth. I'll bring him up, and he'll spurt his venom into both channels of the body of this dear and delightful lady. As long as the traces of this cruel disease persist, the slut will remember not to disturb her daughter while she's getting fucked! (*Everyone applauds; the servant is brought up.* DOLMANCÉ *to the servant.*) Lapierre, fuck that woman. She's extraordinarily healthy! This coitus may cure you! It's a proven remedy!

LAPIERRE. In front of all these people, Monsieur?

DOLMANCÉ. Are you afraid to show us your dick?

LAPIERRE. Not at all! It's gorgeous! . . . C'mon, Madame! Will you be so good as to prepare yourself.

MADAME DE MISTIVAL. Oh, just heavens! What a dreadful condemnation!

EUGÉNIE. It's better than dying, Mama! At least, I'll wear my lovely gowns this summer.

DOLMANCÉ. Meanwhile let's have some fun! My idea would be to flagellate all of us! Madame de Saint-Ange will thrash Lapierre, so that he'll fuck the hell out of Madame de Mistival. I'll trounce Madame de Saint-Ange, Augustin will thrash me, Eugénie will thrash me and be very vigorously whipped by the Chevalier. (*They arrange themselves. When* LAPIERRE *has fucked the pussy, his master orders him to fuck her up the ass, and the servant does so. When everything is completed,* DOLMANCÉ *goes on.*) Fine! Now leave us, Lapierre. Here's ten louis! Damn it all! That was an inoculation worthy of the finest physician!

MADAME DE SAINT-ANGE. I believe it is now crucial for the

venom circulating in Madame's veins to be kept from escaping. Eugénie must therefore meticulously sew up her mother's cunt and her asshole, so that the poison remains concentrated, less subject to evaporation, and that it more promptly burns out the bones.

EUGÉNIE. Come on, come on! Needles and threads! . . . Spread your thighs, Madame, so I can sew you up, and you won't give me any more brothers or sisters! (*MADAME DE SAINT-ANGE hands EUGÉNIE a huge needle with a thick, red, waxen thread. EUGÉNIE sews.*)

MADAME DE MISTIVAL. Oh, God! What pain!

DOLMANCÉ (*laughing like a lunatic*). Damn it! What an excellent idea. It honors you no end, my darling. I would never have come up with it!

EUGÉNIE (*from time to time, she pricks her mother's vaginal lips, inside the pussy, and in the Venus mound*). It doesn't mean anything, Mama! I'm just testing the needle!

CHEVALIER. The little slut is going to cause a bloodbath!

DOLMANCÉ (*MADAME DE SAINT-ANGE jerks him off while he watches the procedure*). Damn it all! How hard it makes me! Eugénie, sew more stitches so that it holds better!

EUGÉNIE. I'll sew over two hundred if necessary. . . . Chevalier, jerk me while I sew!

CHEVALIER (*obeying*). No one's ever seen such a little slut!

EUGÉNIE (*very excited*). No invectives, Chevalier, or I'll prick you, too. Be satisfied with tickling me as you must! A little in my ass, my angel, please. Do you have only one hand? I can't see anything now, I'm going to stitch any which way! . . . Look how far my needle wanders. . . . All the way to my thighs, my tits. . . . Ah, fucking! What a delight! . . .

MADAME DE MISTIVAL. You're tearing me to shreds, you dirty slut! How embarrassed I am for giving you life!

EUGÉNIE. Oh, give us some peace, little Mama! It's done!

DOLMANCÉ (*with his stiff cock he leaves MADAME DE SAINT-ANGE's hands*). Eugénie, give me her ass, that's my area of expertise!

MADAME DE SAINT-ANGE. Your dick is too hard, you'll martyrize her!

DOLMANCÉ. So what! Don't we have written permission? (*He lays the mother out on her belly, grabs a needle, and begins to sew up her asshole.*)

MADAME DE MISTIVAL (*shrieking like a devil*). Ow! Ow! Ow!

DOLMANCÉ (*shoving the needle deep into her flesh*). Shut the fuck up, you bitch! Or I'll make mincemeat out of your butt! . . . Eugénie, jerk my dick! . . .

EUGÉNIE. Yes, but only on condition that you prick her harder—for you must admit that we're being far too lenient! (*She jerks his dick.*)

MADAME DE SAINT-ANGE. Work these two fat ass cheeks a little!

DOLMANCÉ. Patience! I'm about to lard her like a side of beef! You're forgetting what I taught you, Eugénie, you're re-capping the head of my cock!

EUGÉNIE. It's because the sufferings of that slut inflame my imagination so intensely that I don't quite know what I'm doing!

DOLMANCÉ. Fuck it all up! I'm starting to lose my mind! Madame de Saint-Ange, tell Augustin to please fuck your ass in front of me, while your brother fucks your pussy! Above all, I want to see those butts! That tableau will finish me off! (*He sticks the needle into her ass cheeks while the other partici-pants assume the assigned positions.*) Here you are, dear Mama, take that and take that! (*He pricks her in two dozen different spots.*)

MADAME DE MISTIVAL. Oh! Forgive me, Monsieur, forgive me thousands of times! You're killing me! . . .

DOLMANCÉ (*swept away by delight*). I wish I were! . . . I haven't had such a good hard-on in ages! I'd never have guessed after so many orgasms!

MADAME DE SAINT-ANGE (*assuming the assigned position*). Are we lying right, Dolmancé?

DOLMANCÉ. Augustin should turn a bit to the right; I don't see enough of his butt. Let him bend over so I can view his asshole.

EUGÉNIE. Ah! Fuck it! The bugger slut is bleeding everywhere!

DOLMANCÉ. It doesn't matter. Come on, are all of you ready? I'm about to pour the balm of life on the injuries I've inflicted!

MADAME DE SAINT-ANGE. Yes, yes, my darling! We're reach-ing our goal at the same time as you!

DOLMANCÉ (*who has finished his operation, having multiplied his needle pricks on his victim's buttocks and coming*). Ah! Fuck it all to hell! My sperm is running! . . . It's lost, God damn it! Eugénie, direct it to the ass cheeks that I'm torturing! . . . Ah, fuck it! It's done! . . . I can't anymore! . . . Why must such intense passions be followed by feebleness?

MADAME DE SAINT-ANGE. Fuck, fuck me, my brother, I'm coming! . . . (*To* AUGUSTIN.) Get moving, you fucker! Don't you know that you have to get into my ass as fast as possible while I'm coming? Oh, sacred name of God! How sweet it is to get fucked like this by two men! (*The group disbands.*)

DOLMANCÉ. Everything's been said! (*To* MADAME DE MISTIVAL.) Whore! You can get dressed now and leave whenever you like! You realize that your very own husband authorized us to do everything we've done. We told you so, but you refused to believe us! Read the proof. (*He shows her the letter.*) May this example help to remind you that your daughter is old enough to do as she wishes. She loves to fuck, she was born to fuck, and unless you want to get fucked yourself, the best thing would be to let her do as she likes. Leave! The Chevalier will escort you home. Say good-bye to the company, you whore! Kneel before your daughter and ask her to forgive you for your abominable conduct toward her. . . . Eugénie, slap your mother twice very hard, and when she reaches the threshold, kick her the hell out of here! (*Everything is carried out.*) Good-bye, Chevalier! And don't fuck Madame en route! Remember that her holes are sewn up and that she's got syphilis! (*When everyone has left.*) As for us, my friends, let us dine and then all four of us in one bed. What a splendid day it's been! I never dine better, I never sleep more peacefully than after sufficiently wallowing in what morons call crimes.

THE STORY OF PENGUIN CLASSICS

Before 1946 . . . "Classics" are mainly the domain of academics and students; readable editions for everyone else are almost unheard of. This all changes when a little-known classicist, E. V. Rieu, presents Penguin founder Allen Lane with the translation of Homer's *Odyssey* that he has been working on in his spare time.

1946 Penguin Classics debuts with *The Odyssey*, which promptly sells three million copies. Suddenly, classics are no longer for the privileged few.

1950s Rieu, now series editor, turns to professional writers for the best modern, readable translations, including Dorothy L. Sayers's *Inferno* and Robert Graves's unexpurgated *Twelve Caesars*.

1960s The Classics are given the distinctive black covers that have remained a constant throughout the life of the series. Rieu retires in 1964, hailing the Penguin Classics list as "the greatest educative force of the twentieth century."

1970s A new generation of translators swells the Penguin Classics ranks, introducing readers of English to classics of world literature from more than twenty languages. The list grows to encompass more history, philosophy, science, religion, and politics.

1980s The Penguin American Library launches with titles such as *Uncle Tom's Cabin* and joins forces with Penguin Classics to provide the most comprehensive library of world literature available from any paperback publisher.

1990s The launch of Penguin Audiobooks brings the classics to a listening audience for the first time, and in 1999 the worldwide launch of the Penguin Classics Web site extends their reach to the global online community.

The 21st Century Penguin Classics are completely redesigned for the first time in nearly twenty years. This world-famous series now consists of more than 1,300 titles, making the widest range of the best books ever written available to millions—and constantly redefining what makes a "classic."

The Odyssey continues . . .

The best books ever written

PENGUIN 🐧 CLASSICS

SINCE 1946

Find out more at www.penguinclassics.com

Visit www.vpbookclub.com